SAVIOR

BOOKS BY AJ EVERSLEY

THE WATCHER SERIES BOOK THREE

SAVIOR

AJ EVERSLEY

SAVIOR
THE WATCHER SERIES BOOK THREE

For my amazingly supportive family who always encouraged me to dream big.

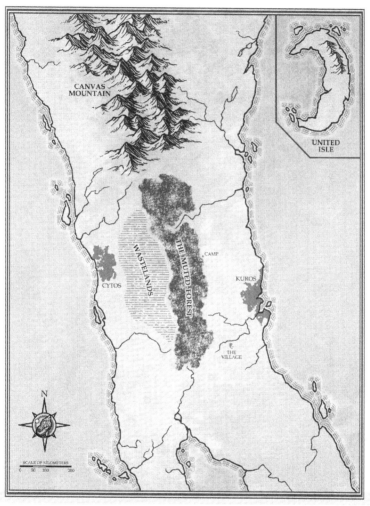

WARNING: UNMARKED AREAS HAVE NOT BEEN FULLY MAPPED AND DOCUMENTED.
SUCH LANDS ARE CONSIDERED *TERRA PERICOLOSA.*
TRAVELLERS TO PROCEED AT OWN RISK.

ONE

There was no escaping the nightmares. I couldn't run fast enough. I couldn't hide from the darkness consuming me. It followed me even in the daylight. Screams echoed in my ears and disturbed my soul.

The crisp winter air stung my cheeks as I ran through the forest. A thin layer of soft snow covered the leaves and twigs. My footprints were the only things disturbing the calm whiteness surrounding me.

This was the closest I'd get to escaping—the only place where my mind seemed to settle. I allowed my legs to do all the work, taking me away, even if only for a moment of peace before the weight of everything came crashing down on me again.

When I reached the edge of the forest, I slowed to a walk. The moon shone, and the village was still asleep, but the sun was eager to make an appearance any moment. Though the sky was turning light gray, darkness hung over me.

My steps were nearly silent as they crunched across the fresh layer of snow. I headed toward the only building still buzzing with activity while staying in the shadows, a habit I could never seem to break. But I wouldn't be joining them. Instead, I slid through the door unseen and made my way to the back room of our former headquarters. It was still pitch-black inside, except for a small sliver of moonlight creeping in through the patched-up wall at the end of the narrow hallway.

I stopped before reaching the bend, and I leaned against the cold cement wall, sliding to the ground and resting my head. I closed my eyes.

His faint breaths were the only sound against the silent night.

He shifted to move closer. "Another nightmare?" Kenzie asked from behind the wall.

"Yeah," I whispered.

"Same one?" he asked.

"Same one."

I'd been there every day for the past two weeks. I wasn't sure why he was the one I turned to. Maybe it was because he was the only one who'd understand. The only one who had lost as much as I. Kenzie understood my nightmares because he knew the man who caused them better than anyone else.

Coleman. He was the reason I'd hardly slept these past two weeks, even if he was never present in any of my nightmares. I knew it was all because of him; everything was because of him.

Every night, I had seen the same scene on repeat. My mother showed me a vision. I witnessed everything through her eyes, and she was trying to show me something. She wanted me to

2

figure it out, but I couldn't focus on anything but the screaming and the blood.

I was in a stark white room. Lena sat strapped to a chair across from me. There was a doctor in the room, one I recognized from Sub 9, and two watchful nurses who hid in the corner, waiting to be called upon.

Lena didn't look scared as she sat still and waited patiently. She looked strong and determined, like the princess I remembered, but that would soon fade.

I always noticed the pails last. Two metal pails rested on either side of her on the floor, just under her armrest.

The doctor walked over to Lena. Something in her hand caught in the fluorescent light of the room, drawing my attention. A sharp blade twisted between her fingers. She leaned over Lena, brushing away a small strand of Lena's golden blonde hair that had fallen across her brow.

This was always when I tried to look away. I begged my mother to close her eyes or to turn around, but she never did. I was forced to watch it.

"This is going to hurt," the doctor whispered into Lena's ear. A menacing smile tugged at the corner of the doctor's mouth.

And then with one swift movement, the blade sliced clean through Lena's wrist, gliding past the layer of Alatonion skin, the wires and structure connecting her hand to the rest of her arm, and out the other side. With a sickening thud, Lena's right hand fell into the pail below.

That was when the screaming began. The blood, streaming from the stub at the end of Lena's arm into the pail below, was a dark contrast to the white room.

The doctor wasted no time as she moved to Lena's other side and removed the left hand.

Lena cried out in pain. Tears rushed down her red cheeks as she thrashed and pulled against the restraints holding her down.

I knew it wasn't only the physical pain that made Lena scream, but also that the internal bond with her powers had been severed.

"The hands are the vessel for your powers," Lena had once told me. Her vessel was gone forever.

The dripping of blood slowly ceased as the Alatonion in Lena's body repaired itself, sealing the wounds at the ends of her wrists shut.

The nurses scooped up the pails containing Lena's hands which were bright red, covered in blood. The nurses left the room, and I—my mom—followed, leaving Lena with the doctor. The last thing I heard every time before I woke from the vision was the sound of Lena begging. "Please, please…"

I shuddered against the cold cement and opened my eyes, shielding them against the bright streak of light peeking through the crack as the sun made its first appearance.

"Did you notice anything different this time?" Kenzie drew my attention back.

"No." I shook my head, even though he couldn't see me.

I wasn't sure why I had confided in Kenzie about this. Maybe a part of me thought he'd have an answer, but even he had no idea what Coleman planned to do with Lena. And though I came daily to speak to him, I'd yet to step around the corner at the end of the hallway and look at him.

I was scared, scared about what I might see, who I might see.

But it was a comfort to hear his voice and feel his energy again.

I dropped my head into my hands. "They're killing her," I mumbled.

Kenzie said nothing. He didn't have to. We both knew it was true. I let out a long breath before I pushed myself back up to my feet. "I should go," I stated. Judging by the subtle rustle of hair against the wall, I think he nodded.

"You can't fight him alone. The people you have—those soldiers—they won't be enough," Kenzie said.

"We have no one else, nothing else," I whispered back.

"Then find more."

I paused, thinking of what Kenzie meant. Who else could we ask for help? We were all that remained of this world.

Without another word, I left Kenzie to his metal confinement and stalked back into the cold winter morning as the guards made their way past me to check on their prisoner. They spared me no glance, and I kept my head down.

Silently, I crept back into my room, kicking off my shoes before crawling over a still-sleeping Max to my side of the bed. He stirred to wrap his arm around my waist, pulling me closer into him. I rested my head on his chest, watching him sleep peacefully.

After a few moments, Max let out a long sigh. "You know I hate it when you watch me sleep," he grumbled.

The corner of my mouth twisted into a smile. "But it's so peaceful and calming."

Max peeked open an eye, and it narrowed into a glare. "It's creepy."

I chuckled and squeezed his side.

Max yawned and stretched his arms overhead. "Is the sun even up yet?" He opened his eyes a crack, wrapping his arms around me once again. He placed a light kiss on the top of my head.

"Just barely."

He groaned. His watchful eyes surveyed me, as he looked me up and down. "How many hours this time?"

"About two," I replied, referring to the hours of sleep I'd managed before the nightmares woke me up.

His eyes grew worried, but I silenced him with a kiss, one on each corner of his mouth before I pressed my lips against his. He eagerly kissed me back.

I was glad he didn't pry, though I noticed the questions written across his face. I'd told him about the vision. The nightmare replayed like a broken record each night, but it was Kenzie who I confided in for an answer.

And I felt guilty for not doing the same with Max, but he wouldn't understand the way Kenzie did. I felt horrible each time I did it, yet I couldn't stop myself. I was betraying him, no matter how many times I tried to convince myself that I went to Kenzie for answers Max couldn't possibly have, it was still wrong.

"Now that you've thoroughly disturbed my sleep, I think there's a way you could make it up to me," Max said. A devilish smile spread across his face.

"Oh, you think so, do you?" My brows rose, and I bit my bottom lip.

"I do," he whispered and pulled me into him, and I let him erase away the nightmare, even if it was only for a moment.

TWO

KENZIE

It was hard for Kenzie to get used to this place. The cement prison smelled of damp stone, and it was far too silent for Kenzie's liking. He pulled at the metal cast around his fist once again, knowing it wouldn't budge, but trying nonetheless. Frustrated, Kenzie slammed his fist into the bar, the metal singing all the way up his arm as it vibrated.

"We had that created by our best scientist," Commander Murray said as he rounded the corner, stepping in front of Kenzie's cell. "It won't come off unless you have the key."

"I'm aware of that," Kenzie snapped, pacing across the small space and rolling his shoulders back.

"Have a good chat?" Murray asked.

Kenzie froze, his glare moving to where the commander stood with a smug smile on his face and his arms crossed over his chest. He didn't reply.

"She is the only reason you're alive. If it were up to me, I'd end you right here and now." Murray shrugged. "You'd deserve it. You know that, right?"

"Then do it!" Kenzie screamed.

Murray twisted his mouth, as if considered to consequences, before he shook his head. "We need information, and you're going to give it to me."

Kenzie rolled his eyes. "I'll give you nothing."

"You'd help him still? After he left you to die?" Murray took a step closer, watching as Kenzie's gaze dropped. "That man called you his son, but he doesn't care about you at all. He has his real family back. You were nothing but a tool for him to wield, and now he's left you here to die."

The muscles in Kenzie's jaw clenched. Murray wasn't wrong; Coleman had left him, and Kenzie knew he wasn't coming back, but that man had given him more than Kenzie could ever repay. Not only that, but he still held a control over Kenzie that prevented him from saying anything even if he wanted to. Right now, he wasn't sure which side he was on, willingly or unwillingly.

Kenzie shrugged. "Are you any better?" he asked. "You lock me up in this cage, preaching to me as if you're better than him. When you're just as bad. You would use Sawyer to save your people if you could—to save your son. And you would tell yourself it was the only choice, that it had to be done, just like him."

Murray's hands curled into fists. "I am nothing like him."

"You all are. *We* all are." Kenzie took a step closer to the bars separating him and the commander. "We tell ourselves we wouldn't do it, but if it was your son's life you were saving, you would have done it, too."

A distant memory flickered into Kenzie's mind. A thought. *So would you, for her.* He shook his head, trying to get rid of the idea. He didn't know her, didn't remember Sawyer or whoever she thought he once was. He wouldn't sacrifice anyone for her because she was his enemy.

Liar.

"And who would you save if given the choice?" Murray asked.

Kenzie clamped his mouth shut as the name sat on the tip of his tongue. *Sawyer.* He rubbed his hand to his temple, a pulsing headache beginning to form as he tried to push the image of her away. He didn't want to remember. He didn't care about her. But he knew that was a lie. He'd begun to hope for the days she'd come and speak to him. Kenzie didn't understand why, couldn't even comprehend how every word she spoke to him felt like a promise and a memory, but it did.

Commander Murray smirked. "Ah, see. That is why you are still alive." He winked before stepping around the corner and out of view.

Kenzie slammed his hand into the bar, screaming at Murray, "You can do your worst, and he'll still kill you all."

A door closing was the only reply Kenzie received.

THREE

"Remind me again why we're out here in the cold?" Tenason asked, as he shivered and danced on the spot, presumably trying to keep his toes warm.

"You said you wanted to help me train," I countered, hiding my shivers.

We were outside in the middle of the village, waiting for Max to return with today's task. Max and Tenason had been helping me train my Carbon abilities, and today's drills had taken us outdoors, much to Tenason's dismay. It was one of the few things I didn't want to ask Kenzie about; it was too personal, too focused on me.

"We have plenty of indoor space to use. Why does Max insist on taking us outside when it's so cold?" Tenason complained.

I chuckled. "Don't ask me. I don't make the rules."

"No, but you do a good job of breaking them," Tenason teased.

I shoved him, rolling my eyes. "This newfound sarcasm of

yours is a bit reminiscent of your brother. I thought you were supposed to be the nice one."

He laughed. "I spent seventeen years with the guy. Some of that sarcasm was bound to rub off." Tenason grinned at the memory of his brother, and I was happy to see that smile.

"Ethan was sarcastic as a baby?"

"Would it surprise you if he was?" Tenason shrugged.

I laughed. "No, it wouldn't."

"Okay, enough chitchat," Max said, as he rounded the corner and strolled toward us. "It's time to get serious."

"Sir, yes, sir!" Tenason gave a mock salute, and I couldn't hide my amusement. Since Coleman's attack, Murray had been working on a way to stop his next inevitable attack. In reality, we had no plans, so I kept my focus on getting stronger and finding a way to harness my abilities.

Max shook his head. "Okay, I've hidden something within the forest. Sawyer, you need to detect it before Tenason finds it. Once you detect it, you still have to beat Tenason to it."

I gave Tenason a challenging smirk, and he stuck out his tongue.

"Whoever gets there first gets to claim the prize," Max finished. "Ready?"

I nodded sharply, and Tenason crouched down as he dug in his heels. We'd remain out of range of the Dred Wulfs, but this forest was still huge.

"On your mark, get set, go!" Max yelled, and Tenason took off.

I summoned my powers to the tips of my fingers, letting them flood the forest, searching for whatever Max had hidden.

I felt Tenason's energy nearby, but I did my best to block him out and stay focused. Even if Tenason was on the right track, I couldn't follow his movements if I had to beat him there.

Beside my ear, there was a loud crunch of an apple being bitten into that drew my attention away from the task. I glanced to my side where Max stood with a large apple.

"Do you mind?" I glared.

"Oh, sorry. Am I distracting you?" He kept his eyes on me as he bit into the apple again.

I growled as I put my focus back into my powers. This was a new challenge for my detection skills, as the forest was full of energy, and the item Max had hidden could've been anything. I didn't just have to find it, but also ensure it was the right item that Max had hidden. The only advantage I would have over Tenason was that I knew what Max felt like through my powers. His energy lingered throughout like a road map I could follow.

Max let out a long yawn beside me. I rolled my eyes but kept my focus on sliding through the forest, winding up and down each tree. Max wouldn't have made it easy for either of us.

A bead of sweat formed on my brow, and the cold winter day began to feel like a sweltering furnace as I used up every bit of energy inside of me. The cuff on my wrist glowed against my pale skin, as it allowed a continual flow of power to seep through me.

I felt a whisper of something, barely anything, but there was something that marked it as different… It reeked of Max's energy.

I took off without a word, following the small tether of

energy pulling me like a rope to the hidden object. I sprinted. The trees were a blur of brown and green. My feet stumbled only a moment on the forest floor before I regained my footing.

Another energy pulsed nearby, and I knew it was Tenason. He was close, so I abandoned the clear path and cut through the thick brush. Using my powers, I pushed the small shrubs aside and snapped the low-hanging branches. I was close enough that I felt each footstep Tenason took, only a few hundred yards ahead of me. Then his footsteps fell silent.

I neared the edge of the trail and heard the crashing waves of a river flowing below. I nearly fell over the edge, skidding to a stop just in time, sending a few pebbles flying. I stared down the steep cliff.

Below, on a rock in the middle of the freezing river rapids, sat a delicious slice of blueberry pie. And beside it, Tenason with a huge mouthful of pie already stuffed in his face.

I sighed as my shoulders slumped. Tenason gave me a cocky little wave and a smile. He had beaten me.

A low chuckle came from behind me. "I even picked your favorite," Max teased.

I gave him a shove before I turned to leave and make my way back to the village.

"Hey!" Tenason called from the rock below. "Isn't anyone gonna help me get back?" He had strung a rope from one end of the cliff to a tree on the other side using his bow and arrow. It had allowed him to glide across and land right in the middle of the river upon the rock. Only now, the rope was too high for him to reach to get back.

I gave him a shrug and waved. I turned back around and left Max and him to figure it out.

"Hey," Tenason yelled again. "You're a sore loser."

"Probably," I shouted over the crashing waves. "But I'm also a dry one." I left before I could hear the choice words Tenason had for me.

The control room was as noisy as ever when I walked in a few hours later. My usual routine each morning was to check if there was any progress on the hunt for Coleman. Murray hadn't spoken much to me in the last few weeks, and I knew he blamed me for what had happened. I had led our enemy right to us. I had shown Coleman exactly where Lena was when he used my mother to trick me with a vision I had thought was real. It had felt so real. I knew my mother wouldn't have done that if there was any other way, still the sting of betrayal lingered every time I saw the way Murray looked at me. I'd revealed our location, and we were no longer safe.

Coleman had used me, and he had Lena—the one thing he'd been willing to move mountains for. He was more dangerous than he'd ever been, yet we still didn't know what his plan was, or where he was hiding.

I had severed the hold Coleman had on me when I let my human host body die. I felt a connection that went deep inside of me break, but there was no way to explain that to anyone. I couldn't make them understand that if Coleman returned, things would be different this time. But I'd tried many times to explain it all to Murray. He listened, but I knew I had lost his trust. It wasn't that he entirely didn't trust me; it was that he'd been burned too many times.

Theresa handed me a warm cup of tea and shoved a muffin in my other hand as she passed with a motherly smile. I took both willingly.

She stepped past me and continued handing out warm drinks and food.

"Any news?" I asked Sam, who had a full mug of coffee steaming beside him.

"None." He shook his head. "We may have—well, I may have—detected where they went. But from there, it's anyone's guess where they are now."

My brows rose.

"See here." He pointed to the screen in front of him. "We were able to follow his ship trajectory… until this point."

I watched as a blinking red dot moved across the screen and then just vanished.

"How did it just disappear like that?" I asked.

Sam threw his hands up. "No clue!" He let out a sigh, as he spun his chair around to face me. "My best guess is that he moved out of range of the satellites we're tapped into. I've checked the others, but they all cut out at the same place."

I watched as his forehead creased, and he bit the inside of his cheek. "What is it, Sam?" I tilted my head.

"Well, there is one person who may be able to give us more information." Sam gave me a knowing look.

Kenzie. He would know where Coleman was hiding out.

Only he hadn't spoken to anyone the past few weeks except me, and that was barely a conversation at all. They'd tried interrogation, anything to get him to speak, but he could withstand more than the normal human, and he gave nothing up. I hadn't joined, couldn't bear to watch, but I knew that I might be the one person who could get him to talk—I just didn't know if I was ready to hear what he had to say.

"I'll see what I can find out." I sighed before turning toward the door leading to the cells where Kenzie was being held.

FOUR

The few conversations Kenzie and I had were nothing more than a personal comfort to me. I spoke to him like I used to, with utter honesty and blind trust, because I needed to get the words out. Again, guilt churned at the realization that Kenzie was the one I'd sought out all this time, not Max. I'd spoken to him, many times about the visions and what to do about Coleman, but Kenzie understood better what it felt like to be the enemy and not want it. That's how I felt—I felt like everyone hated me and saw me as the enemy, and there was nothing I could do to change their minds until I got Lena back and destroyed Coleman. It felt easy talking to Kenzie about that, even when he hardly said much back. Yet today, I was having a hard time even opening the door leading to his cell.

This was different. This wasn't personal; it was business. And it was necessary.

I rolled my shoulders. I set my jaw, pushed open the door,

and walked down the long, cold hallway. I paused at the corner where I usually sat against the cement wall before I took another step and rounded the bend.

He had heard me coming. He leaned on the wall with his free hand pressed against the cold cement. His head whipped up, and his hand dropped as I came into view.

I hadn't seen him since the day he'd almost killed me. I hadn't wanted to see his eyes, the warmth I'd once seen in them gone. They were the same blue I remembered. They lingered on me with a hint of something familiar before he pushed away from the wall and moved to the back corner of his small cell.

His hair was longer than before and stuck up all over the place like he'd just woken up. Stubble grew on his usually smooth face. He seemed older, worn and tired. The smell wafting in the confined space told me he hadn't had a shower in a few days, either.

His left hand was tucked behind his back, but I still saw it. The thick metal casing surrounding his hand molding into a tight fist was hard to miss, even though he tried to hide it. A cage had been placed over his hand, ensuring he couldn't use his powers. He couldn't hurt me, not with his powers anyway, yet I couldn't help the involuntary shiver traveling down my spine.

The rapid beating of my heart pounded in my ears as I took a step closer to the bars.

"Why are you here?" Kenzie asked. His suspicious gaze told me he knew this wasn't a usual visit.

"We need some information, and it's time you start talking." I shoved my hands into my pockets to keep them from reaching out to him. He was so close.

"I've told you before. I can't tell you anything. Even if I wanted to, I can't." He shook his head.

"It's been weeks. Coleman is a long way away. Shouldn't the hold have worn off by now?" I asked. That was how it worked the first time, or at least that's what Kenzie had told me. Maybe that was a lie, too.

His eyes flickered up to me with a cold glare. "He's made some… upgrades." His words were like venom on his lips as he spoke. "I can't tell you where he is. I can't tell you what he is going to do. All I can tell you is to run. Get the hell away from here as far as you can. Because he will be back, and you cannot beat him—not with the army you've got."

I was shaking my head before he'd even finished. "You know I can't do that."

His eyes dropped again. "Yes… I know. You're a fool. You all are."

"How many? How many Carbons does he have?" I tried to turn his attention back to giving me some information, anything that could help us.

He let out a menacing chuckle, and the hint of a smile that was so unlike the one that used to warm his face spread at the side of his mouth. "Thousands. Hundreds of thousands."

I tried to not let my shock show. "When will he be back?"

Kenzie shrugged. "Today, tomorrow. There's no telling when he'll be back."

"But you said he was dying. You said he was infected with a virus of some sort. Maybe he's weak. Maybe—"

"He *was* dying, and then you gave him the one thing that could save him." Kenzie's voice rose as he pushed himself away from the wall and stepped into the middle of the cell. "He'll be back. And he'll be stronger. And this time, he won't stop until every one of you is dead."

Guilt churned at his words. *You gave him the one thing that could save him*—Lena. "Let him try. We've won before." I tried to sound more confident than I felt while I shifted on my feet.

"You think that was his worst?" Kenzie took another step forward. His head tilted to the side with a sneer. "Your mother and I convinced him to only bring a few. We tried to contain the damage as much as we could. Why do you think so many of your men were running in the wrong direction when we arrived? You think your maps accidentally showed the wrong trajectory?"

My throat bobbed, and I couldn't look away from his piercing stare. He took another step forward. I was frozen.

"I did what I could to spare you, to spare innocent people from a fate that is still coming. One they can't just hide from this time." His free hand gripped onto the bar as he leaned in so close I felt his breath on my cheek and saw the fire in his eyes. "Our fates have already been written, Sawyer. And I can't run from it any more than you can. I can't change who I am, what I am. And you can't stop him."

My eyes narrowed. I shook my head. "I don't believe that. I will win, *we* will win." I wrapped my fingers around his, still clenched around the bar.

He flinched as if he would pull back, glancing down at our hands, but he didn't move.

20

"You can fight this. You've done it before, and I believe you can do it again."

Slowly, his gaze moved up to meet mine, and for a moment, it was Kenzie and I again. No one and nothing else mattered in that moment, just us. There was a connection between us, something that went beyond logic, beyond common sense. I couldn't ignore the small part of me still drawn to him—and right now, it was yanking hard, deep in my core.

He slowly drew away his hand, but he didn't move. He reached through the bar toward me. His calloused palm brushed against my cheek and slid down to cup my chin. He pulled me a little closer. His eyes flickered to my mouth and back to my eyes again.

Kenzie's hand slid down my neck, and his thumb gently caressed the soft skin under my chin. Heat rose to my cheeks, and my heart was beating so fast—too fast.

His eyes narrowed. "I can't stop the control anymore, Sawyer. Not like before." He shook his head, and I saw a moment of sorrow—regret. "You put your faith in the wrong people." Then his hand squeezed tight around my throat.

I clawed at his grip as my lungs begged for air. I was gasping, but nothing worked. I kicked blindly toward him, hitting the metal bars between us as he squeezed tighter. My eyes widened as blackness filled the corners of my vision, and my limbs grew weak. How could I have been so stupid? Everything he'd said, every feeling, it was all a lie.

I struggled to pull at my powers, but with the crushing grip of his hand around my throat, I could hardly think straight. I was panicking. Every thought or idea of how to use my abilities to free myself were gone, and all I could do was punch and kick my way free because I didn't know how much time I had.

With one last feeble attempt, I dug into his arms with my nails, but he wouldn't release me. His cold eyes watched as the life drained from me. I knew it wasn't him, it was the order Coleman had given him, the control he still had even this far away and after so much time, but what if part of it was him? What if Kenzie truly wanted me dead, not because he was ordered to, but because he hated me? Darkness consumed me, and my arms fell limp to my side.

There was a muffled voice in the distance and the sound of an electric spark. I was dropped to the ground.

My lungs choked as they filled up with air, and I gasped for more. I peeked open my eyes enough to see Max standing over Kenzie with a long metal rod in his hand that sparked with an electric current at the end.

Kenzie's body convulsed and shook until Max pulled back, and Kenzie remained still on the ground in his cell. Only the soft rise and fall of his back indicated he was still alive.

Max turned his attention to me. His eyes were wild as he reached down and scooped me into his arms. I closed my eyes, letting him carry me away, still struggling to catch my breath. Kenzie had betrayed me, again, and I had been a fool to ever believe I could change him.

FIVE

"What were you thinking?" Max yelled, as he paced in front of where I sat in Doc's office.

"I was trying to help," I whispered. My neck throbbed, and every word felt like knives scraping down my throat.

"You could have been killed!" He glared as he waited for an answer I didn't have. He was right. Kenzie was strong enough, even without his powers, that he could have crushed the microchip at the base of my skull easily. I'd been a fool to get so close.

"I know." I didn't meet his eyes.

"No, you don't know." Max grabbed my shoulders and forced me to look him in the eyes. "I almost lost you. If I hadn't—" His voice cracked.

I couldn't find the words. I couldn't explain what had happened or what I was thinking. I had blindly trusted Kenzie. I had made a mistake and I knew it. I'd let some small memory of the man I once knew take over logic and reason. I'd forgotten it wasn't Kenzie who'd pulled me out of the darkness; it had been Max. I'd forgotten Max. My chest hurt, and I couldn't look at him again, ashamed.

Max's shoulders dropped as he tilted my chin back up to look at him. His voice was softer this time. "He isn't the same Kenzie you knew. You can't trust him as you once did. You can't do that anymore." His thumb stroked my cheek, and I leaned into it.

"I know."

With a long sigh, the anger settled. He leaned down and pressed his lips against my forehead. "Please, don't ever do that again."

"I won't," I whispered into his chest. I meant it. I wouldn't make the mistake of trusting Kenzie ever again.

That night, lying wide awake in my bed and listening to Max sleep beside me, I couldn't get Kenzie's face out of my mind. The cold glare that had filled his features left him a stranger to my memories. The venomous words he spoke were foreign to me. I was left wondering if I ever knew the real Kenzie at all—or if this was the real Kenzie.

As quietly as I could, I crawled out of bed and slid on my boots. I grabbed one of Max's sweaters and headed out the door, careful to not wake him. I didn't know what I was going to say, only that I couldn't leave the words unspoken.

Through the darkly lit village, I made my way back to his

cell. I didn't round the corner this time. I leaned against the cement wall and slid down until I sat on the ground. I didn't want to see him again; I didn't trust myself or him at this point. I wouldn't allow him to see me vulnerable.

"I'm sorry." His voice was barely audible on the other side of the wall.

Silence hung between us before I found the words. "You said Coleman made some upgrades to you?" I paused. "Does that mean the other Kenzie, the one I knew, is completely gone?" I didn't know if I wanted to hear the answer, but I had to know if there was anything left hoping for—even if I wasn't sure what I was actually hoping for. An ally? A friend? More?

"Yes," he whispered and my heart sank.

It was the answer I had expected, but that didn't stop the pain I felt.

"You said once that your heart still remembered me. Was that just a lie then?" My voice cracked, and I swallowed back the emotions rising up. *It's not him. He's gone,* I kept reminding myself.

"No. It does. But my heart doesn't control me. My mind does. And it only sees you as my enemy," he said.

I stood, pushed off the wall, and rounded the corner. I kept my distance from the bars of the cell. Kenzie sat with his back against the wall I'd been leaning on. He glanced up, and I noticed his eyes were bloodshot and rimmed with a wetness threatening to spill over.

I kept my stance strong as I gazed down on him. "This will be the last time I come here, the last time I speak to you." I clenched my jaw, and I kept my words final.

Kenzie swallowed as he nodded. "Good." He looked back to me one last time. "For both you and me."

Before I said anything else, I rounded the corner to leave. Max was at the end of the hallway, his hands in his pockets as he watched me approach. I'd felt him follow me the whole way here. I knew he would come, but I needed him to hear it just as much as I needed Kenzie to hear it, too. I couldn't tell him why I had been drawn to Kenzie, I didn't entirely know myself, but it was over. He was the enemy, he was dangerous, and Max was the man I loved. He was the one I needed to focus on—not Kenzie—and I wanted him to know that, even if I couldn't say the words out loud.

When I reached his side, Max took my hand, and without another word, we walked away from the cold, dark cell. We didn't speak; we didn't have to. Max had always understood me better than I even knew myself, and I would make up for hurting him. Even if he never said that it tore him apart to see me turn to Kenzie, I knew it did. I clung tight to his side, and Max squeezed my hand in response. This was what I needed. The old Kenzie was dead—and so was the old Sawyer.

SIX

I bolted upright, gasping to catch my breath. I felt the cold air against my sweat-covered skin, and it took me a moment to realize where I was.

"You're safe, I'm here." Max was beside me, rubbing my back while I swallowed another breath of air.

The screams still echoed in my ears. Even though I knew it was a dream, it felt so real. There was nothing I could do to help her, nothing I could do to stop Lena's screams.

I dropped my head as my chest caved in, and I slumped into Max's embrace. My body still trembled.

"Have you talked to Doc about them? The dreams?" Max asked, his eyes full with worry.

I shook my head. "He wouldn't understand any more than we already do." I knew this message was meant for me, but aside from the guilt of knowing I'd caused this and that I had led Coleman right to her, I had no idea what I was meant to see.

"He might have something to help you sleep, though."

I knew how it killed Max to watch me shaken and vulnerable. I could tell by the way he held me a little tighter than usual. I shrugged. "They won't go away until I can figure out what I am missing."

Max nodded but stayed silent. Like me, he didn't know what we were missing. They had cut off Lena's hands, removing the vessel for her powers, and thereby rendering her without the ability to use the power that was likely still inside of her. There must've been something I was missing. Something more.

I slid past Max and threw my hooded black sweater over my head. I pulled on thick wool leggings and tucked my feet into my tall boots. "I'm going to get some air." I pushed off the bed and left before Max could protest.

I hated for him to see me this way, to see me weak and helpless.

Resisting the urge to head toward Kenzie's cell, I walked toward the edge of the forest between this village and Kuros down below. The thick green forest was capped in a layer of snow. The abandoned city of Kuros was like a scene in a snow globe gone wrong, like all the pieces had been shaken up and thrown around. The snow made the place seem almost peaceful, though.

Just past the city limits was the dark blue ocean. The sun was making its appearance over the edge, causing the water to look like a sheet of ice, barely moving in the gentle waves.

In the distance, my eyes spotted something. I squinted before my heart leapt with the realization of what it was. Or rather who it was… Captain Lankey had arrived.

"It's good ta see ya, Miss Sawyer." Lankey clapped my back as he and his men reached the snow-covered, sandy shores outside of Kuros.

"You as well." I gave him a smile as we began walking the long trail leading to our village.

Murray and a few of his men had come to greet Lankey and his crew.

"I am sorry ta hear 'bout the princess," Lankey said.

My head dropped. "I'm sorry I couldn't protect her, Captain." The guilt made my chest burn. Lankey had trusted me to take care of his princess and I failed.

"Lena be a strong lass. She be capable of tak'n care of herself. Don't ya' be feelin' sorry for her." Lankey tried a smile, but it didn't quite reach his eyes.

"I wouldn't be so sure of that," I mumbled under my breath.

Lankey's brows knitted together, and I told him of the vision I kept having. I hadn't told anyone outside of Kenzie and Max. They wouldn't understand, and if they thought these visions were somehow another trick from Coleman, I'd just be dismissed—or worse, locked up next to Kenzie. But Lankey would understand. By the time I had finished, all the color in Lankey's face had drained. And his second, Pete, shook beside him.

"But… why?" Lankey asked mostly to himself.

I shrugged, stepping over a log. We had reached the edge of the village. "She's a threat to him. Isn't that obvious?"

"Yes, but still." Lankey shivered. "She be his daughter, his own blood."

I was nodding along with him when it hit me. I stopped, causing a near pileup behind me. "His own blood," I repeated.

Lankey cocked his head as his brows furrowed.

I spun around, searching the crowd for Max. He was only a few feet away, and I rushed over with Lankey on my heels.

"Her blood!" My eyes widened. "They didn't just remove her hands, they collected her blood." They had placed two pails under Lena's hands, not just to catch them when they were severed, but to collect the blood that pooled from the wound. "He's looking for a cure. Kenzie said he's infected with a virus. They took her blood because maybe it's an answer to his problem. Maybe it's the cure?" I felt a warmth in my chest, like my heart knew it was true.

Max nodded. I felt another body hovering behind me—Murray.

"If the girl's blood is a cure, then it's only a matter of time before he's strong enough to attack again." Murray stepped between Max and I, having heard my revelation.

"Yeah." I nodded. "He will be back, and he will be stronger if her blood is the cure, maybe unstoppable." I let my last words hang in the air. "We need help. We need more people to fight with us."

I could tell from the look on Murray's face he was upset I hadn't told him any of this, but right now, that was just another thing on a long list of reasons Murray was upset with me. Still, he said nothing.

"Ye can be sure we're at yer service, Miss Sawyer." Captain

Lankey bowed.

I rested my hand on his shoulder, "Thank you, but I fear that won't be enough. We need more…"

Lankey's men shifted on their feet. They had only just arrived, barely escaping the United Isles with their lives. Now, they will go up against an even stronger enemy, one who had found a way to escape death once again, and was hell bent on our demise. And we weren't enough.

SEVEN

I felt the shift in the air only moments before a distant foreign energy tickled against my own. Max and I stood outside of the control room while Lankey's men became acquainted with their new surroundings. I felt a little tug on my powers calling to me.

My eyes shifted to the edge of the forest not far away from where we stood, then to Max who was watching my every move. He saw me tense at the weird sensation of some other energy seeking my own.

I gave a slight nod toward the forest and made an excuse before I left, Max at my side and my hand on my gun at my hip. Tenason looked up from where he sat a few feet away, and the ever-observant Watcher joined us as we slid around the corner and out of view.

We entered the forest, and I sent my powers ahead of me. I lifted my hand to Max and Tenason, indicating there were three people up ahead.

Tenason clicked off the safety on his gun, and Max unsheathed the large hunting knife from his side. I slowed as we approached, searching for any hint of who these people might be. But they weren't moving, they stood there waiting and tugging gently on my powers. They beckoned me to come.

We reached the last cluster of trees, all three of us ready for anything, but I was shocked at what we found. Releasing the grip on my gun, I stepped into a small clearing.

A few feet ahead stood Aelish, draped in her black cloak. Her long, white hair shifted in the wind behind her. There were two other ladies beside her, the Ladies of the Muted Forest.

The one on her right was tall and beautiful. She had fire-red hair that gently tumbled over her shoulders in soft waves and staggering turquoise eyes. Her strong, corded muscles were evident even under her black cloak. She looked to be about my mother's age. My energy moved toward her, as if she had been the one to call for me.

The other was small and petite with straight, black hair nearly past her hips. She was young, around my age, maybe younger. Her dark gray eyes searched the three of us up and down, pausing on Tenason with a little scrunch of her nose before she looked away.

"I am sorry to have summoned you like this, but I could not wait for night to speak to you," Aelish's hoarse voice drew my attention. "This is my sister, Annia." Aelish nodded to the red-haired lady on her right who gave a sharp nod. I didn't see any resemblance between Annia and Aelish, the white-haired warrior was much older, so I was left to believe they were sisters in arms, not blood relatives. "And this is my granddaughter, Ainsley."

The young, dark-haired girl flashed a toothy grin. She reminded me of Aelish more, and I could see the resemblance in her smile.

We nodded a hello, and Tenason squeaked out an incoherent "hi" before clearing his throat and looking down at his feet. His face was the same shade of red as Annia's hair.

"This is Tenason." I pointed to the still red-faced Tenason on the other side of Max, the only one I was sure the ladies wouldn't know. They likely remembered Max and I from when they saved us from the horde of Dred Wulfs deep in the Muted Forest.

"We have come here as a warning and to ask for your help," Aelish said. "He will return, within one lunation's time, and he will destroy everything and everyone this time, if we don't stop him." Aelish's voice was eerie and foreboding. It sent a chill down my spine. "The Ladies of the Muted Forest have vowed to help you, but it will not be enough."

Tenason shifted his gaze between Aelish and me before the confusion seemed to take over. "Sorry, but am I the only one who doesn't seem to understand how she knows this?"

"She knows because the stars told her." The young one, Ainsley, glared back at Tenason, who still looked confused.

"Each lady has a gift," Aelish explained. "Much like each Carbon has an ability inside of them, so do we. The nuclear war changed many things within the forest, many years ago. And my ancestors were given access to our gifts because of it." Aelish pointed to the sky. "The gift I was given was from the stars themselves. They speak to me and give me specific information to fulfill their wishes. And now, they warn that all will be lost—including the sanctuary of our forest—if we don't intervene and stop Coleman."

It was clearer to me how Aelish had guided Max and I to the cuff wrapped around my wrist, and how they knew we needed help when we were faced with the Dred Wulfs.

"I see." Tenason's throat bobbed as he swallowed. "And what's your gift?" He nodded to Ainsley.

Her glare never left her face as she closed her eyes and moved her hands in front of her. As soon as she did this, she disappeared, clear out of view. Tenason gasped, and there was an eerie chuckle where Ainsley once stood.

"I can blend into my surroundings, cloak myself and others," she stated bluntly, as she jumped back into view.

Before we asked, Aelish answered our next question. "Annia has the gift of hearing and can summon anyone's energy to hers, though she cannot speak." The mute nodded beside her.

Tenason seemed satisfied with the answer, though his cheeks were still a soft shade of pink.

"We have come to ask for your assistance," Aelish said.

"How can we help?" Max asked.

"There are two tribes that live within the forest. The Ladies of the Muted Forest and the Mountain Men, our brothers in arms. We are not permitted to ask for assistance from the Mountain Men on behalf of anyone else. It is a sacred vow our ancestors made a long time ago. We need you to come with us to ask for their assistance in the battle that approaches. They will only accept it if the request comes from the ones in need, even if this war will affect all of us soon enough. And they will be necessary to win the war that is coming."

Tenason rubbed his face, loosing a long breath. It was a lot of new information to gather, and even I was a little confused.

"I assume the Mountain Men live in the mountains, quite far from here, right?" I asked.

"Yes, they live in Canvas Mountain, a few days travel, and we will take you there."

I recalled Canvas Mountain, having seen it on a map what seemed like years ago. I wondered if Murray had known of them before? It wasn't close to here that was for sure. "Coleman knows of Canvas Mountain," I stated, recalling information I was forced to give him long ago.

"He may know of its presence, but you can be sure he cannot enter the mountain unless the Mountain Men were to allow it," Aelish said.

I looked to Max, who had already made up his mind. He trusted Aelish without question and would go anywhere she asked him. To his right, Tenason looked nervous, but he gave a shaky nod, and I knew he would join us if I asked.

"We'll help you as it seems we're in need of more soldiers." I turned back to Aelish. "But if you are going to help us, and possibly these Mountain Men, I think it's time for a little introduction. I would like you to meet Commander Murray."

Max looked ready to argue, but I put my hand up to stop his next words. "It is only right that he knows the people who will be fighting on our side, risking their lives for us. And we've kept a lot from him already, so we need to try and build that trust back," I stated and Max nodded.

"Let's go then. We don't have much time to waste." Aelish gave another sharp nod, and I led the Ladies of the Muted Forest to our village.

EIGHT

It took more than a few tries to explain it all to Murray, Lankey, and their men. We were gathered in the control room where Max and I had done our best to explain Aelish and the Ladies of the Muted Forest, along with the mission we'd soon be going on.

The men around us couldn't keep their eyes off of Annia and her beautiful, strong frame. Many blushed each time she turned her gaze on them, and even I couldn't ignore how stunningly beautiful she was. To her credit, Annia didn't balk away from their prying eyes, as she stood tall at Aelish's right side.

"So, you can see the future? Can you see my future?" Sam's eyes lit up with childish excitement as he asked. He'd been the one asking the most questions, and Aelish had been surprisingly patient, answering each one.

"Only if the stars show me." She gave a soft smile.

"Cool." Sam grinned from ear to ear. "You'll tell me if they

38

do, right?"

"No one is to know their own fate. I am given the knowledge, and in return I must never reveal it to anyone, or their fate may change."

Sam pouted and crossed his arms. "Well, that's no fun."

I chuckled as my eyes shifted to Murray. He had sat silently as we spoke. He hadn't said a word while Max told him of Aelish, and how she had saved him from the Dred Wulfs many years ago when Max was a child. Murray didn't ask any questions when Max had told how Aelish had been the one to train him for six years while Max was hiding in the forest. In fact Murray's eyes hadn't left Max the entire time. I could see the guilt in his face, the realization that he'd left his son to the forest, and someone else had taken care of him—trained him and taught him how to be a man. That was supposed to be a father's role, but he'd left him.

"So…" I shifted uncomfortably on my feet, glancing around to Murray and then to Lankey.

It was the latter who spoke first. "I'd be think'n we'd take all the help we be given. And we'd be much obliged with your assistance, my ladies." He took his hat off to reveal his sparse, thinning hair, as he did a little bow.

I smiled a thank you to Lankey before I sucked in a breath, waiting to see what Murray would say. He took his eyes off Max and glanced up to Aelish. He stood up and walked over to stand in front of her. Instinctively, I stepped a little closer to them and rested my hand on my gun. The room tensed as Murray looked upon Aelish for an uncomfortably long time before he spoke.

"When I sent my son into the forest, I thought I was keeping him safe and away from the grasp of Coleman. And for six years, I feared I had made the biggest mistake of my life." His voice cracked as he spoke. "My men searched for Max every day for six years, and when I finally received word that he'd been found and he was alive, I vowed to keep him safe until my last breath."

I glanced at Max, who was leaning against a wall with his hands shoved into his pockets, listening to every word his dad spoke and looking like he was barely breathing. I wanted to move to him, to hold his hand, but I remained where I stood.

"I have regretted every day the horrors I put him through. The nightmares he faced in that forest, alone and scared. And I never knew how to make it right, so I distanced myself because maybe that would keep him safe if Coleman were to return. I was certain one day it would happen, Coleman would find me, and he'd use anyone close to me as punishment for betraying him, and I couldn't bear to think of that happening to my own son." Murray shifted, glancing back at Max, his face scrunched and pained. "I have been a terrible father. I sent you away, twice, and both times I put you in harm's way." Max opened his mouth to speak, but Murray stopped him. "To find out you had help, that you were protected, taken care of, by her…" He turned back to Aelish. "As a father, I cannot begin to express my gratitude toward you."

Murray pulled in Aelish and embraced her. The old woman hugged him back as she whispered something in his ear, to which he nodded.

Murray took a step back and cleared his throat as he composed himself. "My men and I are at your disposal. And we humbly accept your offer to help us."

My mouth gaped open as I took in the tender moment.

"We thank you." Aelish gave a small bow. "We will leave in the morning, and I will return them safely in one weeks' time." Aelish nodded to Max, Tenason, and I, who would be joining the three ladies to meet the Mountain Men.

Murray nodded, his gaze moving back to Max, as the rest of the men dispersed back to their posts. I led the three ladies to the room they'd be staying in for the night, just as Max brushed past me toward his father. When I turned to close the door behind me, Max had pulled his father into a strong embrace, and for the first time since I'd met him, I saw Murray begin to sob.

After showing Aelish and the ladies to their room, I stalked over to Adam's office to gather a few things. As soon as I opened the door, my energy sparked. I felt a twinge deep within me, almost as if something was searching for me.

"You feel it, too?" Adam caught my troubled look as I entered.

Bandages covered him as he was still healing from the burns he'd received from the fire of Coleman's Carbon only a few weeks ago. I was glad to see he was back to working. "What is it?" I asked, still feeling my energy pull.

"No idea. Been feeling this weird... energy since Coleman

attacked. I thought maybe I was going mad, or it was the pain from the burns making me loopy." Adam brushed his hand through his gray, coarse hair.

I glanced around the room, sending my powers searching for the source. It lingered on a cabinet beside Adam's desk.

"What's in there?" I pointed.

Adam followed my gaze and reached up to unlock the cabinet. "Only that box and cuff you gave me."

I hadn't asked Adam any more about the cuff since I'd found them, and we'd been so focused on finding Coleman that none of us had bothered to search out more about it. I should have asked Aelish as soon as I saw her what it was, what it all meant, but I'd forgotten. This close, I could feel almost an electric pulse moving from the cabinet doors.

"You feel it, too?" Adam asked. "Like static electricity or something, tickles my skin some days."

I nodded.

Adam moved to open the door and pull out the box. As soon as the door opened, I felt a blast of energy pulsing from the box like a heartbeat all-around me. A chill slid down my spine as if the energy swam through me, leaving a tingle on my skin. It was almost overwhelming, and I covered my ears.

"Close it!" I screamed.

Adam's eyes widened as he scrambled to close the cabinet door. "What was that?" he muttered, and I knew he'd felt it, too, only I didn't know how or what it was. Only when it was shut did it stop. I dropped my hands, and a new sound echoed in the distance.

Screaming.

Earsplitting sounds with pain that reverberated through the entire building. I exited the office, and I could tell where the screaming was coming from—Kenzie's cell.

NINE

The guard at the door was covering his ears and shaking his head. "I don't know what happened. He won't stop screaming."

My pulse quickened as I turned the corner to find Kenzie crouched on the floor. His arms covered his ears as he cried out in pain.

"Kenzie," I shouted, but he couldn't hear me. "Open the door," I ordered.

The guard hesitated at first but he opened it. I pushed through, hearing the click of the door behind me.

I knelt down beside Kenzie, my hand hovering over his body, before I rested it down on his back. He started at the touch, and his eyes flashed open. He was boiling hot, and sweat dripped from his brow as he pushed himself up and staggered away from me into the corner of the cell.

"What was that?" His eyes searched mine. "Where is it?" His breaths were ragged and his hands trembled.

He looked around me, as if searching for the source of what had caused him so much pain.

"What did you feel?" I asked, moving a step closer and resting my hand on his arm. This time, he let me.

"Broken. Like a piece of me was ripped apart and something was missing. Like I wanted it back… needed it back, desperately." His eyes focused on mine, and his breath evened out. "Did you feel it, too?"

I nodded. "Yes, not quite like that, but I felt it, too."

"Sawyer, I need it. I can feel it calling me. It's a part of me, whatever it is." He squeezed my hand, begging me to repair something broken in him that he didn't even understand. I wanted to help him, I wanted to fix this, but I knew I couldn't.

I stood, stepping back to the door where the guard opened it only enough for me to squeeze through.

"Sawyer…" Kenzie's brow furrowed with confusion.

"I'm sorry, Kenzie, but I can't give it to you. It's not safe." Kenzie opened his mouth, but I turned and left before he said another word.

It made sense. The other cuff, the one with the lightning across the surface, it was meant for Kenzie. His powers were like a lightning storm, electric and dangerous. If the cuff did for him what it did for me, we'd be giving our enemy a weapon. That was something I couldn't do, no matter how much it called to me and begged that I give it to its owner. I wouldn't do it.

Aelish sat between me and an unhappy Max. I had told him about the cuffs, and I had come to Aelish for some answers.

"Where exactly did you get those cuffs?" I asked, as Aelish took a bite of bread.

She chewed and swallowed before she answered. "The stars led me to a man in Kuros, a scientist, Mr. Chou, to deliver something to him. He had been working on an item that would help circulate blood flow within the body to carry medication to patients unable to do it on their own quickly enough, and keep the medication circulating until the disease or illness was nonexistent." Aelish's gaze rested on my wrist where the small Alatonion cuff clung to me. "Each cuff was matched specifically to a person's DNA. Only the person whose blood matched it could utilize the cuff."

She paused. "What he didn't know was that each person's DNA also carried the C-node code, their gifts. And these cuffs would allow those gifts to flow through a person with no end. The source of the power would never cease or run dry."

I glanced to my hands, feeling the energy move through me like a current.

"So the other cuff, it's meant for Kenzie?" I asked.

Aelish nodded, confirming what I already knew.

My brows scrunched again. "But how? How did he make these cuffs for us when I've never met him?" I wasn't sure if Kenzie had ever met Mr. Chou, but I doubted it.

Aelish glanced at her sister, Annia, who stood a few feet away, watching us talk. She gave Aelish a nod to confirm we were alone.

"Your fates, Kenzie and yours, have been intertwined long before you were even born," Aelish began. "I have only been to Cytos two times. Both times, the stars sent me to a birthing room. On the first occasion, I was only asked to take a small vial of blood from a newborn baby boy. I knew the stars would reveal its purposes eventually, so I did as I was asked. The second time, nearly two years later, was on the day of your birth." My heart beat so fast, and my mouth hung open while I listened as Aelish spoke.

"On that day, I was again asked to take a small vial of blood, but I was also asked to do one more thing." Aelish reached over and touched the small star pendant that hung from the necklace around my neck. "I was to give two star pendants to the mother, and instructed her that a day would come when she was to give the two pendants away. One to a young boy with blue eyes like the ocean, and the other to the baby girl sleeping in her arms."

I shook my head. This couldn't be—this was impossible. I wrapped my hand around the star pendant, the one my mother always used to wear. The one that had been the key to stopping Coleman, to freeing the human hosts he had been using, and to beginning our fight back. This had been given to her from Aelish? How could it be? How could she have known to give the other to Kenzie?

My mind was a fog filled with questions, and I felt as though the room was spinning around me. Max wrapped an arm around my waist. "How?" I breathed.

"The stars have willed it to be, and so it is." Aelish shrugged and rested her hand on my shoulder. "This is the fate you were born for. It has been written in the stars long before you drew your first breath, and it will continue until you take your last."

"The vials of blood, you gave them to Mr. Chou? And he made these?" I looked down to the cuff on my wrist.

Aelish nodded.

"But, what are they meant for? Why me?" I mumbled.

"The stars see something inside of you that will one day be the answer to ending all of this. But only you can decide if you will use it, this gift," Aelish said.

I watched as Aelish slowly walked away. My mind ran wild with what all of this meant, and how someone's fate could be decided like this before they were even born. How could anyone have known this would happen? And how could I possibly be the answer to stopping it all?

Once again, my fate was tied to Kenzie, only now he was the enemy. There was no way he would help us, he'd already stated that he couldn't, but Aelish spoke as though we would need him to win. Why couldn't I get away from him? Why couldn't this just be easier? I knew why… Some part of me had always known I was meant for more than just a simple life, a simple task. I became a Watcher to save people, and I would become what fate needed me to be to save them again. I always would—in every lifetime, in every situation—I would choose to save humanity.

TEN

The moon still hung in the sky the next morning when we readied ourselves to head out. I hadn't spoken much since Aelish revealed everything last night. I wasn't even sure what to think. A big part of me wanted to run away and hide from all this.

My life had never been easy, and I'd always known I was meant for more, meant to be more, but I'd once thought I made those choices myself. Now, all of this made me feel as though I wasn't even in control of my own life. It terrified me. To think my fate was already written before I was even born set my pulse racing and my mind reeling. It felt as though I'd been robbed of a choice, and now everything I thought I'd chosen myself was tainted. Everything but Max…

"Are you going to tell him?" Max asked, as he packed his bag. He hadn't said anything about all this since yesterday. He'd given me time to process before he reminded me that I did, indeed, have to do something, and I couldn't run from this.

I shook my head. "Not yet. Not until I am sure which Kenzie I'd be giving the cuff to."

Max slung his bag over his shoulder before he came to my side and rested his hand over mine. I hadn't even realized it'd been trembling. "I'm right here. I'll always be right here," he promised.

My heart swelled, and for a moment, I was glad that despite everything going on and everything I had to do, Max was there and that gave me comfort. He loved me and I loved him. I wasn't alone.

"You slept better last night." Max moved on to fill my bag with more supplies.

I scrunched my brow. He was right. Last night was the first time I hadn't dreamt of Lena, the first night in weeks I hadn't woken up with her screams in my ears.

"That means we were right about Lena's blood. That's what Mom wanted us to see." I zipped up my pack and tossed it onto my back. It weighed me down, but we would need everything in that bag where we were going, and as a Carbon I was strong enough to carry more if I had to. This time when I entered the forest, I made sure I brought my guns.

If Coleman was cured or could be cured, and Aelish's warning was true, we needed all the help we could get. That would be my only focus—find an army to beat Coleman, because he was coming. He'd be back.

This morning, we'd start our trek to the Canvas Mountain where the Mountain Men lived.

Max stopped me before I reached the door, pulling something

out of his pocket. It was small and made of silver and copper, woven together into a circle in his hand.

"Figured I should get you something for your birthday." Max placed the little ring in my hand. I opened my mouth to say something, but he answered my question before I spoke. "Sam. He has access to everyone's records, including birth records."

I'd never discussed my birthday with anyone. It seemed pointless to celebrate at a time like this, but my chest warmed as I looked at the little silver-and-copper ring.

"It's nothing big, just something to remind you that no matter what, I'll always be there for you. We're intertwined together just like this ring, and it's never-ending, no matter what happens. It's just you and me." He brushed his finger against the ring, and a smile spread across my lips.

No matter what was going on or how hard the journey seemed, he was always there for me, able to pull me out of the pit of darkness and bring me back to life.

I placed the ring on my pinky. It fit snug and comfortable. "Thank you," I said.

He pulled me into his warmth, wrapping his arms around me. His lips were soft against mine, and I melted into him and tugged him closer. I didn't want to leave or move away from his comfort and safety.

With a reluctant sigh, Max pulled away. He held the door open for me, and I stepped out into the dimly lit village that was still sleeping. The sun poked through, sending scatters of gray and silver light over the stark white, snow-covered ground.

Aelish, Annia, and Ainsley waited with Murray, Lankey, and

Tenason in the middle of the courtyard outside of the control room. Tenason would join us on the journey while Murray and Lankey were there to see us off.

"We should reach the mountains in only a few days. Then we are at the mercy of the men to make their decision," Aelish told Murray.

For the first time in a long while, Murray didn't look like the weight of the world was on his shoulders. He'd realized he could use a little help, as his son had received from Aelish.

Murray's eyes shifted to Max as we approached. He rested his hand on his shoulder. "Please be safe, son."

Max, to his credit, didn't take offense or get upset that his father was worried about him. Instead, Max gave him a crooked smile and pulled in Murray for a hug. "I will, Father."

Murray gave me a nod, and Lankey tipped his hat to say goodbye, and then we were off into the forest once again.

"How many days' walk is it to Canvas Mountain?" Tenason asked, as we settled into a single line, trekking through the snow.

"Walk? Over ten days. But we won't be walking," Ainsley said over her shoulder.

Tenason paled. "How… how will we get there then?" he asked.

Ainsley turned around with a devilish smile on her face, just as the sound of rapids crashing hard against the rocks hit my ears.

"The river." Ainsley grinned, and Tenason became even paler.

Three small wooden canoes were secured to the banks where they rocked gently against the river waters. A few yards away, the crashing sounds came into view as the wild river smashed through sharp rocks and snaked through the narrow canal.

I glanced over at Max, who looked about as excited as I was to get into one of the small boats Aelish was untying. But Tenason, he was ready to run in the other direction. His eyes were wide, and his face was the color of his hair, snow white.

"Um, I think maybe I'll just walk. I'll meet you guys there." Tenason's throat bobbed as he swallowed hard.

"You can't walk there. The river's the only way in and the only way past the Dred Wulfs," Aelish said. She tossed Annia the rope of her boat and gestured for Max to hop in.

"I'd much rather take my chances with them." Tenason took another step away from the edge.

Ainsley huffed as she rolled her eyes. "Don't be such a baby."

"I'm not a baby. I just don't like the looks of those boats. They look… unsafe," Tenason argued.

Ainsley grabbed his wrist and pulled him toward her boat with a surprising strength. "You'll be fine, little baby. I'll take care of you, promise."

Tenason looked to me for support but I shrugged.

"Just hold on tight and don't fall in."

"Oh, is that all I'm supposed to do?" Tenason replied.

"You're wasting time." Ainsley pushed him forward again, and he nearly tipped right into the river.

"Okay, okay. I'm going. Just hold on a moment, crazy woman." Tenason tested the stability of his boat before he put in one shaky foot and then the other. He sat on the front rung, gripping the sides with white knuckles.

Ainsley hopped in behind him, causing the boat to sway. Tenason leveled a heavy glare in her direction. She smirked at him.

Annia pushed off the shore first, and she and Max rowed full steam into the rapids and around the first bend, out of view. Ainsley and Tenason were next. I stepped tentatively into the boat Aelish steadied for me, sitting down on the hard wood bench at the front.

"Not too fast, okay?" Tenason begged, but the wicked smile spreading across Ainsley's face told me it was going to be anything but gentle.

With a push off the shore, all I saw was bobbing white hair against the dark rapids. I heard Tenason's scream echoing through the forest, followed by Ainsley's gleeful laugh.

ELEVEN

By mid-morning, we had gone through the worst of it, and we settled into a smooth current that pushed us toward our destination. Tenason had regained a little color, and his grip had softened on the edge of the boat.

I shifted my pack behind me and leaned my head back, allowing the soft waving of the boat to relax me.

"Well, I'm glad someone's enjoying this little trip," Tenason said to my right, as Ainsley pulled up beside Aelish and me.

"Oh, come on. It's not that bad." I gave him a smirk.

"You weren't riding with a crazy woman. I nearly died. Twice!" Tenason glanced over his shoulder, and Ainsley stuck her tongue out.

"Were you scared? I couldn't tell. Is that why your hair is so white, little baby? Did you scare all the color out of it?" Ainsley teased. I couldn't hide my amusement.

"What?" Tenason touched his hair. "No. It's white because…

because… it just is, okay?"

Ainsley grinned. "Is everything else on you just as white? Do you lay in the snow and disappear?"

Tenason's cheeks flushed red. "No. I'm not all white. And even if I were, it's a sign that I am rare. I'm unique."

"My grandmother's hair is white. You're not that unique, little baby." Ainsley nodded to Aelish behind me, who did indeed have long, white hair under her hood.

"But she wasn't born with it." Tenason went to turn around to glare at Ainsley but thought better of it when the boat swayed. "And stop calling me 'little baby.' "

The corner of Ainsley's mouth curved into a smile. "Until you prove me wrong, that's your name."

Tenason threw his hands up in frustration. I couldn't help laughing.

"I like the nickname. It suits you," Max said from over his shoulder a little way ahead of us.

"Oh, shut up," Tenason yelled. "Nobody asked you!"

We pulled off the river and started a small fire around suppertime. Annia had caught a few fish while we drifted down the river, and that would be our food for the night. We were safe on the shore during the daytime, as long as the sun still hung in the air, but we'd be back on the river before the sun set and the Dred Wulfs came out. The air was staggeringly cold already, and it'd only get worse the farther north we went. I had a blanket wrapped around me and sat as close to the fire as I could.

Ainsley lay in her boat, which was still tied to the shore, having a nap with one leg propped over the edge before we had to depart again. Across from me, Tenason looked ready to push her downstream as he glared in her direction.

I looked down to my wrist where the soft current on my cuff moved with the river beside me. My energy still pulsed within me there, but within this forest, it was muted. I didn't feel drained like I did the last time I was here, but I also didn't feel my powers working. I tried to test them on a fallen tree nearby, but it didn't even quiver.

"Your powers will not work in the forest, even with the cuff," Aelish said, as she watched me from across the flames of the fire. "The very thing that has opened our gifts here in the forest, it mutes your own. It is to keep the forest safe, to keep us safe."

"Why?" I asked. "Wouldn't my powers be helpful to you in here?"

"Your powers maybe, but others do not enter this place with the same intentions you do," Aelish answered.

I understood what she meant. If one of Coleman's Carbons were to come here, like the one who had nearly burned down our village, the Ladies of the Muted Forest wouldn't be safe.

"Tell me more about the Mountain Men," I said. Max passed me a piece of bread.

"They are our brothers, our fathers, our grandfathers," Aelish began, and I noticed Ainsley sat up to listen to the story. "Many years ago, after the war that nearly ended the world, my people still lived in this forest, though we could all feel the change. My great-grandmother was the first to understand this was a gift from the stars, and in return we would do as the stars asked us to.

"My great-grandfather felt a pull to the mountains, to his mountain. They journeyed for many days to get there, and when they arrived, the men of the tribe felt the strength within the mountain coursing through their veins, like the river we travel on."

I watched as the calm, smooth river moved down the winding path and through the thick forest. I knew this seemingly calm river was powerful and destructive when it had to be, like we'd seen when we set off hours ago. Now, it was peaceful, the water moving steady through the wide valley, but deep below where the current roared, it was still a force to be reckoned with.

"The Ladies of the Muted Forest were called back, where their gifts were the strongest," Aelish continued, "and so my great-grandparents split the tribe, so we could serve the stars to each of our best abilities. There are parts of the forest and villages within the mountain range where both the men and women live, but we are stronger deeper in the forest, and they are stronger deep within the mountains."

Annia's eyes softened for the first time since I'd met her. I thought of my mother then, wondering if she was still alive. I hadn't had any visions from her since we discovered what Coleman had wanted from Lena, and for some reason that thought terrified me.

Max furrowed his brow. "Not to sound stupid or anything, but how do you guys... procreate if the men and women are separate?"

Tenason's cheeks flushed at the question.

"Not all live apart, but we give up some of our strength and abilities when we are not fully within our own homes— surrounded by the Earth's powers given to us by the stars and the lands. For us, with our gifts and the way the nuclear war that once ravaged the forest changed us, it is harder to procreate. The stars sometimes show us who has the best chance to birth a child, to keep our two tribes alive, and most listen to the calling, as it is our duty to trust the stars," Aelish explained. "It is a great honor if it happens, but it often does not. Ainsley was the first child to be born in more than twenty years." I glanced back to Ainsley who looked maybe fifteen or sixteen years old, but she puffed her chest out, proud and honored.

I couldn't imagine what that would be like, to have the fate of the entire race resting on that one moment. And to think they were chosen and pushed together with no choice in the matter. It bothered me.

Aelish must have noticed my confusion, as she said, "Not all men or women are chosen in their lifetime, and we are free to love whomever we choose. There is no shame or dishonor in choosing love over duty, and many have found love in their own brothers or sisters just as often as the stars have brought together a pairing that defied what the word love even means— fate. But we believe the stars have chosen who is best for us, who is our perfect match, and who is our equal in all things. And it is that trust and that faith that makes us accept the calling if it were to come and accept who the stars place in our lives."

"But what if you choose someone to love, and the stars pair you with someone else?" I asked.

She smiled. "That does not erase the love. That does not mean you must stop loving each other. It means the stars see something you do not yet see, something more—bigger. And in time, you will see as they do. If it is written in the stars, then there is no escaping it, no matter how hard you try to hide from it."

I stared into the dimming fire, taking in Aelish's words. As much as her way of life confused me, I understood loving more than one person. I'd loved Kenzie with all my heart, but I had lost him, and I'd lost that love. But then Max showed up, and that love was different. It filled my heart in a unique way, but it was still love.

"The stars place many loves in our lives. The love of family, the love of friends, or the love of a mate. But sometimes, family comes and goes. We make new friends and lose others." Aelish poked a stick into the embers of the fire, and it roared back to life before it settled again. "And sometimes, the stars take away the love we think is true, that we think is ours... to show us a greater love. But it never erases it, never takes it away from our hearts, only our lives."

I glanced down to my interlocked hands with Max and noticed him watching me. A small smile crept onto my face, and he squeezed my fingers.

But as we returned to the boats and continued drifting down the river toward the setting sun, I couldn't help thinking about what Aelish had said. "The stars see something you do not yet see." I wondered if the stars saw the man in front of me as my equal, or the one whose fate had been intertwined in mine even before my birth.

It was unfair to even think that I wouldn't be given a choice if the stars deemed one over the other to be more worthy. I had chosen Max. I loved Max. And nothing would change that. I glanced up at him, our eyes locking from across the river, and I knew he worried the same thing. That even if I chose him, he might not always be mine. I released a breath, giving him a soft smile. He would always be mine, no matter what the stars decided, he was mine and I was his—always.

TWELVE

KENZIE

Kenzie's entire body was on fire, causing every fiber in him to scream, but nothing silenced the pain. His hand itched, trapped in the steel cage, stopping him from using his powers. His wrist was sore from the weight of the metal wrapped around it, and the edges chafed the delicate skin around his wrist, making it raw.

But it was the burning deep inside of him that was making him go mad. A clench in his stomach caused him to double over in pain.

The source of the burning was unknown to him, much like everything these days. He didn't understand his own thoughts anymore. Even his actions didn't feel like his own. He felt like a mad man, unable to understand who or what he was, and he hated it. He hated the control still over him, hated that he couldn't fight it. He hated Coleman and every lie he had believed, even as he knew there was nothing he could do about it, even when he kept reminding himself that Coleman had saved his life. Kenzie was a weapon—that much he knew—but a part of him fought it, or tried to at least. It was futile.

He had longed every day to see her again, to apologize and somehow make it right. Well, his heart did, and the memories that kept filtering in wouldn't let him rest. He knew the moment he laid eyes on her again, the command—the kill order—would take over. And he had been right. It no longer mattered what his heart wanted, or what he tried to ignore. He'd been ordered to end her, and that was what he would do. He hated the idea that she had once comforted him, that hearing her voice calmed his beating heart, but he couldn't stop it. Part of him didn't want to. *You need her*, a voice kept whispering. But it wasn't safe for her—and it killed him every time he thought of what he'd almost done.

Because of that, he couldn't risk seeing her again. But this burning didn't come from her. It went deeper into his soul, into the pit of his stomach. Like a raging fire, wild and out of control, ready to consume anything in its path.

A creak came from a door opening, and the footsteps that followed told Kenzie it wasn't her. He lifted his heavy eyes to the man standing on the other side of the cell.

"You don't look well, son." Murray's gaze scanned him from head to toe.

Kenzie looked about as good as he felt. He hadn't showered in days. A thick layer of stubble covered his jawline, and a light sheen of sweat coated his brow.

"Been better," Kenzie breathed, his body slumped down onto the cot, and he rested his head against the cold cement wall.

"If you were to promise to keep yourself in check, I'd be willing to allow you a little freedom." Murray crossed his arms as he leaned against the metal bars.

Freedom, Kenzie thought. Freedom was the last thing he needed. "Last time we spoke, you said you wanted to see me dead… Now, you offer freedom?" His gaze flickered up to the Commander. "I don't make promises unless I intend to keep them. And you know I can't." Kenzie wouldn't risk it, no matter the cost. He wouldn't give his mind the chance to betray him again or hope for such things like freedom.

Murray nodded, knowing all too well the feeling of not having control over your mind. He, too, was once a prisoner in his body, but not anymore. Kenzie no longer remembered what that felt like. It was just another dream he knew would never become reality.

"Then I need to ask you a favor without being able to offer anything in return." Murray shrugged.

"You may ask, but it's unlikely I can be of any help." Kenzie knew his command—his orders from Coleman—had bound him to silence. He couldn't reveal anything to his enemies.

"I won't ask anything of you that I'm not certain you are able to give." Murray tilted his head, staring down at Kenzie sitting on the cot. "Have you heard of the Ladies of the Muted Forest? Or the Mountain Men?"

"No."

"Good." Murray nodded. "And does Coleman know of any weapons we might have?"

"Only the ones he's seen. The usual weapons, guns, grenades…" Kenzie watched Murray as a smile spread across the Commander's face. "It's not enough. Whatever you have isn't enough to stop him."

"Oh, we know, and we're remedying that as we speak." Murray was still smiling.

Kenzie narrowed his eyes. "He will send his Carbons, and they will annihilate every one of you. His entire base is filled with them. Tens of thousands, each stronger and faster than any one of you."

Murray didn't balk at the number. He knew the risk. "Yes, his thousands outnumber our few hundred trained men, probably ten to one, maybe more."

Kenzie leaned forward, studying the keen commander. "Do you not get it? You will all die. There is no stopping it. There is no stopping him!"

"Perhaps," Murray mused, as he pushed away from the bars and readjusted his shirt. "But then again, maybe not."

Kenzie's eyes flashed with anger; he didn't understand why Murray wasn't understanding. He wanted to scream that Sawyer would die if Murray continued to blindly believe they could go up against Coleman and live, but he bit his tongue and pushed the thought aside, because he didn't even understand why he cared. Instead, he said, "You would send your men to the grave knowing full well they will not return."

Murray leaned in closer to the bars, and his eyes settled on

Kenzie. "I can see from the look in your eyes that you care if she lives, even if you try to hide it—even if you can't stop the order to kill her. And the very fact that you would care what happens to her tells me so much more than your words ever could have."

Kenzie's heart stopped as he watched the Commander step back. Murray shoved a hand into his pocket. "I know what you seek, what you long for." Murray's voice was a mixture of warning and promise. "And though I don't know what it may do, the old lady told me to trust her. And seeing as I have to do that for the safety of my own son, I will."

Murray turned to walk away.

"But can you trust me?" Kenzie's voice was nearly a whisper but Murray's feet stopped. He'd heard.

"When the time comes, I believe I can." The Commander left.

A few hours later when sleep overtook him, Kenzie let a familiar image soothe his mind and settle his rapid beating heart. He'd stopped fighting it, stopped fighting the moment when he'd finally let her into his mind, the memory of what it'd felt like both familiar and foreign to him. As his eyes drew heavy, a small amount of control lifted, and he saw her for what she really was—his salvation. *He stood before the girl with amber brown eyes. Her details were blurry, but now he was certain it was Sawyer. He always noticed her eyes first and the calmness filling them, filling him.*

Behind her, a storm raged. Lightning shattered the night sky, but he wasn't scared; he wasn't worried. She comforted him. When he would wake in the morning, this feeling and this calm would disappear. But for now—he reveled in it.

And together, they became that storm, fast and sharp, calm yet fierce. Together.

THIRTEEN

My body was tired and ached from sitting for so long, but I expected no less after three days on the boat's hardwood seat as we drifted downriver. Our nights were left sleepless as the Dred Wulfs stalked us, but just as Aelish had said, they didn't dare enter the river to attack. The current was too strong and deep for even the Dred Wulfs to swim through. We were safe if we kept to the middle of the river.

The narrow rushing path of the stream had opened to a wide, slow-moving river. Aelish said we were getting closer when the first ice drift floated by.

Today, we had reached the end of the river. The ice blocks had become so thick we were forced to hack away at the large ones drifting by just to keep moving until the ice chunks formed one big frozen lake.

Max was the first to test the ice. He took a step forward, away from the edge where it creaked and groaned. Once he was far enough away, he dug his hunting knife into the ice, the blade took its time going through, but it never reached the other side. The ice was too thick, which made it safe to travel on.

Max offered me a hand, and I took it, balancing myself on the slick surface. Annia, Aelish, and Ainsley reached the edge, followed by a thankful Tenason, who hadn't grown fond of the little boat.

"How much farther?" I asked, once we had gathered our supplies and began walking across the frozen lake. I'd pulled out a second cloak from my pack, though it did little against the frigid cold. My fingers were numb in the thin gloves I wore, and the scarf wrapped around my face didn't prevent the wind from seeping in.

The waters below were a dark blue, clouded against the thick ice above. The lake extended on farther than even my Carbon eyes could see, surrounded by a dense forest trailing its way up the snow-peaked mountains. The mountains were so high I couldn't see some of the peaks as they were hidden in the clouds.

"That one there." Aelish pointed to the large middle peak of the three mountains ahead of us. "That's where we're going— Canvas Mountain."

"And you're sure Coleman can't reach us there?" I worried for more people I'd be putting at risk by asking for help.

"No one can enter Canvas Mountain unless the Mountain Men allow it," Aelish assured me, "even us."

"Wait, what?" Tenason slipped on the ice as he tried to catch up. "Nobody thought to ask these guys if we were allowed to come before we set out on this little adventure?"

Ainsley snorted behind him. "Are you just as scared on solid land as you were on water?"

Tenason glared at her.

"The men determine who is worthy to enter their home, but I would not bring you here if I didn't think you were worthy." Aelish gave Tenason a warm smile, and his body relaxed a little.

"This one may need to do a little convincing." Ainsley nudged Tenason as she smirked and took up the lead, leaving Annia to secure the back.

Tenason rolled his eyes. "I think she wants me," he whispered to me.

There was a choked burst of laughter from Ainsley, as she turned around to face Tenason. "I am a warrior, a Lady of the Muted Forest. What would I do with a white-haired baby like you?"

Tenason's cheeks blushed, but he didn't look away. "I'm not so useless, you know?"

Ainsley turned back around and said over her shoulder, "Until you prove me wrong, I have more use for the chipmunks sleeping in the trees than I have with you."

Tenason rolled his eyes once again but kept his mouth shut this time.

The sun looked ready to set when we were only halfway across the lake. Aelish had already told us we wouldn't be making camp tonight. We couldn't risk being out in the open for that long. To keep moving was our best option.

"If the freezing cold doesn't get you, the beasts will," Ainsley warned.

"Dred Wulfs?" Max asked.

"Worse." Ainsley's eyes narrowed. "The Ice Bears."

"Ice Bears? They sound lovely." Tenason's voice dripped with sarcasm.

"There are not many left, and most are controlled by the Mountain Men, but a few are free. And right now, we are in their territory." Aelish scanned the lake around us, and so did I.

Max had his hunting knife out already, and Tenason had pulled out his bow. My hand rested on the gun at my hip, knowing I should only use it as a last resort, but I was willing to if the time came.

The three ladies made a perimeter around us, a tight triangle with us in the middle. The sun was nearly hidden behind the mountains up ahead, and the shadow of it covered the lake in darkness.

Aelish lit a torch and passed one to each of us.

"What are they like? Can we kill them?" I asked, always wanting to know the enemy I was about to face.

"They are white as snow and sharp as ice," Aelish said. "Though large, they move swiftly like the wind. And unless you are like Annia and can hear even the mice yards away, you will not know they are there until you see the blood—your blood."

Tenason gulped beside me, and Max squeezed my hand. A smooth breeze swooped past my head, and I ducked as a large, winged bird landed on Annia's shoulder.

The bird chirped and whistled to her. She nodded, and the

71

bird flew off, out of sight against the near black sky. Annia moved her hands as she signed a message to Aelish and Ainsley.

"They're here," Ainsley said at the same time something began to tickle in my chest, a warning, like a sixth sense screaming—*Run!*

FOURTEEN

We were easy prey out in the middle of the lake, our torches like mini-flares leading the Ice Bear straight to us. I couldn't hear them, I couldn't see them, but even my quieted energy screamed, *they're coming*.

"Can't you cloak us or something?" Tenason asked Ainsley.

"It wouldn't do much good when the Ice Bear can smell us from a mile away. It doesn't need to see us to devour us," she whispered.

Annia slashed her torch to the right, hearing something in the distance even I couldn't hear. Aelish and Ainsley formed a wall in front of us while we backed away from where Annia had pointed.

There was the subtle crack of ice. Annia lunged forward, her torch sweeping in wide waves in front of her. In the remnant glow of the torch, I glimpsed its face. Two sharp fangs glistened in the firelight, dripping with saliva. Its top lip was pulled back in a snarl, and its beady black eyes narrowed in on us. The remainder of its enormous frame seemed to disappear against the ice and snow-white backdrop.

Annia hissed an inaudible warning to the bear as Ainsley stepped forward. Her voice was a low growl as she spoke to the Ice Bear, "Go on, get out of here."

The bear fixed its eyes on her as she waved the torch as a warning. It growled low and took a step forward. She growled in response.

"I said leave!" Ainsley bellowed.

The bear paused, and its ear twitched as it surveyed Ainsley. With a little sniff from its nose, it inclined its head and began to turn around. I loosened a breath as the bear looked ready to leave us alone.

But before it had turned its head, there was movement to my left. Tenason lost his footing on the ice and fell.

The bear spun back around and let out a ferocious growl, setting its eyes on us.

Ainsley waved her torch again before she screamed over her shoulder, "Run!"

I reached down and grabbed Tenason's wrist, jerking him up as we scrambled to run. Max grabbed the sleeve of my jacket, and we took off, running blindly in the direction I hoped was the edge of the lake.

Soft footsteps followed close behind as Aelish, Annia, and Ainsley chased after us, the Ice Bear hot on their trail.

"Move!" Aelish yelled, and I picked up my speed as best I could against the slick ice. The ice groaned and creaked as the Ice Bear clamored behind us, no longer silent as the beast roared while bearing down on us.

My foot tripped on a small snowdrift, but Max caught me, tucking his arm around my waist as he pulled me along.

"We're almost there, aim for the edge." Aelish was right behind me. Her hand pushed against my back.

Up ahead, we had reached the edge of the lake where there was a thick line of trees. My lungs burned with restraint against the cold, thin air. The forest stifled my Carbon body's superior ability to heal.

"Keep going that way. Light those trees," Aelish ordered before she darted the opposite way, making as much noise as she could to draw the bear after her. There was a thin line of trees along the edge of the lake, not close enough to the rest of the forest to burn the whole place down, but enough to form a barrier to hide behind.

Max and I reached the edge and dove over the large snowdrift. The snow was deep, so I had to crawl toward the trees. Max reached them first and used his torch to light the first row. The dry limbs caught fire, the flames sparking their way up the trunk. I reached for the next one and lit it as well.

I turned back around to find Aelish and Annia had distracted the bear, but it had changed targets and stomped toward us.

Only then did I notice Tenason, a few feet away, at the end of the snowdrift and the lake. His foot had broken through the thin ice at the edge and it was stuck. He grunted and pulled. It wouldn't budge. I tried to crawl back to him, but the snow was so deep, and the bear was much closer to Tenason than me.

"Come on," I mumbled under my breath, begging Tenason's foot to release.

His eyes widened as he looked back to the bear and then to me. Fear filled his expression as he realized he couldn't get his foot free, and I wouldn't reach him in time.

I fumbled for the gun on my hip, but in the panic and ensuing chase, I'd somehow lost it. I swore under my breath and pulled out a knife, knowing it was way too short and wouldn't do nearly enough damage against the thick hide of the bear.

I tried foolishly to reach for my powers, but there was no answer from them.

Time paused. The Ice Bear moved in slow motion toward my friend I was still crawling toward. I was powerless to stop it. I chucked my knife at the bear, and it stuck into its shoulder, but it didn't slow the beast down.

The bear's mouth opened, and its sharp fangs sparkled like glass. It took two more steps forward. It was nearly on top of Tenason. There was a sharp cry from just beyond the bear, and then there was a roar from the beast as he stumbled over his feet, brought down by something I couldn't see in the darkness. It dropped to its face with a booming thud that shook the ground, and its body fell limp as it slid across the ice toward Tenason, stopping only inches from him.

"Get up, you clumsy baby." Ainsley stormed out of the darkness as her body reappeared against the snow she'd blended in with. A sling hung from her hand, and it was then I noticed the large rock lying beside the Ice Bear. She'd done that—she'd stopped the bear. Ainsley pulled Tenason to his feet with a yank, his foot soaking wet. "Get behind the fire. He won't be down for long."

Tenason's eyes were wide as he looked up from the bear to Ainsley. "Y-you saved me," he stuttered.

Ainsley gripped him under his arm as she pulled Tenason through the snow. "Don't flatter yourself. I didn't even know you were there, little baby." Ainsley shoved him behind the wall of flames we had created in the tree-lined edge of the lake. "You're lucky the stars gifted me as they did, or you'd have been that bear's dinner tonight."

Tenason was shaking. He swore under his breath as he watched her walk away gracefully through the thick snow to light more surrounding trees. I reached Tenason's side, bending down and removing his wet boot, but he hardly noticed, as his eyes never left Ainsley.

"I almost died," he muttered.

"Yeah, you did. And if you don't snap out of it, you're going to lose your foot to frostbite or worse, wake up that hungry bear," I said, pulling at his boot.

He blinked, glancing down at me before moving to untie the lace. I dug into his pack on his back for a spare pair of socks.

"Shit," he breathed, fumbling to remove his boot. "That was way too close."

The flames roared between us and the bear still lying prone at the edge of the lake. Ainsley said that it wouldn't be down for long, and I didn't want to know when that'd be.

Tenason paused. His wet sock was discarded in the snow, and his bare foot looked as if it were already turning blue, but he was staring towards Ainsley controlling the fire surrounding us.

"I think I love her," Tenason whispered.

"I'm not so sure the feeling is mutual." I shook my head, tossing him a fresh pair of socks. "Come on, hurry up. If that bear wakes when you're barefoot, I'm not waiting for you to catch up."

That moved Tenason into motion and he quickly pulled on the clean sock, doubling the one soaked foot with both socks, and shoving his feet into his still wet boot. It would have to do for now. But even as the reality that he'd almost died seemed to settle in, his body still trembling with both fear and cold, Tenason couldn't seem to keep the goofy smile off his face.

FIFTEEN

The fire surrounding us kept the Ice Bear at bay. It woke a few hours later from the blow Ainsley had aimed its way with a large rock at the end of her sling. The Ice Bear was dazed and stalked away as the sun rose over the mountaintop.

As the lingering flames were extinguished, Aelish directed us back onto the lake where it was easier to walk, but we stayed closer to the edge this time.

We had moved a little off course, but by mid-morning, we were on the other side of the lake at the base of Canvas Mountain.

"The trail gets a bit steep from here." Aelish pointed to a sharp incline ahead of us.

I huffed a laugh, staring nearly straight up before I followed Annia up the path. It was a single-person track that at times ended upon a steep cliff we'd have to climb up, and at other times the rocks were so loose and slippery, we had to go one at a time to avoid kicking rocks onto the person below us. One by one, we'd travel to each checkpoint, remaining hidden from falling rocks as best we could. Even though my powers were muted, my Carbon body was strong. Still, the trek was dangerous for me.

By the time we stopped for the day, my hands ached, and there was blood and dirt under my nails. I leaned against Max, closing my eyes. He wrapped his arms around me and pulled me in.

Annia and Aelish were making supper, and Tenason was doing a good job of annoying Ainsley, as she set up a shelter that we'd stay in for the night.

"How are you holding up?" Max whispered.

It felt like weeks since Max and I had been alone or even had a private conversation.

"I'm okay," I answered, glancing up at him. "You?"

"I'm okay, too," Max said, but his eyes told me there was something else bugging him.

I raised a brow.

He sighed. "It's just all a bit… overwhelming. With my dad, I mean."

Guilt tugged in my chest when I realized that with everything going on, I hadn't even asked him how he was feeling about it all. I was too focused on myself to even check in with him.

"I guess I just always thought he saw me as weak or useless. I never thought how he must've felt all those years not knowing where I was or if I was safe." Max paused as he considered it. "I mistook his overprotectiveness for doubt in my abilities—in me. He just didn't want to lose me again, like he thought he once had."

I squeezed his hand, as he gave me a crooked smile. "He cares about you, a lot." I kissed his cheek. "So do I."

He tugged me closer, lifting my hand to his lips where he kissed the silver-and-copper ring on my pinky. "Do you?" A devilish smile spread across his face as Max brushed his nose against my cheek, and his lips met my neck in a tender kiss.

I tilted my head to the side and sighed. My eyes drifted closed.

There was a throat clearing behind us, and my eyes shot open as I turned toward the sound.

"Could you guys at least get a room?" Tenason teased, as he stood a few feet away with his arms crossed. "Food is ready." He shook his head at us before turning away, and I blushed a little with embarrassment.

I made to stand up, but Max pulled me back down for one more kiss and said, "I wish we had a room."

I tried to hide my smile. I jokingly pushed him away and headed toward the others, but he caught the quirk of my lips. The flutter in my chest also wished for the same thing.

My sleep was restless as the bitter cold and the winds kept me awake. By the next morning, we were all exhausted and still had one more steep cliff to climb.

Annia went first, setting out the path for us and securing a rope with anchor points. I did my best to not look down, but staring straight up the icy cliff wasn't much better. Aelish was next, with Max and me to follow. My fingers were already frozen, cracked, and bleeding, but I followed their path carefully as I climbed higher. I wasn't sure how many of my healing abilities were working; they could be muted just like my powers, because everything ached endlessly.

Below me, Tenason was arguing with Ainsley about who would go next.

"Ladies first," he offered.

Ainsley crossed her arms. "You first. I need to be sure you make it all the way up."

Tenason sighed. "Fine, but don't say I didn't offer." He followed behind me up the cliff.

Annia had reached the top and was securing the rope as we moved along. We all had a strap around our waists attached to the main rope, but if any of us were to slip, the rope wouldn't hold us all for long. So I took each step with care as my shoulders screamed with every inch I pulled upward.

"Wow, you can see forever from here," Tenason marveled from below. I chose to not look. I'd wait until I reached the top. "Are you seeing this, guys?"

I mumbled under my breath for him to shut up, but it was Ainsley who said, "Just keep moving." The tension in her voice told me she was as uncomfortable as I was.

Aelish had reached the top, and Max was only a few feet away.

"What? Are you afraid of heights?" Tenason called down to Ainsley.

She gritted her teeth. "Not heights. The fall."

Tenason chuckled as he continued up. "Well, I'm glad to see you are human after all."

Ainsley growled at him but kept her focus on the climb.

Max had reached the top, and I was only a few feet away when I heard a distant rumble. We all stopped and listened to the sound. It was almost as if a thunderstorm was nearby, but there were no clouds, and the sky was clear blue.

The rocks around us shook, and it only took me a second to realize what it was. An avalanche.

"Move!" Aelish cried as Max stumbled to climb back down the rope. I squished down farther, running into Tenason below me, who was also trying to scramble down.

The thunder grew louder as the avalanche neared. I was beside Tenason, clinging to the rocks as Aelish and Annia climbed over the edge and hugged the rock wall. Max was above both of us, his gaze fixed on me as he reached down to help, but he was too far up.

"Stay tight to the rocks and hold on," Aelish yelled over the booming snow slide coming our way.

My breaths were quick and shallow as pure terror filled my every thought. The rocks shook, and small pieces crumbled under my hands. I gasped, reaching, and I gripped a new hold as the one I had previously clung to broke apart. My gaze locked on Max who was searching for a way to reach me. He wouldn't make it, and if he continued to move down, he'd be exposed to the snow slide rumbling towards us.

"Stay," I managed to scream out.

He hesitated, glancing up as small drifts of snow began to

fall over the edge. He pulled himself closer to the wall.

My heartbeat was raging in my ears, and the thunderous sound of the avalanche drew closer. My mouth felt dry and every terrifying thought spilled into my mind. The drop below us. The crushing of the snow. Being suffocated underneath it, trapped with no way out. I couldn't catch my breath.

The first larger chunks of snow flowed over the edge, sending mists of cold ice and rock into my hair and down my jacket. Below me, I heard a scream, and the rope around my waist tightened. I had barely enough time to dig my feet into the cliff before the weight of Ainsley would've taken me down with her.

She had lost her footing and was dangling from the cliff side; her body swung precariously away from the shelter of the rock wall, right into the path the snow pounding down on us would take.

"Sawyer, hold tight!" Tenason ordered as he climbed down toward Ainsley, and the full weight of her became my burden.

I grimaced and dug my nails into the rock that was becoming brittle and slippery under my fingers. I tried to steady my breaths as panic began to make my vision spotty. If Ainsley were taken down, she'd take all of us with her.

"Hurry," Aelish called from above.

I glanced down to see Tenason only a few feet away from Ainsley, but the rope had pushed her away from the cliff. Tenason couldn't quite reach her. Their hands swiped for each other as the snow rolling over the rock became thicker and harder. A large ice block crashed down and narrowly missed Tenason.

"Reach, come on!" Tenason screamed, but Ainsley was too

focused on the fall and the snow coming down on us. "Don't look down, look at me. Ainsley, focus on me."

She drew her attention away from the ground and met Tenason's eyes. She reached a hand out, and Tenason yanked her into him. He shielded her between him and the cliff as the thick snow swept past us so quickly the wind threatened to take me with it.

I held my breath, closing my eyes, and I was sure I was screaming, but all I could hear was the roar of snow and rocks and debris passing us. Then everything went still.

As quickly as it came, the avalanche stopped. An eerie silence hung in the air. I glanced down to find the line of trees below us gone. The entire path down to the frozen lake was nothing but a stark, white trail of snow.

I released a shaking breath, and as the adrenaline seemed to dissipate, my body suddenly felt tired and exhausted. We had to keep moving.

Tenason still held Ainsley, who hadn't taken her eyes off him. "You're okay, I've got you," he said.

I looked up to see Annia testing the snow above us. She shook her head.

"We'll have to go around it," Aelish said, as they began climbing to our right, following the cliff to a narrow opening the avalanche hadn't filled.

Max hesitated, waiting for me, but I knew if I was tired and drained from the climb, so was he. I nodded to let him know I was okay, even though my heart still beat way too fast, and he began following behind Aelish. Below me, Ainsley regained her composure and climbed ahead of Tenason, who was only a few feet away and watched each step she took. I did my best not to look at the drop, not to see the strong, tall trees destroyed, and think how that could have been us.

Finally, we reached far enough over that we could continue our climb up. When I reached the top, Max pulled me the rest of the way, and I nearly fell over from exhaustion, as my arms and legs were heavy and throbbing. Max helped Ainsley and Tenason over the edge before we all sat down in the snow, catching our breath.

"That was close," Max mumbled to my right. "Are you okay?"

I nodded as I dropped my head down and took in a deep breath. That was way too close. This trip was becoming more and more dangerous, and I just hoped it'd be worth it. It had to be.

I shook my head, letting out a long breath as I tried to remove the image of the fall and what could have been from my memory. The others were just as shaken. Ainsley still clung to Tenason's side, and he watched her with concern, but he didn't dare move.

"Now where?" I asked, glancing around us. We were nearly at the top of Canvas Mountain. A small cloud hit the sharp, pointed edge, and the white trail from the avalanche cleared a path to the top. There was no distinct entrance to the mountain, and I wondered where the Mountain Men would be living in a place like this.

"They will come for us," Aelish said.

I narrowed my eyes, about to ask what she meant, when a small prick pinched the back of my neck. I reached for my neck where a small, feathered tip stuck out, revealing a needle. Before I had a chance to get any words out, I saw the same feather-tipped needle pierce the others, and within seconds, they fell to their sides.

I stood on shaky legs. My mouth didn't work, and my lids grew tired. I reached for Max, who was limp in the snow beside me. A second pinch met my arm. I looked down to find another needle sticking out. I pulled it from my arms as my limbs grew weak, and I fell to my knees. The needle was like a tiny dart, and as I held it up to investigate, my vision doubled and became blurry.

The third and final dart hit me in the back, and I fell face first into the cold snow as everything went black.

SIXTEEN

My eyes were heavy. I tried peel them open, but the sunlight burned through them. My head was pounding. It took me a second to realize I was lying on the floor, and that the floor was solid stone, not snow.

Clumsily, I pulled myself to my knees. My head rested in my hands as the room around me spun and went in and out of focus. Blinking a few times, my eyes slowly focused on the figure in front of me, a tall man dressed head-to-toe in white with a white fur vest across his broad chest and a tight white shirt beneath that almost looked like it was made of leather. His blond hair fell over his shoulders and looked as though it weaved into his long, white beard. Piercing violet eyes stared down on me.

"Where am I?" I tried to look around me, but my head pounded with the movement. A heavy headache formed at my temples. I went to stand but found there were chains around my ankle.

Panic set in as my vision narrowed in on my surroundings. I kicked against the chain around my legs. "What is this? What's going on?"

A muffled sound came behind me, and I turned to find Max and Tenason on their knees a few feet away. They were tied up around their ankles, wrists, and waist, so they couldn't move their arms. A gag was wrapped around their mouths, so their words were muffled.

I shot up, lunging toward them, but I was pulled down as my chains tightened, and I was out of reach. Max's eyes widened as they darted from me to the men who stood behind me.

I spun around, throwing my elbow to the side of one of their legs, making his knee wobble. Two strong arms reached me before I could inflict any more pain on his counterpart. The arms pulled me to my feet, so I was facing the man in white.

"We are told you are the leader of this group?" he said with the same subtle accent as Aelish.

I glanced around me, my vision finally focusing to find I was in a cavern I assumed was inside the mountain. On one side of the cavern were the Mountain Men, hundreds of them, all in white. They watched my every movement. To my right stood Aelish, Annia, and Ainsley. They weren't tied up like Max and Tenason, but two men stood on either side of them.

"What do you want from me?" I asked, turning back to the man.

He raised an eyebrow as he surveyed me. "I believe it was *you* who wanted something from *us*."

I huffed. "Is this normally how you treat guests seeking help?"

"Yes," he said with an expression as unmovable as stone.

I glared at the men holding me. They held tight before they released their grip and stepped only a few inches away, still within arm's reach. I shook out my arms and rubbed my neck, sore from the dart that had knocked me out.

"We came to ask for your assistance. There's a war coming, and if we don't stop them first, they will destroy the entire world, including your mountain here," I said.

"We can take care of ourselves," the man said.

"No, you can't." I took a step forward, and the chain tightened again around my ankle, so I stopped a few inches away. "They have an army of thousands of elite Carbons. Human-like machines that are faster and stronger than any human."

"We are strong."

"Not strong enough." I let out a frustrated sigh. "Two of their Carbons destroyed an entire island. Three nearly took out our village. The next time they come, they will bring every one of them, and that number is in the thousands. We don't stand a chance alone and neither will you. The only way we can all live is to work together."

The man in white turned to the rest of his tribe. No one said a word, but they all individually nodded a yes or a no.

Finally, he turned back to me. "We do not help those who are unworthy, and so far you have shown us nothing." He nodded to the men surrounding me who went to take me away.

"Wait," I shouted, pulling against the strong men holding me back. "You haven't even let me prove that I am worthy."

They stopped, and I shrugged off their hold again moving

closer to their leader. The chain stopped me once more, and I growled at the man holding the other end. "There has to be some way I can prove to you that we deserve your help."

The old leader thought before he gave a reluctant nod. "There is one way. We will let you rest for the night. The trial will start in the morning."

The chain around my leg tugged again, yanking me away. "Trial? What trial?"

"It will be a fight to the death," Aelish said when the men had left us to our cell. We were brought down a flight of stone stairs into a room built into the side of the mountain. There was a solid steel door on one side and stone surrounding the remaining sides. No windows or way out except for the door we were shoved through.

"To the death?" My mouth gaped open. My fingers stumbled as I helped Max remove the chains tied around him.

"Don't do it. Let's just leave. Tell them we changed our minds, and we don't need their help anymore," Max suggested.

"Viktor won't let you leave now," Aelish said. Noting my confusion, she continued, "Viktor, the man you were talking to is the leader of the Mountain Men. When he has made a decision, it is set in stone. They will not go back on their word."

"Great," I mumbled, slumping to the rock floor and resting my head back. "Who will I fight? Viktor?"

"No, they will choose the strongest one. Probably one of the younger men," Ainsley clarified as she sat next to Tenason, who was quick to notice her presence.

"I'll do it. I'll fight whomever they send." Max paced in front of me, stepping around a sprawled out Annia who seemed to be taking a nap.

"You can't. He has chosen Sawyer, so she must fight," Aelish countered.

Max let out a frustrated cry. "Why did you bring us here? Did you know beforehand they were going to do this?"

Aelish gave Max a weak smile. "I would never bring you into a danger I did not think you were capable of overcoming. The Mountain Men are necessary for us to win this war, and I know Sawyer is worthy of their help. She will show them tomorrow."

I wasn't so sure. Those men were twice my size and had the strength of the mountain behind them. I didn't even have my powers to help me. My Carbon body was strong, but I was weak and tired from the trip, and that didn't give me confidence I'd have any advantage against someone equally as strong. I suddenly felt like my former self, Sawyer the Watcher, yet I didn't feel as confident or cocky as I once had.

I grabbed Max's hand as he tried to pace past me, tugging him down to the seat next to me. "What's done is done. We'll just have to wait for tomorrow to see who my opponent is, and I hope I can beat him."

SEVENTEEN

KENZIE

The cell around him was pitch black, and the walls seemed to be closing in on him. He hadn't eaten in four days, and not because he wasn't given food, because he couldn't keep it down. The burning pain running through him wouldn't settle enough for him to eat.

It was because of this Kenzie was certain the vision before him was a hallucination. Even his twisted mind couldn't come up with something as horrifying as what he kept seeing. The vision was slowly driving him mad.

It started out simple with an image he was familiar with. He was walking down the metal hallway of Coleman's space station toward Sector 7. He didn't know why he was going there, or what for, but an internal tug called to him, leading him there. He continued his march forward down the bare, silent hallway. The only sound was the echo of his footsteps.

As he rounded the last corner, something changed. The lights flickered low, and the hallway before him was dark and stale. He took a few more steps forward before he hit something. A glass wall divided the hallway, so he couldn't move any farther.

Kenzie's hands searched the smooth glass before he tried pounding against it with his shoulder to break through. Where did this glass come from? It was never there before.

A movement on the other side of the glass caught his attention. He paused. The end of the hallway was pitch black. He had to squint his eyes to see what was hiding in the shadows, but his eyes couldn't fix on anything.

"Who's there?" he called out. "Show yourself."

He waited, but no one answered his call. A chill traveled down his spine, and Kenzie had the weird feeling of wanting to flee, but his feet wouldn't move.

The shadow moved again. Inhumanly quick, the black, mutated body scrambled on twisted limbs toward the glass, slamming into it so hard that Kenzie jumped back, falling onto the floor. Kenzie scrambled to get away from the glass.

The thick glass held strong against the mutated being as it pounded its fists. The creature's mouth opened, and a gutteral scream came out, rattling Kenzie's eardrums and sending a shiver down his spine.

Cautiously, Kenzie stood to his feet and took a tentative step forward. He tried to get a better look at the unusual beast before him.

The creature was covered in the same black scales like Coleman had, only they covered every inch of its body. Its arms and legs twitched and quivered with each movement, and its mouth revealed broken, rotted teeth. Kenzie smelled the stench of rotting skin from his side of the glass.

Kenzie stepped an inch forward as the creature looked up to him, only its eyes didn't meet Kenzie's—it had no eyes. Where its eyes should've been were two deep gouged holes pitted with dry, black blood instead.

With a hitched gasp, Kenzie took a step back as his eyes fixed again on the dark hallway before him… Where dozens more black creatures stepped out of the shadow.

A bolt of white lightning blasted through the beasts, racing across the pack of wild creatures like a strong wind, and they were all gone. Swift and brutal and quick.

But the fear remained.

EIGHTEEN

The man who stood before me might as well have been an Ice Bear. He was as large as one, wore the same glare, had the snarled expression of one, and he wore all white like the other Mountain Men. His white fur vest hung thick against his bare, veined muscles.

He was to be my opponent, and I was regretting this whole trip.

"The fight will continue until there is only one left," Viktor said. He stood at the center of the cavern where I'd woken up the day before.

A cool breeze filtered in from somewhere, but torches lined the cavern walls, bringing in not only light, but heat. Overhead, a stalactite hung from the ceiling, sparkling almost iridescent in the firelight that bounced off of it. There was a subtle smell of sulfur from somewhere, and only one exit that I could see from where I stood.

The rest of the Mountain Men circled around us, and both Max and Tenason were tied up again, although this time they at least didn't have a gag over their mouths.

Viktor spoke again, and I drew my attention back to him. "Before you are four weapons, you may choose two."

At my feet lay a hatchet, a long spear, a hunting knife, and a sharp, barbed rope. My opponent nodded and made a motion to let me choose first. I went with the spear and the hunting knife, two weapons I was familiar with.

The grin on the ox of a man before me had me second-guessing my choices as he twirled the hatchet in his hand and wrapped the barbed rope around the other.

"I think it's only fair I know the name of my opponent," I said, stalling.

Viktor's eyebrows rose before he inclined his head. "You will fight Vance, the youngest of our tribe, and my son."

My eyes widened. I cursed under my breath, feeling my heart rate spike. I'd be fighting for the assistance of the Mountain Men, but to win them over, I had to kill their leader's son? This wasn't going to go over well.

"Are you ready?" Vance asked. His violet eyes, the same as his father's, glimmered with amusement.

I gulped before I nodded.

I didn't have a chance to say yes before Vance brought the hatchet down hard, swinging for my head. I pulled the long spear up to block it, and the hatchet sliced clean through the wooden handle. Splinters of wood flew in the air.

Vance smirked as the sharp end of the spear skipped away

from me. Great, I had a stub of a stick and a knife left.

I stepped back, light on my feet, as Vance whipped the barbed rope overhead before slashing it down to my legs. It skidded across the smooth stone floor. I jumped over it just in time and dove to the side before it swung back over my head.

"Get up!" Max urged from behind me, and I pushed myself to my feet before the hatchet slammed down upon the spot where I had been.

My focus narrowed on Vance. I was aware of the other men around us, but the cavern walls seemed to be closing in on us, leaving only me and him alone. I could hear Max yelling orders. The rest of the room fell silent.

I darted to my left, leaving a little more room between Vance and I. He glared down on me, the barbed rope whipping wildly behind him.

The rope sliced through the air again, aimed for my head, and I was too slow to get down so I raised my arm up in defense. I screamed in pain as the barbs sliced through my jacket and skin, taking flesh. Blood filled my shredded sleeve, and the wound didn't begin to heal, as the Muted Forest took that ability away from me, too.

Gritting my teeth, I pushed myself to my feet. My heart thundered in my ears, and my shredded arm throbbed with each heartbeat. I lunged for Vance, my shoulder connecting with his stomach, taking the air out of his lungs. He fell with a thud to the ground. I tried to pin him down, but he was too strong for me and tossed me off like a rag doll. I slammed into the hard stone wall and my vision spotted for a moment before

I shook my head, blinking away the slight ringing in my ears. The Mountain Men stood stoic around us. None had moved. They barely flinched at the blood covering the floors or Vance's white clothes. Tenason's eyes were wide and wild while Max was screaming something. *Move. Keep moving.*

I did. I kept advancing, running for Vance and skidding to the ground on my knees. I slashed my knife at the back of his leg when he tried to push off and stand. He grimaced as he swung the barbed rope at me. This time, I was ready and brought the broken half of the spear up to block the rope.

It looped around the wooden rod twice, and with a sharp pull, I was able to rip it out of Vance's grip. He growled. I tossed the rope and broken spear far enough away that he couldn't retrieve it, behind the first row of men still watching. He was forced to fight me in close quarters.

He might've been bigger and stronger than me, but I was quicker.

Vance circled. The hatchet spun nimbly in his hand as he searched for an opening. He limped on his wounded leg, only a bit, but it was enough that I used it to my advantage.

All around me, the room was silent. A quick glance told me that wasn't true, the Mountain Men were shouting, cheering, but I heard nothing. I could only hear Max, so I focused on him.

"Keep your guard hand down, Sawyer," he shouted. I readjusted my guard, making sure to not expose my ribs. "He steps back before he lunges. Watch for it!"

I did as Max said and watched as Vance took a step back before lunging. He swung the hatchet through the air. I spun to my left and narrowly missed being decapitated by the sharp blade.

Vance turned on me again, and this time when he took a step back, I lunged first. My knife sliced for his midsection, and he pulled away just in time. My momentum carried me closer, and with my free hand, I grabbed his wrist, keeping his arm and the hatchet from coming down on me. I locked my shoulder and secured my arm to ensure he couldn't move, but his sheer strength caused my entire body to shake.

I jabbed my knife at him, but his arms were longer than mine, and he was just barely out of reach. He gripped my wrist holding the knife, twisting it hard. My face contorted with pain as he brought my wrist down against his knee. He smashed it once, twice, and on the third try, the knife flew out of my hand. I was sure my wrist was broken.

It was me, him, and the hatchet. He had the upper hand.

I brought my foot down on the inside of his knee, and it buckled, falling to the ground. Even kneeling he was enormous, his head at my height now. Using my busted hand, I pushed back on his arm, which was still pulling the hatchet closer to my head. With one last kick, I aimed a knee to his chin, but it only slowed him down for a second before he smiled a bloody, toothy grin. He narrowed his eyes.

I had to stay close. There was no way to escape him if I let go of his arm. That hatchet would be dug deep into me within seconds, and my only chance was to try to turn the table.

In one swift movement, I dropped to my knees, loosening my hold on his arm and causing the hatchet to hammer down and embed in my shoulder. I grimaced in pain but I didn't stop. I spun around with a quick push off of my outside leg, and I took the hatchet with me. It burned as I ripped it out of my shoulder. I twisted around, now at Vance's side, and aimed the bladeless end of the hatchet for the back of his head.

He dropped down hard, blood seeping from his head wound and drenching his white-blond hair crimson.

I dug my knee into his back and aimed the hatchet for his exposed neck. I swung to bring it down on him, but I stopped only inches from his death.

"Yield?" I asked.

Vance twisted his neck around to see me. His eyes widened as he looked from me to the hatchet, inches from his skin. His mouth opened, but he didn't know what to say. He froze.

"There is no yielding. There is only one winner," Viktor said a few feet away.

The Mountain Men had gone silent. Max had gone silent. The only sound was our panted breaths and the soft whistle from the wind outside.

I aimed a glare at Viktor, pushed off of Vance, and stepped back. I took the hatchet and tossed it at Viktor's feet. "I'd rather not kill my best ally," I said.

Viktor looked surprised and confused. Vance didn't know if he should move or say anything. He stayed on the floor where I left him, but his eyes were focused on me.

Viktor looked to the hatchet before he kicked it toward Vance. "Then you finish it, son."

Vance looked from me to the hatchet. His hand gripped the handle, and he pushed himself to his feet. His hand trembled, and I kept my eyes locked on him, hoping, praying I had read him correctly.

His eyes darted from me to his father before he dropped the hatchet. "I yield," he said.

Viktor's violet eyes filled with fire. The Mountain Men who circled us voiced their confusion as Vance looked to me and gave a sharp nod.

"Enough!" Viktor yelled, his voice echoing so loud I swore the mountain shook, and the crowd grew quiet. "Seeing as there was no winner, we will have to discuss if we will or won't assist you. We will give you our answer in a week's time."

"But Father—" Vance started, but he was cut off by his father's glare.

"A week is too long. We can't sit around here waiting for you to decide," I argued. "You wanted me to prove I was worthy. Well, I just did. I proved I could be both strong and merciful. I proved I am deserving of your help."

Viktor watched me from a distance as he thought it through. "One week's time is what I am offering you and that is all. You are free to leave. We know how to find you." He glanced to where Aelish, Annia, and Ainsley stood a few feet from Max near the back of the room.

"Only a coward would go against his own word," I spat as Viktor turned to leave. He turned around slowly, and his cold glare met mine.

"Only a coward would be unable to finish his enemy. A coward who just might do the same in a battle where many more lives would be at stake," Viktor scoffed. "A true leader considers all of his men. And will sacrifice any one of them for the greater good, even his own son. A leader does not lead his men into a battle they cannot win unless all of them are willing to die for it."

With that he turned, leaving me standing defeated in the middle of the Mountain Men, even though I had won.

NINETEEN

By the afternoon, we were packed and ready to head back. The Mountain Men were gracious enough to provide us with a little food, but they wouldn't give us an answer. We had to leave knowing the entire trip may well have been a waste of our time. My wounds were hastily patched by Aelish and still stung.

Max was furious and angry I'd been put through all that just to be sent home with nothing. He'd wrapped my shredded arm and shoulder as best he could, using his own shirt, while Aelish splinted my wrist. The pain reminded me I wasn't entirely invincible and it humbled me.

The Mountain Men had also provided us with a quicker way home. They'd guide us to the edge of the forest on the backs of the Ice Bears they controlled.

I stood before an enormous bear that looked capable of eating me in a single bite, but the tame animal stood quietly and still. Vance reached down to help me up.

I gripped onto his strong arm. Vance was careful to hold onto my forearm as my wrist was still bandaged and broken. I would have to wait until we left this forest for it to heal properly, along with the deep gouge in my shoulder that stung every time I moved. Vance pulled me up to sit behind him. The bear moved, and I was forced to wrap my arms around Vance for fear that I'd fall off if I didn't.

Vance let out a low chuckle.

Max was on a bear behind me watching me with caution, followed by the rest of our crew, including a very uncomfortable Tenason, who was on one of the larger bears. He was squished between Ainsley and one of the men. Ainsley lounged on the bear with her arms resting behind her head.

"Could you please sit up?" Tenason growled over his shoulder. "We're both going to fall off if you keep lying like that."

Ainsley didn't move an inch. "You worry too much, little baby," she said, and the burly man at the front chuckled as he nudged Tenason.

"Little baby!" He laughed.

"Great. Now everyone's going to call me that," Tenason grumbled.

I couldn't help but smile as we made our way down the mountain toward the frozen lake.

The journey was much quicker on top of the Ice Bears. They covered twice the distance we did, even in the deep snow they were walking through. And when night fell, the bears continued.

"You can sleep if you'd like," Vance offered. He hadn't said much as we traveled, mostly asking questions about Coleman and his army of Carbons.

"It's fine. I'm not tired." I stifled a yawn. "How did you guys ever manage to tame these bears?" I sat taller and reached down to stroke the side of the enormous beast below me. It huffed through its large nose, and Vance chuckled, patting the side of its neck.

"My great-grandfather was the first to encounter one of the Ice Bears. He was on a hunting trip one day in the dead of winter when he stumbled upon the wild beast staring down on him from a peak above. He had nowhere to go, the path he had taken was steep and dangerous. Running would've been futile. So instead, he stood his ground, and he fought the bear." Vance's voice was low as the others around us slept. The only sound that filled the silence was the heavy paws crunching through deep snow. "On the third day, the bear and my great-grandfather were both clinging to life. A large storm swept through. Both knew they could not survive on their own, so on that day, the Ice Bear and my great-grandfather made a pact. The bear dug a deep hole in the snow and the rocks with its clawed paws, enough for both it and my great-grandfather to wait out the storm in. And then my great-grandfather lit a fire to surround the cave in warmth, and he tended to the bear's wounds."

Vance smiled at the thought of the pledge between the two.

"So, now all Ice Bears and Mountain Men live in harmony together, working together?" I asked.

"Yes. Each bear is paired with one of our men, and the bond

between the two is as close as family. When we are born, we are given a cub to grow with us, to learn and train together for the rest of our lives. If a Mountain Man or a bear were to die, it would be a wound deeper than death to lose the other. They could never replace the connection they once had," Vance explained.

"That's so sad." I frowned. To think of losing a bond like that had my heart clenching, and it brought back my memory of Chevy, with whom I had little time, but he was as close as family to me. I understood how hard it would be to replace that, to find another.

"It is not sad in our culture, for the Ice Bears live forever within us. Even when they are gone, they provide for us." Vance glanced over his shoulder at me, tapping the warm fur vest across his shoulder. "They are always with us. This vest protects us when the Ice Bears cannot. This vest, this layer of thick protection, was from my father's bear, that died two years ago after living a long and full life. These vests have been passed down to each man, to protect them and keep their strength with them, no matter where they go."

I pressed my hand against the vest, the thick fur was soft and warm, but beneath the fur was a layer within it. It felt as strong as Alatonion. That layer of protection made the Ice Bears hard to take down and protected the Mountain Men.

There was silence before Vance spoke again, "My father is a good man, and he will see that we need to help you. I will make sure of it."

"I hope so," I mumbled. "It's not just for our safety or our people… it's for you guys, too. There is no stopping Coleman and his army if they get through. We have to work together; it's the only way."

Vance nodded before he went quiet.

My lids were slowly drifting closed when Vance said, "Thank you."

"You don't have to thank me for not killing you. You didn't deserve to die, even if that makes me a coward," I said.

"No." Vance shook his head. "Thank you for not backing down and for fighting for what you know is right. A true warrior knows who his enemy is, and I am not your enemy."

"I know you aren't."

"I owe you a life debt, Sawyer, and the Mountain Men always pay their debts," Vance said. His words made me realize this trip hadn't been a waste. No matter what his father decided, I'd made an ally in Vance, and that was worth every moment of this journey.

We arrived at the edge of the village three days faster than when we had left. We'd avoided the Dred Wulfs territory on the other side of the river as best we could, and on the nights when we continued moving and came closer to them, I heard howling, but Vance assured me they would not dare cross the Ice Bears.

Dropping down from the bear, I gave it one last rub before nodding my thanks to Vance and the other men as they turned to head back to their homes.

"I will be seeing you soon, Sawyer," Vance said over his shoulder.

"I'm counting on it." I smiled.

Max was at my side, and I put my arm around his shoulder, thankful for his warmth against the cold weather. "Do you think they'll come?" he asked.

"I do." I smiled as we turned toward the direction of the village.

"We will be leaving you here," Aelish said. "Ainsley will stay with you. We can get word to her through the birds, or she can send word to us. We will prepare the Ladies of the Muted Forest for the battle to come."

"Thank you," I said. Even though I'd come back worse than when I left, our journey was an important one, and not just to find an ally. I'd found a strength within me beyond my powers.

She gave me a nod before she and Annia left us.

As we stepped into the forest that surrounded the village, just beyond the invisible boundaries of the Muted Forest, my powers once again circulated through me. Like a weight lifted from me as the gentle current seeped back in. My Carbon body healed my earlier wounds, and I was happy to have a sense of power back. I was also glad to know I didn't need them to win. If a time came when I didn't have my powers or they couldn't be used, I wasn't entirely useless. I had forgotten the skilled Watcher I was before I ever had these abilities.

Murray met us at the door when we reached the control room. "Will they help us?"

"We're not sure yet, but I believe they will," I said. Murray seemed to relax at the possibility of another ally against Coleman, even if there was no guarantee it'd be enough.

"You guys are okay?" He looked to my shredded jacket. I had tried to patch up my jacket during our journey, but the injured skin beneath it had already been repaired, along with the broken bone in my wrist mending itself back together.

I nodded.

"Good." Murray pulled me aside while the others headed for Theresa's kitchen to get some food. "There's something you should know. Something happened while you were away."

I narrowed my eyes and kept my voice quiet like Murray. "What?"

"It's Kenzie. He's gone, well, we don't know. But he won't eat or move. Keeps mumbling some nonsense about black creatures." Murray's eyes looked worried, and I wondered how anyone or anything could spook him. "He said he won't speak to anyone but you."

I sighed. Of course he'd only speak to me, because I was the only one who didn't want to speak to *him*.

"He knows about the cuff," Murray said quietly. "Well, he knows about something that is bound to him. I haven't given it to him, but the old lady, Aelish, told me to give it to him soon."

I frowned. "When did she tell you about this?"

"Before you left."

I bit the inside of my cheek before I nodded. "I'll talk to him. But we can't give him that cuff. It will make him stronger, unbeatable. We can't afford to give him a tool he could use against us."

Murray nodded. "I know, but she said we should trust him…"

Again, I frowned, but I shook my head. "Not yet, not now."

Murray gave my shoulder a squeeze before he returned to his post.

Max walked over with a muffin and a warm cup of tea in his hand. He passed them to me, and I greedily drank the whole cup. He watched me before he said, "You have to see him again, don't you?"

I nodded.

"Then I am coming with you," he stated. I didn't argue.

TWENTY

I wasn't prepared to see him like that. I was prepared for a version of Kenzie I'd grown accustomed to, a strong-willed, defiant version, the ever-obedient soldier. That wasn't who sat before me.

Even in only a week of not eating, his face was gaunt, and his shoulders looked boney through his gray T-shirt. He hardly looked up at us when Max and I stepped in front of the cell bars.

I did my best to compose myself and not crumble like my body threatened. "Are you on a hunger strike for a good reason at least?"

The hint of a smile poked through as his gaze settled on me. I noted his eyes focused on the little ring on my pinky, and I shoved my hands in my pocket. Kenzie swung his legs around, so he was seated at the end of his cot, facing me only a few inches from the bar.

"I couldn't eat, the pain was…" He shook his head, unable to explain.

My brows lifted, waiting. I passed him the muffin I had grabbed on my way to him through the bars. It sat in his hand, and he stared at it.

"They told me you would only speak to me," I said.

Kenzie nodded.

"Well, I'll only listen if you eat."

His eyes shifted from me to the muffin. He was so weak it nearly broke me. He was silent before he said, "I'm not hungry."

"Okay then, we'll come back when you are." I stepped around Max and went to round the corner.

"Wait!" he said. I stopped.

Turning back to face him, I raised an eyebrow. Reluctantly, he took a bite of the muffin, and I made my way back to the space in front of him.

"So, what is it you have to tell me?" I asked.

Kenzie's eyes shifted to Max, who stood beside me and leaned against the cement wall with his hands in his pockets. His glare didn't leave his face, and his jaw was locked, as the two stared each other down.

"Anything you have to tell me, you can say in front of Max. I'm going to tell him, anyways." I shrugged my shoulders, making sure it was clear there were no secrets between Max and me.

Kenzie grumbled before continuing, "I've been having visions. Dreams like you said your mom sent you. I think she sent me one, too, and they won't go away until I figure it out," he said.

"What happens in the visions?"

Kenzie shook as he closed his eyes and took a deep breath before he began. "I'm onboard the space station where Coleman is, only the halls are empty. I end up in a hallway divided by a glass wall, and on the other side there are... creatures. Black and scaled, like Coleman was, except they are covered from head-to-toe. It starts with only one, but there were more. So many more." He rubbed his hand over his face, and the muffin fell to the ground.

"Like Coleman?" I wondered out loud. "Do you think the virus he had has spread?"

Kenzie didn't take his hand away from his face as he nodded.

"What else was there? Do you remember where you were? Any other details we might need to know?" I asked.

Kenzie dropped his hand as he thought back to the vision. "I was being pulled toward Sector 7."

"Pulled toward? By whom?" I asked.

"Not who—what. Something was telling me to go there, like a string pulling me toward that hallway for some reason." Kenzie's brows scrunched, as he thought. "It's the same pull I feel here, now." He looked around the cell, like he was searching for something. "You guys are hiding something, something that is mine, and I can feel it calling for me."

I took a step backward at the anger rising in his voice. "I'm sorry, Kenzie, but I can't give that to you."

He slammed his fist against the bar and I flinched. Max had his gun pointed at Kenzie, ready to fire if he even raised a finger toward me. But Kenzie's arm fell limp to his side and he stilled. "The two are connected. You can't keep it from me much longer because whatever those *things* are, the only way to stop them is connected to whatever it is that you're hiding."

I shifted on my feet, unsure whom to trust at this point, knowing neither decision was the right one.

Max took a step forward. "Until you can convince even *me* that you're not going to kill every one of us the second we give it to you, it's staying locked up. So don't even bother asking again."

Kenzie glared at Max, and then his eyes shifted to me, pleading for me to give it to him, to stop the pain and the pull the cuff had over him.

I shook my head. "He's right, Kenzie. You said yourself that you can't be trusted. You have no control over your own actions. We'd be giving you a loaded gun and trusting you to not turn it on us."

Kenzie's head dropped.

I turned to leave. "Wait!" Kenzie cried.

I stopped, looking over my shoulder at him.

"What if I can give you something, something that will help you find Coleman without me having to actually give you the information?" he said.

I inclined my head for him to continue.

"This pull, this… drive, is much stronger than the hold Coleman has over me. I think—I know—I can keep his orders at bay if something else takes its place," Kenzie suggested. "I'm not promising it will be permanent, or that I've broken any hold he has over me, but as long as this drive for whatever you're hiding from me keeps pulling me, I don't think I'd hurt you."

Max scoffed, "You can hardly convince yourself this is true. There's no way we're taking that risk."

I was inclined to believe Max, but there was something in Kenzie's eyes that rang with familiarity, something I was drawn to trust. I glanced at Max, and his mouth hung open.

"No way. You don't believe him, do you?" Max said. "He's a liar and a traitor. He'll wait for you to turn your back, and then he'll stab as deep as he can."

"It was meant for him," I whispered. "Aelish told us it was for him. And she told your dad to trust him. Do you trust *them*?"

Max threw his head back as he paced toward the rear wall. He slammed his fist against the cement. It was silent before he turned around to face me. Max kept his eyes on me while he asked Kenzie, "What do you have to offer? What information will you give us?"

"Access to a back door," Kenzie said.

Max's eyebrows rose with suspicion.

"I can't reveal where Coleman is simply because I don't know. But I have access to all his systems, and I'm sure your men can find a way to hack into their database, so you can track him down. I won't be breaking the control because I was ordered not to reveal anything, and I'm not, it'd be up to you to figure it out."

I gave Max a look that asked him to trust me.

Max let out another long sigh and ran his hand through his hair. "All right, you give us access to Coleman, and we'll discuss giving you the… item." Max was careful to not reveal too much. "We can have Sam over here in a minute. You can direct him what to do."

Kenzie shook his head. "It's not that simple. I need my tablet, one connected to Coleman's server. You won't gain access to anything through your own computers. You need mine. And only my retina scan will open it."

"And where exactly can we find this tablet of yours?" Max asked.

"Cytos. In Sub 9."

TWENTY ONE

"No! No way. There is not a chance in hell we're sending him to Cytos, no matter what he says." Max was adamantly against the idea, and he made that clear to the others sitting around the table. Murray was at the front, flanked by a few officers. Lankey sat across from me in a lazy, slouched position, twiddling his thumbs. Tenason and Ainsley were seated to my right, the latter quietly observing everything.

"We wouldn't send him alone. He'd be watched the entire time," I argued.

Max turned on me. "He could kill a hundred of our trained men in the blink of an eye."

"So we leave the metal cast on his hand." I shrugged.

"This could be a trap. How do we know Coleman isn't just

trying to draw us out into his territory and using Kenzie to get to us?" Max said.

"We don't," I stated. "But at this point, do we have any other choice?"

Max opened his mouth but then clamped it shut with a huff. I placed a hand on his lap, wishing I could wipe away the worry across his face. He knew better than anyone what Kenzie was capable of, the jagged scar on his side was a reminder forever, but I needed him to trust me. I met his gaze, squeezing his leg.

"They're building an army, one that is bigger, stronger, and faster than every one of us. If we don't have some sort of inside track as to what Coleman's plans are, or when he will arrive, we don't know how to prepare," I said. "This is no longer about trusting *him*, Max. It's about what will help us out in a war we know is coming."

"I think Sawyer is right, Max," Murray said from the end of the table. He'd kept quiet the entire time we'd explained everything to them, but I noted how he was watching Max. "If there was any other way, we'd have done it already. But without knowing where Coleman is, we're just sitting ducks out here. Exposed now that he knows exactly where we are."

I watched as Max's shoulders deflated but he didn't argue. His hand rested on mine where it still sat on his leg, and he held it tightly.

"Bring Kenzie in. We'll find out exactly where it is, and what we need to do to get it. And I'll send in the cavalry if we have to," Murray assured Max. The officer on his right stalked out of the room, returning only a moment later with a chained-up

Kenzie between him and another guard.

"Well, son, what's your plan to get us this tablet of yours?" Murray asked.

Kenzie shifted awkwardly on his feet, and I wanted to offer him a seat. He looked so weak, but I stayed where I was. Just the thought of being concerned for his wellbeing left a tinge of guilt in my gut, and I held tighter to Max's hand.

"Sawyer and I will go in and retrieve it. It's in my quarters of Sub 9. We'll be in and out in less than an hour, assuming you guys have transport from here to Cytos."

Max stood up, releasing my hand and nearly knocked over the table. "Oh, come on. You really think we're going to send just you and Sawyer? You think we're that stupid?"

"Apparently so." Kenzie narrowed his eyes. Tenason had to jump between the two men before Max tackled Kenzie.

"Sit down," I said, pulling on Max's sleeve.

He sat, shaking his head the entire time.

"Kenzie, we'll be sending as many men as we can carry."

"They can't come." Kenzie shrugged his shoulders. "Coleman left Sub 9 standing as a backup. The rest of Cytos is destroyed, but that one building still stands, for his use. Which means it is still fully programmed and will sense any intruder in the building."

"Then how do ya intend ta get in there yerself?" Lankey piped in.

"I'm not an intruder. And the system won't be alarmed if a Carbon enters." Kenzie shifted his glare back to Max. "So the only ones who can enter the building are Sawyer and I."

"Well, that's just great." Max threw his hands up, looking at the ceiling. "Why am I not surprised?"

My chest clenched as Kenzie met my stare. We'd be going into Sub 9, alone. I swallowed, unable to decide if this was a terrible decision, and I should back out now, or trust the man who had already tried to kill me more than once. What if we were wrong, what if I was wrong, and this was a trap? This didn't feel right, but Kenzie held my stare and gave me a small nod, as if to say *trust me.*

"You won't be going in there unguarded, son," Murray said to Kenzie. "We'll be outfitting you with a few items for insurance purposes."

Kenzie gave him a smirk. "I would expect nothing less from you, Commander."

Murray nodded. "Good, then we'll get everything set and leave in the morning, if that's all right with you, Sawyer?"

I nodded, numb and unable to speak. *I can do this, we need the tablet, it's the only way.*

"Great, then it's settled." Murray dismissed the team.

Max pushed his chair back and stormed past me before I could stop him. He paused only inches away from Kenzie. "You're looking a little frail to carry all the weight we're going to add to you. I hear exploding vests are a bit heavy." He patted Kenzie on the stomach before he left the room.

I stormed behind Max to catch up to him, feeling Kenzie's gaze trail me the entire way. Once we were outside, I grabbed Max's arm. "Will you just stop already?"

He jerked his arm out of my grip and continued walking away.

"Don't you trust me?" I stopped in the middle of the crowded courtyard.

To my surprise, Max stopped, too. He dropped his head to his chest before he turned to face me. He closed the distance between us and gently grabbed my hands.

"I don't trust him, and I don't trust this plan. Ever since we got back here, we've been blindly listening to everyone else tell us what to do and where to go. That's not like us, that's not like *you*," he said. "It feels like we have no control, and it doesn't feel right."

"But you trust me, right?" I asked. "And you trust Aelish and your dad?"

He nodded, looking down with shame at our hands.

"Then please, just trust me. If he steps out of line, if anything happens, I'll take care of it. I can do it this time." I didn't want to say the words but I had to. And this time, I meant it—I truly meant it, even though it killed a part of me. I had trusted Kenzie over and over again, but I wouldn't be tricked again. If he tried to kill me, if he betrayed us again, I would end him. I just prayed I didn't have to. "We are desperate, Max, and we need to find some sort of upper hand. If getting this tablet will give us even the slightest advantage, then it's worth the risk."

He pulled me into his chest and wrapped his arms around me. I locked my arms around his waist and took a deep breath of his scent. Like the forest we came out of, it smelled of pine and maple.

"I'm sorry," he whispered. "I just don't want to lose you."

I tilted my chin up to face him. "You won't," I said. I knew it was a promise I shouldn't have made. There was no way to guarantee I'd be able to keep it, but it was a promise I was willing to fight for. One I'd do everything in my power to keep.

TWENTY TWO

Max wasn't kidding when he said he intended to load up Kenzie with everything he could to ensure that if he stepped out of line, he'd regret it. Max had a heavy vest laid out for Kenzie with electric shocks throughout—the trigger was in my left pocket. The metal cage around his hand would stay, and three more chains would be added. One around each ankle to ensure he only had enough room to walk, and another to secure his wrists to the chain around his waist, so his arms couldn't go higher than his shoulders.

"Is this all really necessary?" I asked, as I fitted my guns into my belt.

"This is only half of what I intended to give him. Adam made me put the rest back as he pointed out a bomb on Kenzie could cause you some damage, too, if you were too close." Max shrugged.

I rolled my eyes as the door behind us opened.

Secured between two heavily armed guards was Kenzie. They had allowed him to shower and given him a razor to remove the patchy stubble across his face. A weird twinge in my stomach churned as the man standing before me brought back so many feelings—too many feelings. I shook them away. They were nothing anymore but memories and a reminder that the Kenzie I once knew was gone forever. He was my past. Max was my future.

I went back to checking my guns.

The guards brought him over to the table. "Arms up," a guard ordered. Kenzie obeyed. His eyes watched me the entire time as they placed the vest over his head. They secured the chains around his free wrist, waist, and ankles then attached the last chain to the metal cast on his left arm.

"If you so much as touch a hair on her head, I swear to God," Max warned Kenzie, who took his time turning his attention to Max.

"Won't touch a hair, I promise." Kenzie gave Max a smile that didn't quell the mood.

"Let's just get this over with." I brushed past the two men, trying to ignore the tension, and headed out to the courtyard where a shuttle was powered up and ready to go.

Sam handed me an earpiece that I shoved in place. He gave me something I never thought I'd see again—the Eye. The small lens fit perfectly over my right eye, as it had back when I was only a Watcher—when life wasn't so confusing.

"Testing, testing. Sawyer, can you hear me?" I winced at the volume as Sam screamed into his mic only steps away from me.

"Yeah, I hear you," I said.

Sam gave a thumbs-up before he skipped back into the control room. "We'll monitor you from here. The Eye has been outfitted to see through Alatonion, so you'll see any advanced Carbons if they're in Cytos. And I've got you guys outfitted with location trackers, so with that and the Eye, we can watch your progress the whole way," Sam said through the earpiece.

"Great," I mumbled. "Nothing like being watched while you work…"

I stepped up the ramp of the shuttle and took a seat against the far wall of the compact space. Max joined me a moment later, and the guards placed Kenzie across from me.

"We'll be dropping you guys off just on the outskirts of the city. This shuttle is too heavy to land on the rooftop, and we're not sure if there's any other clear ground within the city limits," Murray said, as the shuttle doors closed, and the shuttle rumbled into the air. "That will be our meeting point. We'll drop you off and meet back in one hour."

Kenzie nodded, still watching me. I looked away quickly, swallowing the lump in my throat as his stare left me with an uneasy feeling, as if he were a predator assessing his prey.

"We'll be close by in case you need us for anything, all right?" Max whispered to me. "Just give us a call, and I'll come running."

I gave him a confident smile. "It's just a quick grab and go. Shouldn't be any trouble." I winked.

I should've known to not say this was going to be an easy job. We ran into trouble the minute we tried to land.

"Uh, guys, we can't land here… We can't land anywhere," the pilot spoke from the front of the shuttle.

I glanced out the window. Thick mud lined the entire perimeter of Cytos beyond the wall that once protected the city. There was no way to tell how deep it was. The only dry patch was a few feet from the wall, not nearly enough room for the shuttle to land.

"Find another spot," Max ordered.

The pilot shook his head. "It's all the same. Big storm must've hit recently."

In the distance, sticky black mud covered the ground. Small ponds of water remained from a heavy storm that must've recently passed by.

"Then turn around. We'll come back when it's dry," Max suggested.

"We don't have time to waste," I argued while I looked out the window for a solution. Even if they put us down away from the mud, we'd have to get through it, and I didn't want to risk getting stuck. I pointed to the small dry patch near the wall. "Get us as close to the wall as you can. We'll jump the rest of the way."

I stood. Max grabbed my arm to yank me down. "We won't be able to pick you back up from there. We should just wait, even a day."

I shook my head. "We'll be fine. You guys can drop a rope for us when we're done."

Max didn't look convinced, but I reached down and placed a kiss on his lips. I felt that familiar tingle on the back of my neck telling me Kenzie was watching, and I had to resist the urge to pull away.

"I'll be right back," I said softly, pulling my arm away from his grasp. "Come on, let's go." I nodded my head to Kenzie, who stood and followed me to the edge of the shuttle.

I pressed the button to open the shuttle door, lowering the ramp enough for us to get a clear view of the ground where we had to jump.

"I can't hover in one place with this shuttle, so you'll have to jump as I go by," the pilot shouted against the roaring engines as he circled back around for another pass.

"Ready?" I asked.

Kenzie nodded.

I grabbed onto the collar of Kenzie's vest and pulled him with me as we tumbled out of the shuttle.

It was a lot higher than I'd first thought, but as soon as my feet touched the ground, I tucked into a roll and shielded my head. Kenzie did the same a few feet away as best he could with the chains holding him down.

I stood and brushed off the dirt before I helped Kenzie to his feet. The shuttle swooped past one more time, and I gave them an all-clear wave before they headed farther out where the ground was solid, and there was no mud.

"Lead the way." I gestured to Kenzie, and with a smile he

stepped into the former city of my broken home.

Releasing a staggered breath, I followed. We had returned to Cytos.

TWENTY THREE

The city was nothing like I remembered, and yet it was so familiar to me. It reminded me of my parents, of the last time I was inside Sub 9, when I watched my father die right before my eyes. I missed them both. The city had been demolished when Coleman's Bots blew it up. It was all gone, except for Sub 9, which still stood in the distance like an annoying cockroach that wouldn't die.

My chest grew tighter and tighter the farther into the city we moved. It wasn't like before, there was no danger, even though I kept looking over my shoulder expecting something, but there was a pull into the city that made my heart clench with child-like yearning. Wishing for a time before this war, before everything was destroyed, but it was all gone.

Cytos was in ruins long before Coleman had finished it off, but it was like walking through a ghost town. The streets were quiet—what was left of them anyway. It was hard to tell what was street and what were former buildings with everything gone, but we followed a path towards Sub 9. Even the wind didn't make a sound. Not one building we passed still stood. It was a crumbled pile of metal and glass. Debris and concrete covered every inch of the path we took, causing us to climb over large boulders at times, slowing our progress as Kenzie struggled with the chains around him.

Kenzie shuffled beside me, taking quick steps to keep up with me, despite the chains around his legs. He kept glancing my way until I gave him a look. "What is it already?"

"You have it with you," he stated, not a question.

That was why he was looking at me so intently. It was the cuff tucked into my jacket pocket he was looking for. There was the smallest bit of disappointment at the realization, but I swallowed it back.

I nodded.

"Good." He turned his attention back to Sub 9, which we were nearing. "That will be the only thing to keep me in check. Not this electric vest or these chains."

I chuckled. "Max will be disappointed to hear that."

Kenzie rolled his eyes. "A bit overprotective, that boyfriend of yours."

I took a moment to choose my words, and I found myself absently playing with the ring on my pinky. "He was the one who was there for me in my darkest time. He just doesn't want to see me hurt like that again."

A frown marred Kenzie's brow, as he tilted his head to the side, as if he didn't quite understand what my darkest times were. I realized it was because he didn't. My ribs felt like they were clenching, and it made my heart hurt—*he doesn't remember.*

I rubbed at the back of my neck. "When I thought you died… I wasn't exactly myself for some time."

Kenzie's body became tense and he was quiet. "I'm sorry you had to go through that. I… I didn't know."

"Yeah, I know. You don't remember any of it." I shrugged my shoulders, trying my best to act like I was over it, like it still didn't break my heart every time I thought of that day.

He watched me before he left it alone.

We slowed down as we reached the front of Sub 9. It was weird to see it unguarded and untouched. We walked right through the front doors and into the main lobby without any alarms or interruptions.

"We've entered Sub 9, heading up to the thirtieth floor now," I said in my earpiece and clicked on the Eye. It blinked to life, clearing the view all around me. Luckily, nothing blinked green to indicate anyone else was there. For now, we were alone.

"Roger that. We have you up on our screens," Sam chimed. "Place looks a bit run down, doesn't it? No one there to keep up the household chores?"

I put the earpiece back on mute before I had to listen to more of Sam's babbling.

Kenzie nodded to the stairwell. "Power's been left off. That means heading up the old fashioned way."

I groaned as I took my first step up toward the thirtieth floor. The stairwell smelled musty and old.

We stopped twice when an eerie quiet set me on edge, but there was nothing else there. My eyepiece didn't indicate otherwise. There was nothing we could see, anyway. To his credit, Kenzie kept up with me despite the extra weight holding him down, and the chains that made it difficult to step.

Once we had reached his floor, Kenzie led the way down the hall to his quarters. He held the door open while I slipped in.

It was a small room with a single bed against the wall and a desk pushed against the other. At the end was a glass window spanning the entire wall.

Kenzie opened the top drawer of his desk and lifted the bottom to reveal a secret compartment underneath. He pulled out the tablet and a small journal with his name on the front. He shoved the journal in his pocket.

"Hand it over." I put my hand out, waiting for the journal.

He sighed before he shoved it in my hand. I peeled open the dusty cover to reveal messy handwriting and scribbles across the book. A date on each page. "This was yours?" I questioned, and he grabbed it away from my prying eyes.

"Now that you've seen it's nothing special, I'll be keeping that with me," Kenzie said. A little heat met his cheeks, though he tried to hide it.

"Whatever." I shrugged my shoulders. "Let's just get out of here."

We stepped back into the hallway, and I clicked my earpiece back on. "Sam, we've got the tablet, and we're heading back,"

I said.

"Uh, Sawyer, not to alarm you or anything, because it might not be anything. In fact it probably isn't anything, and our system is just acting weird, seeing as we're so far away from you guys and all," Sam babbled.

"What is it?" I asked. Kenzie frowned as he heard only one side of the conversation.

"Well, our systems are picking up someone else in Sub 9 with you. Or rather *something* else…"

I froze. "What do you mean something else?" Kenzie watched my expression change from confusion to horror.

"I'd suggest maybe you guys… run?"

I looked for an exit and took off, running toward the stairwell we came from. Kenzie shuffled behind me, the chains keeping him from doing much more than that. I pushed open the door, and not only did I hear it, I smelled it.

The smell of rotting flesh filled the entire stairwell, and hundreds of footsteps brought it closer.

I peered over the edge and down the stairwell just as Kenzie burst through the doors. My eyepiece lit up. Little dots of green blinked into view, hundreds of them converging on us quicker than anything I'd seen before. They were black as night, running with an inhuman speed right for us.

"No," he whispered. "How?"

I shook my head and pushed him back into the hallway.

Kenzie was frozen with fear; he wouldn't move. I shoved him out of the way, pulling the door shut behind me.

"Sam, we need a way out," I yelled, as I grabbed a heavy desk and flipped it on its side. I tore off the thick metal leg of the desk with every ounce of power I had in me, and I shoved the metal rod through the door handle.

"Um, we're looking for something, but it's not looking good if I'm being honest." Sam's voice did nothing to quell my fear.

Kenzie couldn't take his eyes off the door. The things on the other side scratched and clawed at the barrier. Dark hands that were scaled and black reached through the small crack under the door. They pulled at it, but my makeshift lock held strong. I left Kenzie there and sprinted to the other end of the hallway where a second door stood to a mirroring stairwell.

"There's more, a lot more," I said, peering over the edge of the railing. My eyepiece blinked to life again. I couldn't catch my breath; it hitched in my throat, which was suddenly so dry. I felt my hands trembling.

The entire stairwell was filled with them. They closed the distance to me faster than I had time to react. Using my powers, I shoved the *things* back, pushing them into each other. A few toppled down the stairs, but others crawled over them. *This can't be real. This is a nightmare.* But it was real, and I had to move.

I barely had enough time to shove the door closed before the black creatures pounded against it, trying to claw their way through. My heart was beating so fast, too fast, and I could hear it thundering in my ears. I shoved myself against the door as a hand reached through. I severed it with a sickening crunch, and I shifted away from it as it thudded by my feet.

"Kenzie!" I screamed, but he still hadn't moved. The door in

135

front of him banged and rattled as the creatures tried to break through.

I pushed myself against the door, trying to keep it shut, but more of them pressed against it. I wasn't going to be able to hold on much longer. *No, no.* I had to hold it. I had to get Kenzie moving.

I used my powers to pull over a heavy cabinet. It scrapped against the ground, metal against cement floor as I pulled it closer to me, one hand stretched out.

I brought it close enough to try to secure it against the door, but in order to do that I had to move out of the way. If I did, it might allow the creatures in before I had time to get the cabinet in place. I cursed under my breath, closing my eyes and trying to figure out a way out of here. *Think, Sawyer. Focus.* I took a steadying breath, calming down my raging pulse. I needed Kenzie's help, but he seemed to be in a fog, frozen with terror. Then I remembered what I'd shoved in my pocket only hours ago.

"Damnit, Kenzie. Snap out of it!" I pressed the trigger button Max had given me to control the vest across Kenzie's chest. I only pressed it once, but it was enough to get his attention.

Kenzie blinked before he rushed over, and while he held the door shut, I moved the cabinet in the way.

Stepping back, I surveyed the hall. "Are there any other access points?" I asked. Kenzie stared blankly at me. "Kenzie. Is there any other way in here?"

He shook his head.

I sighed with relief. "Sam, we're locked in the hallway on

the thirtieth floor. Please tell me you guys have a way to get us out of here?" I swallowed back the image of those black things clawing at me, their screams still echoing behind that barricaded door. I could still smell their stench, and it made my stomach churn and nausea rose in my throat.

"We're working on it. Hold tight," Sam assured me, but I was anything but assured.

"How the hell did those things get in here?" I wondered.

"It was empty," Kenzie said, still in a daze. "There was no one else… nothing else here." He shook his head.

"Well, there is now. And unless you want us both to die a horrible death, I'd suggest you start helping me secure these doors better." I moved anything I found to block the doors at both ends of the hallway.

It wasn't until I was sure they couldn't get through that I allowed myself to sit down. My head dropped into my hands, and my entire body shook.

Kenzie sat across from me, a horrified look on his face. "He sent them here."

"Who? Those creatures?" I asked.

Kenzie shook his head. "No, Carbons. He sent them here to clean up the mess and make sure nothing was damaged, but I never thought to ask why they hadn't come back."

"I guess now we know." I shrugged.

"Whatever this virus is, it's spreading. Rapidly," Kenzie warned. "How long has it been? Three weeks? A month?"

"Yeah, about that."

"Well, these Carbons were sent down here only a few days

before we attacked. This was his backup location if something prevented him from reaching the station," Kenzie explained. "That means that in less than a month, this virus spread and took every one of them. And if Coleman is the carrier of the virus, that means he must have known these Carbons were infected before they left—he knew what would happen to them."

I tried to not think of them as a shiver traveled down my spine. The screaming had gone silent.

If there was a virus affecting the Carbons, I was at risk. Even Kenzie wasn't what I was; he was more Bot than Carbon. He could be spared from that fate if this virus were to infect all Carbons. My skin crawled at the thought of turning into one of those creatures. I'd already turned into a monster of a different kind, but this was a new horror I hadn't imagined.

It was clear why Kenzie had spent the last week not eating. I couldn't think of food without my stomach rolling with nausea.

"Sam? Anything?" I begged.

"Yes, sort of. Well, we think it might work—"

"Sam!"

"Right, sorry. Adam thinks he can turn on the power to Sub 9 from here, if Kenzie can patch us in," Sam explained.

"What good will that do us?" I questioned.

"You'll be able to access the elevator from there," Sam said. "Of course you won't want to take it down. There's more of those things on the ground level. So, the only choice is up… only there are still more up there, too, although less than the bottom, and you'll have to climb your way up to the rooftop where we're planning an extraction…"

I sighed. "When do you suppose the power will be back on?"

A rustle in the mic came before a new voice spoke through the earpiece. "Hey Sawyer, Adam here. I'm working as fast as I can, but there are many security checks in place that Sam is working through with me. And if you could get Kenzie to open the system to us, that'd be a big help as well. But I'd suggest you get comfy for the night," Adam said.

I groaned.

"I could've said that," Sam said on the other end of the earpiece.

"Yeah, but you didn't. I did," Adam argued.

"I'm the communications guy. It's kind of my job to do these things, you know," Sam spat back.

"Okay, just let us know when it's ready, all right? I'll get Kenzie to patch you guys in, and I'm turning off the Eye to save power." I cut Sam off before he had a chance to argue. I put the earpiece on mute and shut down the Eye. Turning to Kenzie, I said, "They need access to the system here, which you're going to give them."

He didn't argue. He just nodded.

I swallowed the lump in my throat, trying to sound like my next words didn't terrify me. "It looks like we're spending the night."

TWENTY FOUR

It was weird to look out on the dark, broken city of Cytos, my former home. From the window in Kenzie's old quarters, I saw everything.

Crumbled buildings that once stood tall across the city were reduced to nothing. The sunset-stained sky glowed red and pink in the distance, but dark clouds were rolling in. It seemed like even the sun didn't want to stay in this place for too long. It was like a gray landscape of death and destruction on one side, and the calm before the storm on the other. The home I once loved, completely gone.

The sky was covered in dark clouds, and the moon, nearly a full circle, tried to peek its way through the misery. The dim light covered the dark streets and the rubble below in eerie shadows. Beyond that was more of it as far as the eye could see.

We'd barricaded ourselves in Kenzie's room after he managed to patch Sam and Adam into the system at Sub 9, but that was the best we could do. Kenzie didn't have anything but his tablet to help us, so we had to rely on the others to get us out. We had pushed the small desk from Kenzie's room in front of the door for good measure, not that it would do much to stop those things.

I sat cross-legged on the bed, looking out the window while Kenzie sat in the chair across from me. We were both quiet for some time.

Our last check-in with Sam told us we still had at least another eight hours before the power could be turned on. There was nothing more we could do but wait. I had kicked off my boots and removed my jacket and gun belt a while ago. Kenzie was still chained up with the vest secure.

I watched him for a minute as he squirmed in the chair, trying to get more comfortable. He gave up and slouched down.

"Here." I reached into my pocket and pulled out the key to his chains. I started with the ones around his ankle and then moved to the ones on his wrists and waist.

He watched me untie them and let the chains fall to the ground. "You sure you trust me enough for that?" he asked.

"Right now, you need me to stay alive if you want to get out of here, and I'm banking on you not wanting to die." I shrugged, taking a seat on the cot.

Kenzie rotated his wrists before he moved to remove the vest. He unlatched one side, but the other side couldn't be reached with the metal cage around his hand. *That* I wasn't removing.

I rolled my eyes at his pathetic attempts before I climbed up to help. I had to lean in close to reach around his back and unlock the latch behind him. I couldn't help noticing the heat radiating from him or the way his body tensed where I touched it.

When I pulled back, my gaze snagged his eyes and I paused. My breath caught in my lungs for a long second.

But I blinked and it disappeared. As I sat back down, I pushed myself farther into the back corner of the cot, playing with that silver-and-copper ring in my hand to avoid his stare.

Kenzie lifted the vest over his head and let it fall to the ground.

We were quiet again before I noticed Kenzie reach into his pocket and pull out the journal he'd hidden away in there.

"When is it from?" I asked, as he thumbed through it.

"It begins a few weeks after I was brought here." He flipped to one of the last pages. "Until after… after my family died." His shoulders dropped as he read his last entry.

I decided to not probe, giving him the space he deserved, considering the fishbowl he'd been living in the past few weeks.

He squinted closer, struggling to read against the diminishing sunlight before it disappeared. He was forced to close the journal and put it back in his pocket.

I watched him in the new darkness, wondering what the child version of Kenzie was like.

"I was so mad when it happened," Kenzie said, and I waited for him to explain. "When my family died, when he let them die."

"Coleman?" I asked.

He nodded. "I begged him to bring them here. Begged him to spare their lives but he wouldn't." He stared out the window before he continued, "I'd forgotten what that pain felt like. I had promised them I'd get vengeance for their deaths, but I forgot about them."

His shoulders slumped, and in the darkness I couldn't tell if he was crying. I reached out for him. I gripped his hand and squeezed it, but he didn't flinch back, his fingers just curled around my hand gently.

"There's still time. You can still keep that promise," I said. His head moved up to meet my gaze.

"I can't beat him," he whispered.

"You already have." I looked down to where our hands were connected, and the way he gently held onto me, not like he did before, not like when he was trying to kill me.

Kenzie shook his head and moved to pull his hand away, but I didn't let him. "We don't know that… I don't know that I won't hurt you again," he said.

"You won't," I assured him. I wasn't sure how I knew, but I felt a shift in him. He wasn't the same Kenzie from before, but he was somewhere between the two, somewhere that still felt safe to me.

He gazed at our hands. "You should rest. I'll sleep on the floor," he suggested, as he gently pulled his hand away from my grasp.

Kenzie reached past me and grabbed a pillow and a blanket. He moved the chair out of the way before he lay down on the floor at an awkward angle where he couldn't even straighten his legs.

I gave him a crooked smirk. "You can't sleep there."

"It's fine. I've slept in worse places." Kenzie squeezed his eyes shut, but I noticed him fidgeting to get comfortable.

"Oh, come on. There's plenty of room for both of us up here." I slid over on the small bed to allow him to see how much room there was. Not much at all, but enough for two people at least… if neither moved. I tried not to think about what it felt like with Kenzie lying beside me. This was just to get some rest. If we were getting out of here tomorrow, we both needed our strength.

"I don't think that's a good idea, Sawyer." Kenzie scowled.

"We've slept in a bed together before and it was fine."

Kenzie tensed before I realized he didn't remember. My stomach dropped, and I ignored the tinge of disappointment. There was a small bit of worry that by even offering my bed to Kenzie, I was betraying Max, but I wouldn't do anything, and neither would Kenzie. We'd just sleep.

"Just get up here already before you make me feel guiltier for the way you've been treated all day."

Kenzie let out a long sigh before he sat up and lay down on the bed beside me.

"Goodnight." I tried to sound as casual as I could, fiddling with the ring on my pinky as I closed my eyes.

"Night," Kenzie mumbled.

The scene was anything but comfortable. Both of us were fully clothed, lying side-by-side on our backs, and pretending to sleep. One of my shoulders was squished against the wall while the other was pinned under Kenzie's broad shoulder.

I stared at the ceiling, counting my breaths slowly and deliberately while I tried to ignore the spark of energy tickling my skin where Kenzie's shoulder met mine.

I had to blink my eyes against the sun blaring through the window of Kenzie's room. I went to stretch out my arms. I discovered I was face-to-face with the wall with no room to move. It took me only a moment to notice the warm chest pressed against my back.

I stilled, trying not to move as my mind caught up with where I was and what had happened. Sometime during the night, I had turned onto my side, and Kenzie had done the same. He was pressed up against my back, and his arm was draped over my side.

Soft, even breaths pressed against the nape of my neck. Every part of me touching him was awake and on fire. My pulse raced. I didn't know how either of us managed to fall asleep with those monsters just beyond the hallway, but we had—and it seemed like for a long while, as the sun had already risen.

I moved only an inch, and that was enough to wake Kenzie. He shot out of bed so fast he nearly fell face-first onto the ground.

"Sorry… I…" he mumbled, as he ran his hand through his tangled, messy hair.

I shook my head, fumbling with the blankets as the cold air met me where his warmth once was. "We should get going.

They probably have the power on by now."

I reached over for my earpiece I had left on the desk, trying to shake the image and the warmth of Kenzie's arm wrapped around me. My skin felt itchy, and there was a pain in the back of my throat as I realized I still missed the way it felt to be near Kenzie. *What am I doing?* I loved Max. He was the only one who'd never hurt me, never betrayed me, and here I was in the arms of another man, thinking of him while Max was likely worried sick about me. *He's not the same Kenzie, Sawyer. He doesn't remember you!*

"Sam?" I called into the earpiece. "Are we ready yet?"

"Sawyer! Thank God. We've been trying to get ahold of you for hours. We were pretty certain you were still alive seeing as your location trackers still showed you guys together in a little room, but when you guys didn't move or answer, we got a bit spooked," Sam said. "Max was ready to break down the wall to get you guys out."

I blushed at the thought of what Max would've said if he'd seen Kenzie and I as we'd been in the bed. Again, I tried to shake the image away. "We were sleeping, sorry. Is the power on?"

"Yup, you guys are good to go. The shuttle will be leaving in five minutes, so you have twenty minutes to get to the roof before they arrive," Sam said. "Sawyer, good luck. Be careful."

"I always am."

TWENTY FIVE

Kenzie was already putting the vest back over his head when I turned around.

"You don't need that anymore," I said.

"The others will disagree," Kenzie countered.

"I don't care. We need to run and move fast. Leave it."

Kenzie shrugged before he dropped it to the floor.

I strapped on my belt and my guns, and then I pulled on my boots and put my jacket on. I secured the Eye in place and turned it back on. Kenzie watched me with a frown.

"What?" I asked.

"I think we should cover you up more. We don't know how that virus is spread, through touch or the air. We should cover your neck and face as best we can," Kenzie suggested.

Unfortunately, he was right. I glanced for something to cover my face, but I came up empty, unless I wanted to wrap a blanket around me, which I didn't.

"Here." Kenzie pulled his shirt over his head and ripped the bottom half. I couldn't help staring at his bare chest until I realized that back at the control room everyone was seeing what I was seeing.

Blinking rapidly, I grabbed the piece of fabric he'd torn off and I turned away. I wrapped it around my face, covering my mouth and nose, so only my eyes were still visible. The fabric smelled like him, fresh and almost warm, like summer, and I found it hard to breathe as memories flooded back to me. The feeling of his body against mine and his lips grazing my neck. *Stop!*

"You okay?" Kenzie asked.

I'd been standing in a silent daze for way longer than I should have. I nodded, not trusting my voice. *What is wrong with me?* It wasn't real, none of it was, and it didn't matter if some part of me still longed for him, I loved Max. That *wasn't* a lie—that was real.

Kenzie moved the desk away and opened the door only enough that we saw the hallway was still empty.

At the end of the hallway, our makeshift barriers had worked, but barely, as it seemed the metal table against one door was cracked and nearly split in two. I tried to not think about how strong these creatures must've been to nearly rip apart a metal table.

Kenzie pressed the button for the elevator, and it slowly made its way up to us.

I handed him a gun. "Here, just don't use it on me," I said.

He smirked. "You know my arm could do a lot more damage than this gun could…" He glanced down to his hand still trapped in the metal cage around his fist.

"Yes, I know. That's why you're only getting a gun," I teased as the elevator dinged, and the doors slid open.

There was a flash of black and the sound of a gun going off before I even knew what had happened. The creature lay twitching on the ground, straddling the threshold of the elevator. Kenzie had put a bullet through its skull.

I shuddered as Kenzie kicked it out of the way, and I gave him a thankful nod.

"Must've snuck in here before the power went off," Kenzie said, as he stepped into the elevator.

"We're heading up," I said to Sam when I'd turned the earpiece back on.

"Roger that," he chimed back. "There are quite a few on the top floor where you'll be heading. They're all jumbled together, so it's hard to say how many, but quite a few is a good guess."

"Helpful," I said.

"The shuttle is fifteen minutes out. They will meet you at the rooftop for extraction," Sam explained. "The stairs are at the back corner of the office, so unfortunately you have to get through those gross black things to get there. I bet they smell awful. They look like they'd smell as bad as my Aunt Lily. She was *not* a lily, let me tell you. Had no sense of smell and farted like a—"

"Sam, I'm sure you're trying to be helpful, but this is not helping," I said.

"Right, right, sorry," Sam said. He went silent.

"Ready?" I asked Kenzie. He nodded and raised his gun to face the elevator doors. I pressed the button for the top floor and the smooth, quick elevator rose.

My ears popped as we climbed higher. The elevator slowed down, making my stomach do a jump. My powers were on the tip of my fingers, waiting for me to unleash them. I managed one deep breath before the elevator dinged, and the doors slid open.

All in front of me was black. Black limbs and distorted bodies ripped at each other to get to us. I shoved my powers out, and the creatures were blasted back. But there were more.

The entire room was a black wave of mutated figures. With every figure I pushed back, two more came at us.

Kenzie pushed me out of the elevator as he released every bullet in his clip. We were surrounded. It felt like the room was closing in, and I couldn't see anything but the wave of black surrounding us.

I held my breath against the smell. It was so strong I staggered back a step, trying to shake off the dizziness and bile that stuck in my throat. I pushed the creatures back, keeping them out of reach, but they clawed at the air around us in a flurry of limbs. There were too many.

Kenzie's gun clicked its final bullet, and he tossed it away before he retrieved the second gun at my back, unleashing it on the creatures behind us. They fell down, but they didn't all stay down. *Move, move, move,* I ordered myself.

We'd barely made any progress, and my powers couldn't find anything on these *things* to grab hold of. There was no microchip, no wires, or Alatonion—it was as if it'd all melted from their bodies leaving this black misshapen mess in its place. I could only push them out of our way before they jumped back up and attacked. There was nothing but rotting flesh and a drive to slaughter us. *Focus, stay focused.* I released a breath and kept moving, pushing my way through. My chest felt like it would crack in two as my heart pounded against my rib cage. For the first time in a long while, there was true fear we might not make it.

I managed to clear a path to the rear stairwell, grabbing Kenzie's arm and pulling him with me. We reached the door as Kenzie finished his second set of bullets. He swore under his breath and used the back end of the gun to shove them back, but they were too close to him. We had to hurry.

I sprinted up the stairwell, removing the few creatures occupying the space with a swipe of my hand. I ran into the door at the top of the stairs leading out onto the rooftop.

"Dammit. It's locked," I said, turning to my powers to push the door open. I needed to keep the door intact; otherwise, we'd have a horde of black creatures with us on the rooftop.

I managed to break through, taking some of the wall with it. It was the best I could do.

"Go!" I yelled at Kenzie, who was still halfway up the stairs fending off way too many of them.

I shoved him through the doorway and followed him. We slammed it shut behind us, but these things were relentless. I tried to gulp in air, feeling my pulse racing too fast, threatening to explode.

The door pressed against our backs, as we held on as tightly as we could. I looked around the rooftop for anything I could use to block the door, but there was nothing.

"Sam! We need an extraction *now*," I yelled.

"They are five minutes out," Sam called back.

"We don't have five minutes," I screamed, as the top bolt on the door broke free.

I used my powers to add some pressure against the door that was ready to buckle. The metal door folded down like a can of tuna being opened. There were too many of them pressing against it for us to hold them back.

In the distance, I heard the shuttle racing toward us.

"They can see you. Almost there," Sam said.

The shuttle neared and circled around the rooftop. We waited for them to drop down and land but they kept circling.

"Sam, why aren't they landing?"

"Um, the pilot says the rooftop is too small. They won't be able to land on it. They'll drop down a ladder for you guys."

The side door of the shuttle slid open, and a rope ladder dropped. From the door of the shuttle, Max watched with his gun out. He stood ready to cover us. He waved for us to go.

I shifted away from the door for only a second, and instantly the second bolt broke off. I couldn't move without these things getting out at the same time. We wouldn't make it to the ladder if I couldn't hold on longer.

"Go," I yelled to Kenzie, who shook his head. "I can hold it with my powers a bit longer, just hurry or neither of us will make it out."

Kenzie frowned as he looked ready to argue. We didn't have much time, and my powers were strong, but they were faltering against the sheer number of these monsters. I couldn't hold on for long, but I could at least give him a head start.

He sprinted for the ladder. The door buckled again, and black arms reached around the metal, gripping my arm and ripping through the fabric of my jacket. I pulled back. I couldn't let it touch me. The arms threatened to rip my whole limb clean out of its socket. Blood dripped down my sleeve as sharp claws tore into my arm. *Shit.* I grimaced, trying to hold onto the door just a little longer. Using a small amount of my powers, I pulled out the knife from the inside of my boot and severed the hand trying to rip off my arm. I shook off the clawed, black hand still clenched to my jacket, praying the virus hadn't touched me on its long, sharp nail.

Kenzie had made it to the ladder and was slowly climbing his way up. The shuttle circled around the rooftop, unable to hover in one stop for too long.

The last bolt on the door burst off, and I was out of time. I sprinted for the ladder dragging across the rooftop, away from me. Using my Carbon abilities, I raced as fast as I could, but the creatures were also once Carbons and equally as fast.

The shuttle had reached the end of the rooftop and looked ready to circle back, but that would lead Kenzie and I right back into the horde of creatures only inches behind me.

"Go! Keep going!" I waved the pilot on while I chased the ladder.

I was almost at the end of the rooftop, and the ladder hung

153

a few feet over the edge.

I took two powerful strides before I launched myself off the edge of the roof and toward the ladder. I managed to grab hold of one of the rungs, but I only had one hand secure, and the other was already losing its grip.

Blood had dripped down my hand, making my grip slick. I struggled to hold on. Dangling over the edge of the building, I kicked my legs to find a hold. My hands were near the end of the ladder, and there was nowhere for my feet to reach.

My pinky went first, and then the next finger and the next, until all that remained was one finger holding onto the ladder and my body dangling over the city of Cytos. Blood coated my hand and the wrung of the ladder, making it nearly impossible to hang on.

Back on the rooftop, the black creatures that had been so set on reaching me had thrown themselves over the edge and fell to the ground in a waterfall of black.

I grimaced and tried to hold on, swinging my other arm around to grab hold, but my last finger slipped, and I was falling.

TWENTY SIX

I was weightless for what felt like forever, but in reality it was less than a second before a strong hand gripped my arm. Above me, Kenzie had wrapped his caged arm around the ladder and reached me in time before I fell to the ground like one of those creatures.

I'd never been afraid of heights, but at that moment I was terrified of falling.

"Don't let go, please don't let go," I begged, as my eyes met Kenzie's. He tightened his grip around my forearm.

"I won't," he said through clenched teeth.

I glanced below and my heart raced.

"Don't look down, look at me," Kenzie commanded.

I evened out my breaths and my pulse slowed. I didn't look

away from Kenzie's eyes as the ocean blue calmed me like a gentle wave. Kenzie screamed as he tightened his grip once more. His face twisted in pain, but he held my gaze and didn't let go of me.

The shuttle moved, passing the wall and surrounding mud until we found solid ground. The pilot lowered the shuttle as close as he could, and Kenzie released my arm. I tumbled a short distance to the ground. Kenzie was right behind me.

I lie there, trying to catch my breath. Kenzie rushed to me and hovered over my body. His bare chest was heaving, and he held his one arm close to him in an awkward angle. Dislocated. It must've separated when he was holding onto me in the air.

His other hand pushed back the makeshift scarf around my face, so I could take a deep gulp of air. "You okay?" he asked, as he searched my body for wounds. The gash on my arm was already healing, and the blood coating my hand and sleeve wasn't fresh.

I nodded, unable to look away.

Footsteps neared. One of Murray's guards shoved Kenzie out of the way and pinned him to the ground.

Max was at my side, helping me to my feet. "Sawyer," he said, looking me over as Kenzie had.

My attention turned to the men pinning down Kenzie, who grimaced in pain. "Let him go! You're hurting him."

I tried to push one of them off, but Max pulled me back. "They're just making sure he's secure," Max said.

"He's fine. He's not a threat anymore. Didn't you see he just saved my life?" I argued.

He looked to the guards who seemed to be waiting for some sort of order. "Leave him," Max said, and the two guards stepped away.

I bent down beside Kenzie and helped him back to his feet. He was holding his arm tight to his body. There was an odd dip where his shoulder should've been.

"Dislocated." He grimaced.

"We have to get him to Doc," I told Max and he nodded, leading the way back to the shuttle.

"We have one more thing to do before we head back," Max said over his shoulder. He helped Kenzie into the shuttle and secured him in his seat.

I waited for Max to sit beside me before I asked, "What's left to do?"

"Destroy Sub 9," Max said, and his hand clasped mine. He gave it a squeeze.

The shuttle rumbled to a start and shook the whole way up into the sky. It leveled out and soared over Cytos. I did my best to not look down, my stomach still in my throat from the feeling of weightlessness.

"Locked and loaded," the pilot said.

"Fire," Max ordered. The shuttle quivered as missiles launched from it and headed toward Sub 9. They crashed into the side of the building, and it went up in an explosion that filled the sky and echoed throughout the shuttle.

Out the small window, I watched as Sub 9 fell to the ground, resting in the pile of the rubble that was Cytos. There was nothing left standing in the city I once called my home—

including the nightmares.

Max nearly carried me back to my quarters when we arrived at the village. I was more than capable of walking, but he held me tightly under his arm, and I eased into him. I watched as they pulled Kenzie into Doc's office; our eyes met before he was shoved out of view.

Max pulled me into my room where I sat in a daze. I was exhausted, confused, and lost. I blinked, trying to erase the horrors from my mind, but I couldn't get the horde of black creatures to disappear. I closed my eyes and they faded away, even if only for a moment.

Without a word, Max took off my boots. He helped me undo my gun belt and removed my jacket. The shredded fabric from Kenzie's shirt lay on top of the pile of dirty clothes.

Max examined the scratches and bruises on my arms that were already healing. I didn't feel any different, but in the back of my mind, I worried the infection would spread, seeing as those things touched me. I shivered, trying to push the thought away.

Max gently gripped my chin and looked up at me from where he knelt at the foot of the bed. "You're okay, you're safe now." He brushed his thumb against my cheek.

I let out a shaky breath and gazed at Max. His eyes filled me with warmth, and my stomach churned with a sense of guilt and betrayal. I looked away.

"I-I need to tell you something," I started.

"Don't," Max stopped me, shaking his head and pulling my face back up to meet his gaze. "You don't have to explain it to me. I get that he was a big part of your past and letting that go isn't easy. I trust you, Sawyer. And I love you"

Those three words made it worse, and I felt a tear fall down my cheek. "I love you, too," I whispered. "I don't want to hurt you."

He swallowed, pausing for a long moment before he spoke. "If all I got was to hear you tell me you loved me and know you meant it, that's enough."

My throat burned, and I felt more tears filling my eyes. I did mean it, I truly did. Whatever feelings I still had for Kenzie weren't the same. They were what I needed then, when I was the old Sawyer. But Max was what I needed now. I leaned in and kissed him softly.

He pulled me into a tight hug. "Come on, let's get you cleaned up." Max led me to the shower at the back of my quarters, and I spent a long time trying to wash off not only the smell of rotten flesh all over me, but also the shame coating me every time I thought back to the way Kenzie had looked at me… and the way I had looked back.

TWENTY SEVEN

I was glad to see Kenzie was no longer in chains or shoved in the back of his cell. He still had the metal cage around his hand, but he also had a sling across his arm after Doc had put his shoulder back in place. We were settled at the back of the control room where Sam was making fast work of the tablet Kenzie had brought back. Kenzie had already opened it with the retina scanner, giving Sam full access to it.

"Just a few more firewalls to get past, and I should have access to everything Coleman," Sam exclaimed, glancing over his shoulder at me. "So, did they smell as bad as I thought? What did they look like? The Eye wasn't that clear."

I shivered as all eyes turned to me. "Worse. They smelled worse than you could imagine. And their skin was like…

black, scaled, like burnt fish, covering them head-to-toe. They looked like the undead walking, no eyes, clawed hands…" I shivered again, trying not to imagine myself as one.

"Reeks," Ainsley said from the corner of the room.

The space became silent, and her face turned pale.

"You know what they are?" I asked.

She shook her head. "No. But I was told a story once of a creature black as night. Human form in the shadows, but not human at all. You would know them by their smell and the pits where their eyes once were. My people called them Reeks, though I thought it was a myth, a story."

Tenason rested a hand on her shoulder, which she shrugged away.

"Wow." Sam let out a long whistle. "Well, let's hope we don't see any more of those things around."

Ainsley continued speaking about the stories she had heard of the Reeks but I couldn't listen. I strolled over to Kenzie, who was leaning against the back wall with two guards nearby watching his every breath. His face was as grave as mine while he listened to Ainsley's story of the Reeks.

Max monitored me the whole way.

"How's your arm?" I asked.

"Fine," Kenzie said. "It'll be back to normal in a few hours."

Like me, Kenzie healed quickly, and I was glad for it.

"How are you?" He eyed me with suspicion.

"Fine," I lied, not wanting to admit how much those Reeks had shaken me up. But we were far away, and whatever remained of them had died when Sub 9 was taken down.

"Good." Kenzie nodded as he shifted uncomfortably on his feet. "So… can we chat for a minute, in private?" Kenzie eyed the two men on either side of him.

They watched us carefully as I nodded and directed Kenzie to an empty office around the corner. "We'll just be a few minutes," I told the guards, who followed us as far as I'd let them. They stood guard on the other side of the door.

Kenzie made his way to the back of the small room. He leaned against the wall and watched me. I kept my distance, standing with my hands in my pocket and leaning against the opposite door.

"I just… I guess with everything that happened, this seems like a stupid thing to ask. It's just, I can't get it off my mind," Kenzie started.

My palms were sweating. I waited for him to continue, not wanting to say anything before he did. But the way he wouldn't stop looking at me made me wonder if he remembered what we had. I realized then that was what I wanted from him— confirmation that what I had felt wasn't a lie. He'd said his heart remembered me, but it could be remembering the façade Kenzie put up when he was trying to get information from the Watchers for Coleman. It all could have been a lie, and for some reason, that thought alone terrified me… because even if it was over, it hadn't been a lie for me.

"I was wondering if… you were going to hold up your end of the bargain?"

Frowning, I tried to piece together what Kenzie was asking.

"The thing that you have, that you won't tell me about or

show me?" Kenzie watched as realization spread across my face.

The cuff. He'd been looking at me that entire time because of the cuff I had hidden in my jacket pocket. The one that called to him.

Reaching into my jacket, I pulled out the Alatonion cuff, etched with lightning bolts scattered across it. Even in my hands, strong power and energy flowed from it, reaching out to Kenzie. His eyes were wide, searching the cuff in my hands. He stepped closer to me. Reaching out a tentative hand, the tips of his fingers grazed the metal surface.

He flinched as the power vibrated off of him, and the zigzag lines on the cuff flowed erratically across the surface of the cuff.

"What is it?" Kenzie whispered.

I turned it over in my hands. "A tool. Something to help you wield your powers without feeling the burnout. Without dying," I explained, placing it into his open palm. "It's made specifically for you. Only you can wear it, and only you can use its powers."

He looked from the cuff in his hands back up to me. "You have one, too?"

I nodded and lifted the sleeve of my jacket where the etched current of my Alatonion cuff moved smoothly across its surface. My powers reached out to the other cuff's energy beating close by.

Kenzie looked down to his hand still encased in the metal cage, preventing him from using the powers inside of his arm.

"We don't know what this cuff will do to you or to your… directive," I tried to explain. I'd given Kenzie the cuff, but I wouldn't let him use his powers until I was certain he wouldn't hurt anyone or risk hurting himself. I'd promised Max I wouldn't remove the cast on his hand.

Kenzie nodded, knowing there was still a force present within him that he was fighting against. He knew we might never be sure he could control it or his own mind, but he was thankful I had at least trusted him enough to give it to him.

He shoved the cuff into his pocket. "Thank you," he said. Before I could respond, he stepped around me and out the doors, and the electric energy followed him.

"I've got good news, and I've got bad news," Sam said from his spot at the front of the control room. It'd taken him four more hours to break through, but he'd done it. "Well, I can tell you for certain I know where Coleman is. He's in a space station orbiting the earth. Problem is, we have no way to get there. We're not equipped with anything that would take us into outer space, that's for sure."

Murray sighed from his place to the right of Sam.

"But at least now, we can see him. We'll know what he's up to and when he makes any moves," Sam said, trying to add a silver lining.

"See him how?" I asked.

"Through the security feed," Sam said, as he bolted back to his desk and pulled up the live feed on the big screen. "Kenzie had access to all the security cameras in the station, so I was able to tap into them."

The screen filled up with multiple boxes, showing empty hallways, filled bunkrooms, and the occasional guard making its rounds. One more thing caught my eye.

"Pull up that feed." I pointed to a small one in the corner.

The screen popped up and took over the entire front panel. I had to cover my mouth from the scream wanting to escape as I stepped closer to make sure what I was seeing was actually happening. Lena was strapped down on a large metal table. Her arms were chained down. At the end of her wrists, her hands were gone.

Multiple tubes were coming out of her, all filled with a dark red—her blood.

Her cheeks were stained with tears, and her mouth was moving. "Do we have sound?" I asked, even though I didn't need to hear to know she was begging for her life.

"One second… here it is." Sam clicked on the sound, and the room filled with an eerie, echoing voice repeating, "Please. Please stop. I can't… please," Lena begged. My chest caved in, as my heart broke in two.

I was shaking, but I stood strong, not letting the fear inside of me take over. I was powerless to help, and the guilt of knowing how helpless I was burned inside of me.

The screen was blurry as angry tears flooded my vision.

In the corner of the screen, a shadow moved into view. Coleman stood beside his daughter, watching as she begged him repeatedly to stop. His eyes were cold, and his hand twitched at his side, moving up as if to reach for her before it dropped back down and he looked away.

"I'm sorry, dear, but we're almost done. I promise, it's almost over," Coleman said.

Lena screamed, and she fought against the restraints around her, thrashing as she tried to get out of their grasp. She was tied down too tightly.

A sandy-blonde-haired doctor walked into the room, and Lena went still, her eyes still filled with tears. Lena's body relaxed, and her voice fell silent.

"Thank you, Irene," Coleman said.

He gave the doctor a subtle nod before he left the room.

I couldn't watch anymore. I couldn't take seeing Lena like that.

"Shut it off," Max said over my shoulder.

"Wait, can you rewind that last bit?" Kenzie said, as he took a step closer, watching the screen over Sam's shoulder.

Max scowled at Kenzie. "Isn't it enough to see that once?"

But Kenzie ignored him, and Sam rewound the feed again. I turned to watch Kenzie, not wanting to look at the screen.

"There." Kenzie pointed, and Sam paused the screen.

I looked up to the image of Coleman turning to face the camera before he left the room. I spotted what Kenzie was pointing out.

"He's healed. The virus isn't on him anymore," I said, noting his once coal black hands back to their normal white color. His neck, which was once scaled in black scabs, was nothing more than the wrinkled white skin of an old man.

Kenzie nodded. "He's found the cure."

TWENTY EIGHT

There wasn't much time to process what I'd witnessed. I stayed in the control room with Max and Sam, looking over hours of security footage. As we searched, I kept hoping we would see my mother—but we never did. Kenzie kept to himself in the back of the room, but I noted how he watched over everything we did, occasionally giving us general information or locations we didn't have, as much as the control over him allowed.

The space station had twelve sectors spread out around its circular structure. One of them was missing, which Kenzie said would account for the Carbons-turned-Reeks in Sub 9. Each sector housed thousands of Carbons and could travel down to earth at any time.

A second sector was offline but still attached. "Any idea what this could mean?" I called over to Kenzie, who took his time walking over. He leaned on the back of my chair as he looked over my shoulder. I caught Max's scowl at the act, his hand resting on the gun at his hip, but he turned back to the screen. He might trust me, but not Kenzie.

"Which sector?" Kenzie asked.

"Uh… seven, I believe." Sam counted on the homemade image of the station he was working on. "Yes, seven!"

"That was my old training sector. It was empty. Why would they close it?" Kenzie wondered.

Kenzie reached past me to the computer and directed the cameras to that sector. His arm had healed and was out of its sling. He brushed against my side as he leaned over the controls. His brows scrunched as he typed in a code to get past the security system Sam had been trying to override.

"How are you suddenly now able to do that?" Max asked, still glaring at Kenzie.

"It wasn't anything when I left, so there was no reason for Coleman's control to stop me from looking in there," Kenzie said, not even glancing over his shoulder at Max. He pulled up the cameras in Sector 7. I nearly fell out of my chair at the sight.

There were hundreds of Reeks chained to the walls of the room. They pushed and pulled against restraints, and their mouths clicked open with inaudible screams.

"Why are they keeping them?" I asked.

Kenzie shook his head and his brow furrowed. "I'm not sure. Coleman would have no reason for keeping them. This system lockdown wasn't done by him."

"Who then?" I asked.

Kenzie shrugged. "Best guess? Doctor Irene… She covered her tracks good, but even she can't keep this from Coleman. If he doesn't already know about them, he soon will."

Who would want to keep these things? And worse, what were they doing with them?

There was a tap on my shoulder, and I twisted around to find Tenason and Ainsley. She inclined her head for me to follow.

"Be right back," I said, taking Max with me. Kenzie took up the seat I vacated.

We stepped outside where Tenason was pacing, and Ainsley had her arms crossed watching him. As soon as I stepped into view, she pulled me away from the entrance before she spoke. "I have word from Vance," she said.

"And?"

She shook her head. "Viktor will not fight our war."

I swore under my breath.

"But Vance will," Ainsley finished.

I tilted my head in confusion.

"He's bringing his own men, about sixty of them. And they are already on their way," Tenason said.

"That's great news," I said, but I noticed neither of them seemed too excited. "Isn't it?"

"I also received word from Aelish," Ainsley said. "Coleman changed his time line. He'll be here in two days."

This time, Max was the one to swear. "Why?"

"Something spooked him. I'm not sure." Ainsley shrugged her shoulders.

"We did," I sighed. "We blew up Sub 9. He was bound to notice."

The others agreed.

"Will they make it in time? Vance and Aelish?" I asked.

Ainsley gave me a weak smile and shrugged her shoulders. "We hope…"

"I'll tell the others," Max said. He hurried back into the control room.

We thought we had more time. Two days wasn't enough. We weren't prepared. We hadn't even begun to think of a plan.

"We set up the bombs and let them do the work," Murray said, referring to the Megastun bombs Adam had created to stop the Carbons. When set off, the bombs would send out a magnetic energy that gripped onto the Carbons' microchip and ripped them out. But they were untested, and the likelihood of these bombs doing what they were meant for was slim. We needed more fighters. We needed a backup. These Carbons would destroy every one of us if our only weapon was the bombs.

"That won't be enough," Max reminded him.

"We be good n the waters. My ship can send them packin'," Lankey added.

"They won't be stupid enough to get too close to the water this time," I said, remembering how Lankey drove them out when we'd first met in Kuros. We had no way of knowing where they would attack, and I was certain they wouldn't go near Kuros.

"So you make them," Kenzie said from the back of the room.

All eyes turned on him, and he stepped forward, out of the shadow he'd lurked in. His guards followed his steps.

"You don't know where he's going to be, so make the choice for him. Make it so the only place they can land is the one you choose for them," Kenzie suggested.

Murray nodded.

"We should drive them toward the Muted Forest too, split them up," Ainsley piped up. She stood like a warrior at the front of the room beside Tenason, who watched her with a goofy smile on his face. "The forest will mute the Carbon's abilities. They will still be strong and fast, but at least there'll be one thing we won't have to worry about."

I nodded. I knew all too well what that forest did to a Carbon.

"Any idea how many will be coming, son?" Murray turned to Kenzie.

He shook his head. "He could send ten—he could send them all."

That was the factor we didn't have a solution for. There were a couple hundred soldiers in this village. Lankey had another eighty or so. Vance would bring sixty men, and the Ladies of The Muted Forest were a couple hundred as well, but still. One sector on that space station housed thousands of Carbons. I didn't want to voice my doubt, but it was hard to not think about it.

"We'll prepare for thousands and hope for less," I said.

Max gave my hand a squeeze. An all too familiar feeling of doubt took up residence in my chest, and it was hard to breathe. But when I looked at him, my heartbeat slowed and my shoulders relaxed.

That night, I had a hard time falling asleep. When my eyes grew heavy and I was almost asleep, a blinding pain struck my head. The whole room faded to black.

I was standing on the space station in an empty hallway. I recognized it from the security camera video I'd been watching for the past day and a half. I made my way down the hallway, hearing the echo of my feet reverberate through the metal walls and floor.

I didn't know what I was looking for, but I felt a tug on my energy pulling me forward, so I followed it. When I rounded the next hallway, I was stopped by a glass wall. My mother was on the other side.

"Only you can end this. You are their savior now. You can trust him," my mother said.

I pressed my hand against the glass, but she slowly walked away from me, shaking her head. I wanted to say something, to call out to her, but my voice wouldn't work.

Behind her, a horde of Reeks loomed in the shadow. I banged against the glass, warning her to run, but she kept walking toward them. In less than a second, they consumed her in a wild frenzy, and I could no longer see her against the black creatures surrounding her.

I woke up with a jolt, breathing heavily as my heart raced. Max was awake, too, watching me with cautious eyes as he rubbed my back in slow circles.

"Who was it?" he asked.

I shook my head, wondering what he meant.

"You were telling someone to run," he said.

I dropped my head into my hands, trying to steady my breathing. I closed my eyes. My nightmares were spilling over into my reality, and I wasn't sure I was prepared for what was coming.

"We have no defense against the Reeks, or the Carbons for that matter. What if he sends them all?" I whispered.

"We'll make it out alive, Sawyer. I promise you," Max said into my hair, as he kissed the top of my head.

My mom said I was their savior, but who would be mine?

TWENTY NINE

We had one more day to prepare. It wasn't enough time, but it would have to be. The soldiers carried large woodpiles to the middle of the courtyards and any other open spaces a ship may be able to land. When they arrived, we'd light the fires and pray they didn't just smash them down.

The bombs were being carried out to the edge of the forest separating Kuros and our village. Our only hope would be to direct Coleman and his Carbons to a flat opening in Kuros, where we would push them into the Muted Forest or the ocean, trying to separate their forces. The bombs, though potentially useless, would at least keep the Carbons away from the village.

Lankey would take the ocean side of Kuros with his men, and they'd take out as many as they could.

I watched as they carried the large bombs through the forest.

"Will this be far enough?" I asked Adam, who was overseeing the operation.

"Yes, it should be," Adam said. I was to wait in the village until all the bombs had been detonated. Afterward, I'd join the battle in the Muted Forest.

"I'm staying with you," Max said from the other side of me. I went to argue, but he put up his hand to stop me. "Last time I left you alone, things didn't go so well. I'm staying here this time."

I recalled back to when I almost died at the hands of Kenzie.

I glanced over my shoulder where Kenzie stood outside of the control room, watching the progress. He'd been surprisingly helpful, although I'd expected nothing less from the trained soldier he always was. He hadn't spoken much to me outside of orders or information he thought might be useful to win. I wondered if I'd get a chance to ask him if it was ever real—if we were ever real to him. I wasn't even sure why I needed to know, but it bothered me that he could forget something like that. His distance from me still made me wonder which side he'd end up on when the battle was over.

Ainsley came into view as she made her way back from the forest. She had laid out a clear line, so our soldiers knew where the Muted Forest began, and how far they had to run when the Carbons came. She would cloak as many as she could to allow us an element of surprise against the Carbons, but her gifts could only go so far. Tenason was following close behind her. The two had become inseparable the last few days.

"Will they be able to make it?" I asked her.

She gave a grim smile, as she shrugged her shoulders. "Some, not all."

I nodded, knowing there would be casualties even if the plan worked perfectly. More if it didn't.

"Any word from Aelish?" Max asked.

Ainsley shook her head. They would come, that I was certain of. We prayed it was quick enough. Vance and the Mountain Men were also on their way, but the trip from Canvas Mountain was long.

I walked toward the edge of the forest, looking down to the abandoned city of Kuros where our men could be seen setting up bombs and preparing for the attack. Max's arms wrapped around me, and I leaned into him with a sigh.

"This has to work," I mumbled.

"It will," Max promised. I knew he only said it for my sake. There was no way for him to know if it would or wouldn't work, but I was glad he said it.

Night fell upon us when I decided it was time to do the last task I had to complete, before Coleman's inevitable arrival the next day.

I nodded to the guards outside of a tiny house, and they let me pass. I knocked once and waited for the door to open.

He was in a gray sweater that made his eyes seem brighter than before. The metal cage around his hand hung down by his waist while the other held the door open for me.

"I was wondering when you'd come get me," Kenzie said.

I gave him a half smile. "We tried to give you as long as we could."

He nodded and stepped out the door to follow me back to the control room, where the little cell at the rear of the building waited for him once again, though this time he wasn't a prisoner. This time it was for his safety as much as ours. We couldn't risk having Coleman find him and use him. So far, he'd been able to fight it or break it by giving us little bits of information, but we still weren't too sure. There was no telling what he'd do if Coleman gave him an order he couldn't refuse.

The walk seemed long, and Kenzie shuffled his feet behind me at a slow pace. When we arrived, the door was already opened for him and he walked in.

I closed the door and turned the key, shoving it in my pocket.

"If things go bad, if there's no hope and everyone is gone, will you run?" he asked.

I shook my head.

"I didn't think so." Kenzie rested his head against the metal bars of the cage.

"Would you? If you had the chance, would you run?" I asked, tilting my chin up to see his eyes gazing down at me with such tenderness that my breath caught.

"Yes," he said.

I frowned, disappointed at the answer. I looked away.

He reached for my chin and tilted my head back up to meet his eyes again.

"I would run to you. To take you far away from here, away

from this pain and destruction. I'd run for your life, not mine," he said.

I couldn't breathe. My mind swam and I couldn't speak. I didn't understand what any of this could mean, or why I felt my heart beat a little faster at his words. It could all be a lie, another trick to get me to trust him, to let him out. I took a step back, and his hand fell to the space between us.

"Be safe," he said before he stepped away from the cage, sitting on the small cot in the corner.

I nodded, clamping my mouth shut. I didn't trust my voice. I turned on my heels and nearly sprinted out of there away from the heat stuck in my core.

Out in the cold night air, I shivered, but the warmth of his fingers on my skin lingered. There was so much confusion running through my mind. So many questions I wanted to ask and answers I didn't have. But I had to keep reminding myself of one thing.

He wasn't the same Kenzie he was before.

He could betray me at any moment, and I had to be on my guard. I shook my head, rubbing my sleeve against my chin to remove the betrayal stained there, but the warmth wouldn't go away.

THIRTY

The sun rose like any other day, but when it set, I knew the world would never be the same. Sam watched on his monitors for any evidence of Coleman moving, and everyone was stationed in their positions, ready for anything. But the wait was long, and we were beginning to wonder if Aelish had been right.

By suppertime, we were all getting impatient. It was odd that we'd want to rush to our possible deaths, but sitting around waiting for it was even worse.

There'd been no sign of Aelish or Vance, either.

"They'll be here," Ainsley promised. She lounged in a chair with her feet kicked up on the table.

Tenason and Ainsley were in charge of the men at the edge of the forest. They'd be the ones to lead the Carbons to the Muted Forest where more support waited, and I couldn't help worrying for them.

"It doesn't matter where they are. They'll still be in harm's way. Stop worrying and just trust your friends are smart," Max reminded me.

"You know, little baby, if you survive this, you may gain just a little respect from me," Ainsley teased.

"Only a little respect? Come on. I've been pretty useful, haven't I?" Tenason asked.

Ainsley smirked. "As useful as a puppy."

"A puppy? Really?" Tenason's eyes widened.

Ainsley shrugged.

"Okay then, how about we see how well you do without your lap dog?" Tenason stood to leave, but Ainsley grabbed his wrist before he went too far.

"So sensitive… a puppy is still a good companion to have around. A furry friend who makes you laugh when they chase their tail." Ainsley gave a toothy grin.

Tenason glared at the comparison but he sat down. After a moment of silence, he said, "So I'm a friend, then?"

Ainsley rolled her eyes, and I couldn't help smiling.

"We've got movement!" Sam yelled from the front of the room.

I sprinted up behind him to watch as the Carbons on the screen marched toward a sector of the station. There were hundreds of them. No, thousands.

As they passed the last camera, a thick metal door slammed shut, and that section of the station was gone, headed straight for Earth.

Sam pulled up a different screen where his location trackers were monitoring the ships coming our way.

"How many?" I asked.

Sam checked the others. "Two are heading our way, and they look filled to capacity," he confirmed.

My shoulders dropped. We'd been right to assume Coleman would send as many Carbons as he could.

"Is he with them?" Max asked.

Sam again pulled the screen to the security feed where he searched for the location of Coleman. "No," he said.

Max swore under his breath. We'd been hoping Coleman would come with the Carbons, so we had a chance to end this.

On the screen, Coleman stood in his office, looking out a large window to the two sections of the spaceship headed our way. "Make sure every one of them is destroyed," Coleman spoke to an officer standing in the corner of the room with his back to the screen. "I've had enough with their games. This ends now. This ends today."

The air in the room shifted at Coleman's words ringing loud and clear through the speakers of control. This would either be our greatest victory, or it would be our end. But one way or another, this was our moment.

"I don't care what he has to say. I hope he continues to underestimate each and every one of us, because we have something that none of them have…" Murray stood behind us, his voice filling the room. "We have a reason to live. We have something to fight for. They don't. This will not be our last fight, and we will not give up. Ever."

The soldiers all around us cheered before heading out to their posts. They prepared for the Carbons with as much confidence as they could muster.

Murray placed a hand on his son's shoulder and gave him a nod. Neither said goodbye, but the possibility still hung in the air that this could be the end.

I nodded to Ainsley and Tenason, who stood ready to go. "Run fast," I ordered, and Ainsley gave me a devilish smile before they sprinted out of the control room.

It pained me to have to stand by and wait while the others fought our battle, but we had a plan, and I had to be patient. A cool breeze pushed the pine smell of the forest toward where I stood on a hill at the edge of the village, overlooking Kuros. I couldn't even use my powers up here in case the Carbons noticed and turned their eyes on me, ruining all our hard work and planning.

The fires had been set, and the heat from the huge bonfires warmed my back. I stood at the edge of the forest. Kuros lay before me, and the men lined up with their backs to me, ready to run toward the Muted Forest and help.

In the distance, the two ships broke through the atmosphere with a sharp crack, and they came into view. They were much bigger than the last ship Coleman had sent down, and I did my best to keep my legs strong as my knees weakened.

The village around me was quiet and empty, except for the few men who had stayed with Max and I. The civilians who wouldn't be fighting had been sent north, hopefully far enough away from the destruction, if it came to that. It was hard to hide from the inevitable, even if we tried.

In the distance, Tenason and Ainsley were holding the front line, waiting for their moment. Behind them, a group of shadows stepped forward. Out of the forest, a line of warriors took up their places behind our soldiers. The Ladies of the Muted Forest had arrived. I watched as they stepped up to the front with Ainsley before she cloaked them with her gift. All I saw was the edge of the forest. They disappeared right before my eyes, but they were still there.

I let out a sigh of relief. There was nothing more we could do, nothing left that I could do.

"Two minutes out," Sam called into the earpiece I wore.

I watched in the distance where the two ships glided over the ocean. They were circular, and they cut through the air like a ripple in the water, smooth and graceful.

The ships circled around the village and Kuros, and I ducked low against the fierce wind and the dust the ship kicked up. They seemed to be surveying the area before they landed on the only open spot they found, where we had planned for them to land.

So far our plan was working.

My heart was beating so fast as the ramps of the two ships lowered. In unison, the Carbons marched out. They formed organized lines in front of their ships, facing our soldiers and the Ladies of the Muted Forest they couldn't yet see. There were so many of them, thousands of Carbons. They made our small army look like nothing.

From what I saw though, there were no Reeks among them.

The Carbons waited. For what, I wasn't sure, but they stood

their ground, facing toward where our soldiers stood. My only guess was that the Carbons felt them.

The anticipation was too much. I nearly ran for them, but Max gripped my hand. I sighed while I watched, trying to understand what they were doing.

Murray didn't wait for them to make the first move. With an echoing boom that took me right off my feet, he set off the Megastun Bombs that had been placed right where the Carbons stood.

A wave of energy blasted from the bombs, spreading so far that even I felt the effects from here. My knees buckled when I tried to stand and my head pounded. The space around me seemed to be spinning, and voices were muffled and loud all at once.

Before I had a chance to do anything else, Max picked me up and bolted. He tried to get as much distance as he could from the Megastun Bombs before they did their last task—ripping out the microchip at the base of every Carbon skull in sight, which included me.

I was too close, even as far away as I was, not as safe as Adam thought I was. The bombs had reached me as powerfully as if I were standing beside them.

A sharp pull burned at the back of my neck, and I screamed in pain. My eyes filled with tears as I looked up to Max, who sprinted harder.

We were almost at the control room when there was a sharp jolt and a tug at my neck. My entire body fell limp, and my head dropped back.

The last thing I heard was Max crying my name.

THIRTY
ONE

It didn't take me long to realize I wasn't dead, but the time it took to regain function of my body was slow and maddening. The effects of the bomb did more to my physical body than it did to the microchip. When I was able to sit up, I reached my hand to the back of my neck where the microchip was still in place.

Max hovered over me, worried and unsure how to help.

"Did it work?" My voice was raw, and I swallowed at the dryness. "Find out, now."

Reluctantly, Max left me to see Sam while I scrambled to my knees and stood on shaky legs.

I could barely walk straight, and my eyes were seeing double. With each step, I became a little stronger. My Carbon body was bouncing back fast, which meant if the bombs didn't take out the microchips like they were supposed to, their bodies would recover fast, too.

I picked up my pace, nearing the edge and looking down to Kuros where the thousands of Carbons were scattered across the ground. Some weren't moving, but those who were had already regained their strength, just like me.

It didn't work. I hadn't expected it to, but I'd hoped we'd take out a few at least. The hundred or so Carbons who had been destroyed did nothing to sway the numbers as their army was in the thousands.

Our people were taking steps toward them, visible and exposed. A few cheered like they had already won the battle, shooting a few Carbons lying on the ground, but without the microchips destroyed it wouldn't matter.

"Get back!" I yelled, but there was no way they heard me.

I waved my arms frantically, but I was too far away. No one saw me.

There was a sharp sound in my earpiece as Sam scrambled. "It didn't work, get out of there now!" he ordered.

As the order translated down the line, the soldiers quickly moved back. More Carbons crawled to their feet. I caught Ainsley trying to cloak as many as she could. But as they scrambled away toward the forest, they were out of sync and scattered enough that she couldn't cover them all.

A couple soldiers took the opportunity to get out a few shots before they turned toward the forest and sprinted. The Carbons regained their footing and took off after our men.

They didn't stand a chance. Those who couldn't run quickly

enough, and even the ones that Ainsley cloaked, were being caught. The Carbons took them out before they took more than two strides, and they were down—dead. Our people were about to be massacred.

A Carbon at the front of the line was already using its abilities. A strong wind pushed a few of the Ladies of the Muted Forest off their feet, and a rumble in the ground caused the earth to quake. More of our people fell to their knees.

Our fighters weren't even going to get to the edge of the forest if we didn't do something quick.

I looked around me to the bonfires burning strong. I summoned my powers to the top, causing a tingling on my fingertips. I lifted the enormous fire into the air, careful to keep each log in my grasp, and I threw the flames past the forest line. My powers clung to the ball of fire until it crashed down on the Carbons, engulfing everything in its path.

From the ocean side, Lankey let his cannons loose. They blasted at the line of Carbons who turned their attention onto Lankey's men. It allowed a few of our people to sprint back into the forest and out of my view. The Carbons followed, but from there I had no idea how far our people escaped.

Max was back beside me, a hand on my elbow, and we took off. I stayed with him, knowing I could run faster, but not wanting to leave him alone or exposed.

As we reached the edge of Kuros, we found a few Carbons had been taken out by Lankey and his men. They continued to push the Carbons into the forest.

A line of flames burning along the tree line leading to the

village did a decent job of moving the Carbons in the direction we wanted them to, but the sheer number of the enemy was overwhelming.

I made quick work of the Carbons without abilities. Stepping out from the forest, I only had to send out one quick swipe of my powers, one flick of my wrist, and their microchips were in my grasp. They were easy to take down. It was the ones who fought back with their abilities that gave me trouble.

Wind blasted against me like a punch to the stomach, and I was thrown back into Max. He grunted but pushed me to my feet before he pulled us out of the way of another blast.

The Carbon's ability was too erratic for me to hold onto, so I had to take him out another way. I sent two knifes aimed for his head, slicing through the air. He moved before they hit their mark, but one still stabbed deep into the Carbon's side. He stumbled but yanked out the knife. The Carbon sent another burst of air at us.

I ducked behind a tree that creaked and groaned against the storm before uprooting and tearing from the ground. The tree threatened to take out the fleeing soldiers behind me, so I gripped onto it with my powers. Bracing myself and digging into the solid ground beneath me, I grunted as I flung it toward the Carbon.

The Carbon ducked out of the way, but its comrades behind weren't so lucky, and I eliminated a few more.

Just as the Carbon stepped forward to send another blast my way, a large white blur sprinted out of the forest. Before the Carbon could even raise its hands, the Ice Bear that Vance rode on ripped off the Carbon's head.

More followed him as the Mountain Men rode on enormous Ice Bears that tore apart the Carbons, with vicious fangs and sharp claws.

Vance gave me a wink before he set his eyes on the next Carbon ahead of him, his mouth twisting into a vicious smile as he pounced.

"Sawyer!" Max called from behind me.

I looked to where he was pointing. Tenason and Ainsley stood in the middle of four Carbons, trying to fight their way out. Ainsley cloaked them, but the Carbons still aimed where they were, and Ainsley couldn't hold on to hide them. Tenason was limping, and Ainsley had a large gash on the side of her face. My heart stopped as Tenason kicked one of the Carbons away, and Ainsley aimed an arrow at it, but another attacked them.

Tenason looked around, knowing he was surrounded. He took Ainsley in his arms and shielded her with his body, ready to take the blows for her.

But the blow would never reach him; I wasn't about to let that happen.

I stalked toward them, my energy boiling as my rage fueled it. I pushed my powers forward, gripping all four Carbons, but I wasn't done yet.

I stepped past Tenason who was still hovering over Ainsley, as he watched with both horror and awe. My powers were still wrapped around all four Carbons, lifting them into the air as my glare burned through them. I squeezed, and they choked and clawed at nothing. With one more quick snap, I ended their lives and tossed them to the side in a pile with the rest of their dead companions.

Max helped Tenason to his feet when I turned back around.

"Most have gone into the forest, but our people aren't getting far. Murray has already called in everyone from the Muted Forest to help. We can't get the Carbons deep enough into the forest for this plan to work," Max said.

My earpiece had fallen out sometime during the fight, but Sam was still reporting every move to Max and the others. It wasn't good news.

I looked around me where bodies lay lifeless on the ground. Not just the Carbons but ours. For every Carbon we took down, there were ten more Carbons waiting to fight. Even with the Ladies of the Muted Forest and the Mountain Men at our side, we weren't winning.

I shook my head. "What do we do?"

For only a second, I thought it was the end. My powers weren't enough to fight this many Carbons, and too many of our people were going to die if we didn't think of something else.

"We don't give up," Tenason said. He leaned on Ainsley for support but she nodded, too.

"We can't beat them, not like this. We need more," I said. I wanted to sound tougher. I wanted to be tougher, but all I saw was red, and it was our blood.

"I have an idea," Max said. "Stay here."

He went to leave, but I grabbed his arm.

"You trust me, right?" he asked.

"Of course," I said.

"Then trust me now." He reached into my pocket, taking the key I had stashed there, and ran.

THIRTY TWO

KENZIE

He heard the screaming from his cell. Every bomb and shot that went off made him flinch, as he sat with his hand gripping the bar so tight his knuckles were white. Not knowing was what killed him the most. Whose screams was he hearing?

He paced back and forth in the small space. All he could think of was Sawyer. Was she okay? Would she survive? He had found that as long as he kept his distance from Sawyer, tried not to think of her or the memories that kept filtering into his mind on their own, he was able to ignore the kill order. He didn't remember it all or who he used to be, yet there were times when she would move a certain way, or say something that sparked an image. A dark, cement-covered room. The feel of the delicate skin over her collarbone. Those memories, small and fleeting, snuck in sometimes, and it made his heart ache.

He knew the army they were facing. If he was honest with himself, there was no way they could beat them. Their plan was a good one, but Coleman's army was better.

The door down the hallway smashed open, and feet skidded across the floor with haste. Kenzie had his guard up before Max swung around the corner.

He grabbed a key from his pocket and opened the cell door. Kenzie took a step back.

"He's not here," Max assured Kenzie when he saw the fear in his eyes. The thought that Coleman could use him against them once more was running through Kenzie's mind. "We need your help."

Max reached for Kenzie's caged-up hand and pulled out a smaller key from his front pocket. He twisted it into the lock, and the heavy metal cage clanked to the ground.

Kenzie stretched out his fingers. They felt weird and weak, but the power inside of him instantly roared to life, begging to be let free.

"You still have that cuff of yours?" Max asked.

Kenzie pulled the cuff out from his pocket and held it in his hands. It sent a shiver down his spine.

"You're going to need that," Max said. He turned to leave the cell, leading Kenzie with him.

"Is it safe?" he asked, worried more for Sawyer than anyone else, but still he didn't want to harm innocent lives.

"We're about to find out."

Tentatively, Kenzie took the cuff and placed it on his left wrist. There was a slight tingle at first before the cuff latched on and dug into his skin. He winced and hissed through his teeth.

"Oh yeah, forgot to tell you about that part," Max said over his shoulder. He pushed open the door, and the flames burning in the village hit them with a wave of heat. Though his back was to him, Kenzie didn't feel the urge to kill him as he had worried; instead, he felt a pull towards something far away—something waiting for him on the battlefield. His heart raced.

Max stopped at the end of the hallway and turned to face Kenzie. "Listen, I sure as hell don't trust you. And the second you step out of line, I have no problem putting a bullet through your skull. But she trusts you. And frankly, we need your help. So just don't let her down again, okay?"

Kenzie flexed his hands and rolled his shoulders back. Max's words hit far deeper than he had expected, *don't let her down again*. Because he had… the old Kenzie anyway, but the new Kenzie wouldn't do that ever again.

He looked Max in the eyes. "I won't."

The destruction was worse than he'd imagined. Coleman had sent nearly two thousand of his best Carbons, many with abilities even Kenzie was afraid of. Though Commander Murray's team was putting up a good fight, they wouldn't last much longer, and they were heavily outnumbered.

Kenzie slowed as he stepped out of the forest line, still feeling a tug on his energy pulling him onward. He watched the Carbons as they circled and attacked. Coleman had trained them well—he had trained them well. Lifting his hand, Kenzie let his powers lose. His energy deep inside begged for more, having been cooped up for so long. A sharp feeling of electricity ran through his entire body in a way it never had before. The pulse and strength of each burst he released swam through his veins.

Max was to his right, and Kenzie was impressed with how many Carbons he took down with a hunting knife and a gun, but there were still more coming.

Up ahead, Kenzie found Sawyer in the middle of a horde of Carbons. She pushed them back with her powers, sending the Carbons crashing down. She followed with another blow to keep them there, removing their microchips and crushing them in mid-air. The pull intensified towards her. She moved with the grace of a dancer and the determination of a warrior. Her hair had come loose from its usual braid and flowed behind her in a wave of dark brown.

When she turned and found Kenzie standing only a few feet away, her eyes locked on his, and he nearly dropped to his knees.

For months now, maybe longer than that even, he'd been seeing this very image in his dreams. It had soothed the nightmares so many times. A girl with amber brown eyes stood before him, her hair blowing in the wind behind her, and her eyes locked on his. Sawyer was the girl with the amber brown eyes, he knew with all certainty now. He remembered it all so clearly, and yet there was something missing from the picture.

She made her way through Carbons to where Max and him

stood. "Are you going to help us this time? Or them?"

"You," he said.

She glanced quickly to Max before she nodded and turned back to the Carbons coming in droves.

"We have to do something." Her voice was quiet as she shoved a group of Carbons back with the flick of her wrist. Her powers had become second nature to her, but even she knew that wasn't enough.

Sawyer glanced back at him, before taking out three Carbons coming at them from behind. And in that brief moment, he noticed what was missing from his dream. The storm. It wasn't just a dream; it was a vision. For him.

"Do you trust me?" Kenzie asked Sawyer.

She looked over her shoulder, thinking before she said, "Yes."

He put his hand out toward her, aiming it at her chest where she stood a few feet away. Her eyes widened, but she didn't look afraid.

He heard the click of a gun next.

Max was at his side. "What did I tell you?" Max growled, but Kenzie didn't put his hand down.

"I know what you said." Kenzie spared him only a second's glance before he locked in on Sawyer again. "We can do this. We can end this. I've seen it." *I won't hurt you,* he silently said.

Sawyer frowned, considering Kenzie's words before she gave a sharp nod. Max dropped his hand.

"How?" she asked.

"Take it." He gestured to his still outstretched hand. "And wreak havoc on them all."

Sawyer's smile spread with understanding.

"Ready?" Kenzie asked.

Sawyer shifted her weight, turning fully to face him. "Ready."

Kenzie unleashed all of his powers right at Sawyer.

THIRTY THREE

The blast hit me hard, making me stumble back a few steps, but my powers caught the erratic bolt of electricity in time. I felt every spark, every bit of electricity Kenzie sent my way, and I pushed it out, up, and around as it grew. My never-ending source of control held onto every inch of it.

The skies grew dark as my abilities pulled the black smoke from the bonfires with it, as if thick clouds moved overhead, but it was just us, just our combined energy filling the sky above us. The electric wave I sent up into the air pooled in the darkness and delivered thunderous booms all around us as the bolts sparked and crashed into one another. It rumbled the ground and the trees shook.

I kept my eyes on Kenzie, keeping my breath steady and

my focus on him alone. His body was tense, and the muscles on his neck were corded with strain. Everything else around us seemed to slow, all focused on the energy that fused and molded between us.

My gaze caught Max to my right, keeping the Carbons away from Kenzie and I while the storm grew stronger. I let our abilities melt together and form one strong force.

Max dropped to one knee and let out a scream of pain that threatened to break my concentration. A Carbon stood over him. But Max wasn't weak and he wasn't stupid.

He slashed his large knife at the Carbon's leg, cutting clean through the back of its ankle. The Carbon began to drop, standing unbalanced on one leg. With another flick of his knife, Max sliced through the back of the Carbon's head, destroying the microchip there.

As my heart settled, my attention moved back to Kenzie as his energy flooded through me.

It grew, the unnatural storm overhead, and I kept fueling it and building it until there was no more room. The skies were jet black with smoke, and jagged bolts of electricity moved across it like a painting, filling up the dark space with its own white markings. A sweet breeze caressed my damp skin, and my gaze followed the lines in the sky, like lightning bolts waiting to be let loose.

The smoke clouds seemed to grow heavy, and our powers had reached their maximum ceiling. I could fill it no more. There was a pulse in the air and energy surrounded us. It was full and ready to be unleashed.

Kenzie felt it, too, and he dropped his hand, falling to his knees. He kept his eyes on me. His presence was calming, and the threatening storm above us didn't take me with it. I brought my hands up to hold each bolt, feeling the tingle of electricity shivering over my skin.

All around me, I was suddenly aware of each and every energy surrounding us, picking out my enemies from my allies, marking them like a big X across their backs.

The wind pushed my hair all around me as the storm brewed. But inside of me everything grew quiet, and all I heard were two heartbeats. Mine and Kenzie's. He watched me, waiting and ready.

It was time.

My arms burned with the effort. Every muscle in my body tensed. I thought I was screaming, but all I heard was the constant *thump-thump, thump-thump* of our hearts. I dropped to my knees, but I didn't let go, not yet.

I took in a deep breath. I closed my eyes and slashed my hands down like a lightning bolt. Around me, the sharp white bolts came crashing down all at once. I saw the bright flashes of light even through my closed eyes. The sound was deafening as each individual bolt, thousands of them, hit their marks in less time than it took me to blink.

The entire area fell silent.

I opened my eyes and everything was still. The Carbons all around us stood like stones before a soft breeze flickered by. Each Carbon turned to nothing more than ash and dust as they disappeared with the wind before our eyes.

Every Carbon who had once been fighting our people was gone.

I was on my knees when Kenzie knelt before me. My heart was calm, and my breaths were natural and even. His eyes were wild with a fire that seeped into me, warming my core.

He touched my arm, and his skin was blazing hot against mine. A cool breeze sent a shiver down my spine, and I smelled the bonfires still burning nearby.

"You did it." He smiled.

I shook my head. "We did it."

Every last Carbon had been destroyed, along with hundreds of our people. We'd killed nearly two thousand Carbons, but if Kenzie's numbers were correct, that was nothing to Coleman. We had lost nearly a third of our people. Less than a thousand remained. Though we had ended the battle, it was hard to say we'd won with so many of our own lives lost.

I stood rooted in the same spot for who knows how long, watching with horror at the scene around me. Max stayed with me, a calming presence by my side, but he didn't speak. Neither of us knew what to say. Bodies were scattered across the broken pavement near Kuros, and more trailed up toward the forest leading to the village. Moans were mixed with cheers and cries of victory, but I couldn't see past the blood.

When my feet started moving, I didn't know where they'd take me, but Max followed a step behind me. I couldn't stay where I was, surrounded by a victory that didn't feel much like one. If my legs would've let me run, I would have.

A few feet away from the edge of the forest, Aelish knelt on the ground over the body of one of her ladies. Annia was beside her, her lips moving in a silent prayer for her fallen sister. I blinked at the sight, my mind so used to seeing death all around me that my heart was beginning to ice over to the pain and sorrow. Death would never stop; it covered me like a blanket. I was powerless to prevent the ache in their eyes. I squeezed Aelish's shoulder while I passed. Max whispered something in her ear before we kept moving.

More bodies lay beyond her.

I was walking through a dream or a nightmare. Either way, it didn't feel real, and I wondered if my mind didn't truly understand what had happened. Max was by my side and that was the only thing in this moment grounding me to reality. He allowed me to move, even if I had no destination that felt right.

Ainsley and Kenzie helped Tenason back to the village. He had wounded his leg and winced with every step he tried to take, but he had survived. Kenzie caught my gaze, and I noticed the same haunted expression in his eyes that glazed over mine.

So many lives gone in the blink of an eye.

A few more steps down the path, Vance stood before three Ice Bears that had died during the battle. He marked them with his blood as he placed a hand on each of their large heads.

"Thank you," I managed to get out. "And I'm sorry." He had lost many men along with the Ice Bears.

"Never apologize for a war you did not start. We would have

felt this same loss, probably worse, if we had done nothing," Vance said.

I gave a weak smile before I turned back toward the abandoned city of Kuros. The ship those Carbons had arrived on stood still and silent, towering over the crumbled ruins of the city. Smoke and ash swirled past me on a silent wind, but the skies had opened up, and I could see the moon once again.

I didn't know where I was going, but I couldn't be here anymore. I couldn't be around these people who saw me as their savior, when all I saw was death and the ones I couldn't save.

Max gave me space, remaining close, but keeping an eye on me. He limped slightly with a wound on his leg, but he'd heal; he would live. I appreciated his presence, and that he didn't press me for anything.

I sat on large cement block near the edge of the city, overlooking the dark ocean now reflecting the stars and moon overhead. I left space for Max to sit beside me. Lankey and his men had already returned from their ship. They were some of the few who were unharmed through it all, but they had already lost many in the United Isles. Though they were spared today, they weren't without loss.

Silence hung between us for some time.

"They'll be back," I said. "He'll bring more and we'll have less."

Max nodded. This victory would be short lived. We were wounded and beaten down.

Lena had told us a long time ago that her father wouldn't stop. We could kill thousands of his Carbons, and Coleman would send more to replace them. When he ran out, he would come for us in a different way, and I feared a time would come when we couldn't stop him.

"We have a weapon now." Max squeezed my leg. "You have a weapon."

I sighed. Kenzie and I were just that—a weapon. But a weapon could be dismantled. A weapon could be turned against its master. Coleman might still hold a power over Kenzie that he could use to his advantage.

"We got lucky this time that he wasn't there. I don't think he'll make that mistake again," I whispered.

Max agreed. "All we can do is take one step at a time. But this time, we need to make a move first."

I looked over to Max, covered in dirt and blood.

"Thank you," I said.

Max swallowed, waiting for me to continue.

"For trusting me."

Max gave me a crooked smile and pulled me into his chest. He said into my hair, "I will always trust you."

A little bit of the heavy weight lifted from my shoulders.

THIRTY
FOUR

The trail leading back to the village was worn down and covered in speckles of blood. The moon was bright, allowing Max and me to see every drop our men had spilled. No matter where I looked, it was there, all around me.

When we reached Doc's office, the number of injured overwhelmed me. They had added a new wing out the back of his small room, covered with a canvas tent. People were sprawled out on blood-soaked mattresses dragged from nearby houses. It smelled like death and dirt and bile, and there was blood everywhere. It was an effort to not gag at the scent.

My entire body was heavy and drained. Not like last time, not my powers, but my physical body and my mind. I was certain I could sleep for days with the weight of everything pulling me down.

Tenason was near the back, his leg heavily bandaged and coated in red like the rest of the room. He had a bump under his eye that looked to be growing, along with a sling over one arm where his shoulder was wrapped up.

"How is it?" I asked. Max followed behind me, and I stepped around to where Ainsley stood at Tenason's bedside. Kenzie was in a chair a few feet away.

"It's fine. These guys are just making a big fuss out of nothing. Barely a flesh wound." Tenason gave a weak smile.

"I could see your bone from how deep the cut was," Ainsley spat. "That's not just a little flesh wound."

My stomach churned.

"Yeah, yeah. It'll be fine." Tenason waved a hand at Ainsley. She crossed her arms and narrowed her eyes.

I checked Ainsley over once. She had a gash across her cheek that had been hastily patched up and a few scrapes across her arm, but she seemed in good health. Kenzie also looked fine. I was certain the blood covering his clothing wasn't his. He was quiet, leaning against the wall at the end of Tenason's bed.

"That was amazing what you guys did." Tenason's eyes lit up. He glanced between Kenzie and me. "Those Carbons didn't stand a chance. One minute they were there, then the next... poof. Just gone. Unbelievable!"

I didn't have a chance to reply before Kenzie pushed himself off the wall abruptly, knocking into Max's shoulder. Kenzie rushed by like he was trying to get away from someone.

"Something I said?" Tenason asked.

"It's always something you said," Ainsley teased.

I turned to follow Kenzie, but Max stepped in my path. His eyes narrowed on me with a mix of warning and worry.

"I'll be right back," I promised. Reluctantly, Max let me pass.

Outside, it only took me a few minutes to track where Kenzie had gone. He hadn't made it that far. He was pressed up against a wall around the corner of the building. Leaning against the cold metal, he rested his elbows on his knees. His head dropped and he vomited.

I was quiet as I approached. "Everything okay?" I asked.

Kenzie shook his head, wiping off his mouth with the sleeve of his sweater. "I can't believe we did that," he whispered.

"We saved a lot of people today, Kenzie," I said, but he wouldn't meet my eyes.

He pushed off the wall and paced a few steps. "No." He shook his head again. "We killed thousands of them."

Frowning, I moved to stand in front of him, forcing him to stop his pacing or run straight into me. He met my gaze, and his face was as pale as ever. His eyes frantically searched mine, but for what I wasn't sure.

"I can't do that again. I can never do that again." He was shaking.

"I don't understand. They are the enemy. They would've killed every one of us if we hadn't stopped them." I took a step forward, and dirt and snow crunched under my feet.

Kenzie leaned back against the wall, closing his eyes. His head pressed against the metal. His chest rose and fell with a deep breath before he said, "What if one of them was like you… like your mom?"

I thought for a moment. "There's no way for us to know that."

"All I could see out there was you. But when the dust settled, when the reality of what we did settled, what if we just ended a life that didn't deserve the fate we'd chosen for them?"

I sighed, took another step forward, and leaned against the wall beside him. He had a point. If my mom, Lena, and I broke the control Coleman had over us, who was to say these Carbons couldn't have done that, too? But they were the ones who attacked us. They shot first.

"All I've ever been my entire life is a weapon. Something to be used for or against. And even when I do good, even when I helped save so many people, I can't help but feel that the rest didn't deserve to die," Kenzie whispered.

"If we hadn't done what we did, there would be no turning back for anyone. Neither you nor I could live with ourselves if we'd let these people die." I swept my hands out to the village that was still buzzing with life and people, even wounded and marred. "Sometimes, we have to make the hard choices, Kenzie. And sometimes, there is no right or wrong answer… It just is."

He glanced over to me, his eyes tired and sad. He dropped his head. "I can't do that again…"

"I won't make you," I said, squeezing his shoulder before I left him with the haunted memories of an impossible choice he had to make. The consequences were heavy on his shoulders, just as they weighed heavy on mine.

"Well, it seems we pissed him off royally," Sam said from his desk at the front of the control room. For the last five minutes, we'd been watching on the big screen as Coleman tossed the contents in his office all over the place.

With Kenzie's access to the space station, Sam had been monitoring Coleman through the security cameras. I didn't think Sam had slept judging by the full pot of coffee on his desk and his bloodshot eyes.

"Do you think he'll send more right away?" Max asked Kenzie, who was still pale but stood near the front, watching the mayhem.

"No." Kenzie shook his head. "He won't risk it just yet. He's too calculated to be impulsive."

He was right. Coleman may have been a menace, but he was anything but impulsive. Only *we* were the problem, Kenzie and I.

I watched as Kenzie's shoulders tensed with each toss of a book or the smash of a chair being thrown across the room. Finally, Coleman settled down, as he sat on the edge of his empty desk. His chin fell to his chest.

A door in the back corner of Coleman's office slid open, and I recognized the person on the other side. It was my mother.

"Turn the sound up," I instructed, stepping behind Sam.

"Ah, Russo. Hope you don't mind my redecorated office." Coleman narrowed his eyes, and the joke was lost in his cold stare.

"No, sir." My mom stopped a few feet away, her back straight and her face neutral.

Coleman tilted his head to the side as he watched my mother. My knuckles were white, and I gripped the back of Sam's chair, waiting to see what he wanted with her.

"It seems the traitor you found for me before wasn't the only one," Coleman said. I didn't know what he was referring to, but I knew just as well as anyone that my mom was probably the traitor he meant. "Every time I try to end this, someone keeps getting in the way, and I have run out of patience."

There was a small shift in my mother's stance, as she waited for Coleman to continue.

"Who do you suppose could have gotten a message to those people that we were coming? How could they possibly have been so prepared for us to arrive?" Coleman stood up, circling around her before he stopped at her side. His nose was a few inches from her face, but she kept her stare forward. "You wouldn't know anything about this now, would you?"

Again, there was the smallest of shifts, enough that I noticed, before my mother said, "No, sir."

Coleman's eyebrows rose. "No, you wouldn't, would you?" he snarled. "They have a weapon now. They destroyed my Carbons in the blink of an eye, but I wonder how they could possibly have known to use it. To use… each other?"

My mother didn't blink as Coleman moved to stand in front of her. "Your powers are quite unique, Russo, aren't they? The ability to make anyone see what you want them to see." Coleman's eyes draped over her. "I wonder what sort of images you might have put into Kenzie's head—to make him turn on me with such vengeance."

The game was over, and my mother knew it. Her eyes grew glacial as they met Coleman's. "I didn't have to show him anything to get him to turn on you. You did that all on your own. You thought you created an obedient soldier, but you only managed to give him the tools that will be your ending."

"My ending?" Coleman smirked. "Oh, I don't think that'll be coming anytime soon for me, my dear. You, on the other hand, I can't be so sure."

With each step he took back to the desk, my pulse raced. As he turned back around, his eyes didn't settle back on my mother. Instead, they looked into the camera lens from which we watched.

His lips curved into a snarl. "Oh, to be a fly on the wall, watching our every movement. It's not very nice to watch in on people without their consent." His eyes bore right into the camera and right through me. "You want to see what I'm going to do next? You want to know just how far I will take it? Well, congratulations, because now you have a front-row seat to witness just what I am capable of."

The screen went black.

"What happened?" I couldn't keep the panic from my voice.

"I don't know…" Sam frantically tried to pull up the security feeds we'd hacked into, but they were all black. "He's locked us out."

Sam was still attempting to pull up some sort of feed when one screen turned on. My mother walked down the long hallway of the space station, two guards at her side.

The security cameras flickered on as she moved past one

camera's range and into another. Hundreds of black screens filled the front wall of control, as one at a time they turned on, so we could watch my mother continue down the hallway.

"Where are they taking her?" I asked Kenzie, who stood behind me.

I could tell by his tense shoulders he didn't want to say. "I think they are heading to

Sector 7…"

It took me a moment to recall why that sounded so familiar, and when I did, my chest caved in. "No!"

I remembered the abandoned sector filled with chained-up Reeks trying to get away, nearly tearing themselves apart.

"He wouldn't, would he?" Sam asked.

I knew the answer. He would. This was a message to me, to hit me where it would hurt the most. To let me know that no matter what I did, he knew my weakness, and he knew I wouldn't last long.

The final camera flickered on. The Reeks had grown in numbers since the last time I'd seen this room. Chains clung to the walls, and thousands of monsters yanked on them. Some reached out as the guards pulled my mother into the center of the room and chained her to the floor, out of reach of the Reeks.

"Let's see how mad she drives them. Let's see how long it takes before they rip apart their own bodies to reach her. And I'm curious to find out just how much longer you can watch." Coleman's voice sounded through room.

Sam reacted, pulling up our security system on his screen. "He's hacked into my computer. I have to shut it all down but…"

He turned around to me, waiting. There was nothing I could do for her, but I couldn't look away.

Kenzie shifted behind me. "We've got to shut it down before he gets in any farther."

I couldn't look away from the screen. My mother's eyes were wild as she scanned the room, the Reeks clawing and reaching for her, only inches away. The horde grew wilder as they strained against their restraints, hungry for her.

Max put his hand in mine. It was warm against my cold skin.

"We'll find some way to get her out," he promised.

I tore my gaze way from the screen and nodded to Sam. With a sharp crack, the screen went blank, and the room became silent.

THIRTY
FIVE

I couldn't stop thinking about her. Every night, I closed my eyes and prayed she'd give me some vision that she was okay, but all I saw was darkness. The sound of those creatures' guttural screams rang through my ears.

The atmosphere in the village was somber. It'd been almost a week, and many were on the mend, including Tenason. The threat of more to come hung over us.

Aelish and the Ladies of the Muted Forest had left a few days earlier, and with them, Vance and the Mountain Men. Their wounded healed enough to move back into the Muted Forest to a village where the two tribes stayed together. They were close enough to return if we needed them, but they remained within their boundaries, so they could heal and build up their strength.

Vance had sent word to his father they needed the rest of the men's help, but he wasn't confident his father would change his mind.

Ainsley chose to stay with us. She had said her training and knowledge of the Muted Forest would help us communicate with the others if needed, but in truth it was her refusal to leave Tenason's side that kept her in our village. She'd become his crutch in more ways than one and he was hers.

The cold of winter had made its turn from bitter freezing to warmer weather and melting snow. I sat outside wrapped in a blanket, watching Max train some of the villagers. We'd lost many skilled soldiers and even more were injured in the battle. We needed to train whomever was able and willing to help.

"Arms strong." Max walked down the line, testing their stance and pushing down their stretched-out arms as they held their weapons out before them. Men and women, children and the old, all stood waiting for their turn. "Keep your stance wide, knees bent. If I can push you over, you won't last five minutes out there. Your base of support is the most important weapon you have."

It killed me to watch these people forced to fight out of necessity, but if they didn't have any training, it'd be so much worse. Some of our people from the base in Cytos, Theresa and Adam included, joined. We'd lost our source of inside information on Coleman, and we no longer knew what he'd do next unless Aelish was given something from the stars that would help. She'd said there was no way to tell or force it to happen—they spoke when they chose to and that was all she could provide.

"How are they looking?" Tenason hobbled over to my side, one arm wrapped around Ainsley for support, but he was at least able to put weight on his injured leg.

"As good as a beginner group can look at this point." I shrugged, sliding over to give him room to sit.

His leg was still bandaged up from his ankle to his knee. Even though he tried to hide the pain, I noted the wince as he sat as gingerly as he could.

"When they get to shooting, make sure Max lets me know. I want to help," Tenason said.

"You couldn't shoot the side of a house with the shape you're in," Ainsley huffed, as she helped him prop his leg up on a log.

"Ye of little faith." Tenason winked, and Ainsley rolled her eyes.

I had to agree with her. He was in worse shape than he cared to admit. Not just his leg, but his shoulder was a mess, and one eye was still swollen and covered in a black-and-purple bruise.

"All right, pair up and practice balance checks," Max instructed before he stepped over to where we were seated. "How's the leg doing?"

"Oh, it's great. Hardly even feel it anymore." Tenason smirked.

Ainsley reached down and poked Tenason's leg right where the bandage covered his wound. He howled in pain.

"Hardly feel it, hey?" Ainsley raised an eyebrow.

"Well, if you don't touch it, it's fine." Tenason glared at Ainsley before she flashed a mischievous smile.

Max squished in beside me, wrapping the blanket tighter

around my shoulders. I leaned into his warmth.

"How do you have a blanket on? You're boiling." He rubbed my shoulders.

I shrugged and let myself relax into him. I didn't feel warm at all. I was freezing. My body was exhausted, and my mind even more so. I knew the cuff kept my abilities strong, never allowing them to burn out, but the last few weeks I'd hardly slept at all, and I was feeling the effects of it today.

"Any news from Sam?" Max whispered in my ears.

I shook my head. I checked in with Sam daily for any updates on my mom, but so far things had gone quiet. We couldn't risk trying to get back into Coleman's system now that he knew we were there. We'd be welcoming him into our command center, and he'd know any steps we looked to take. Even if we had no plan.

Adam and Sam were trying to get our small shuttle equipped to go into space, but there was of course the matter of who could fly it. There was a slim chance we'd be able to save my mom and Lena, but it was something. Still, there were a few kinks to be ironed out, so for now we were grounded, left waiting for another attack.

In the grand scheme of things, my mother was the last thing that should've been consuming my mind. It didn't matter if she was still alive or not if we had no way to save her, anyway.

"She's going to be all right." Max squeezed my shoulder again, and I appreciated the positive words. They were only meant to comfort me. "I'll be back, stay warm."

The minute Max left my side I shivered at the cold against

my back. My body was too weak to even hold itself up without him to steady me, so I rested my forearms on my knees and dropped my head into my hands. As my gaze trailed him walking back to the villagers, my eye caught Kenzie at the back of the crowd. He was watching and offering a few tips as he went by. Two guards still trailed him as he carried on, but everyone had been more trusting of him since he'd helped save us, Max included.

Kenzie caught my eyes. He stepped back while a young boy and his father continued training, but Kenzie's gaze never left me. My cheeks grew hot, but I couldn't look away.

Beside me, Tenason and Ainsley were arguing about something. Their voices were muffled in my ears, and a subtle ringing began.

Seconds later, my pulse quickened as heat flowed through my body with a sudden jolt. My hands trembled, but it was like they weren't even a part of me, like my body was foreign. I couldn't understand what was happening. I blinked as my vision doubled, and I tried to shake away the weird feeling threatening to overcome me.

Kenzie was so far away, and only a breath later, he was right in front of me, his hands against my cheek. He was calling my name, his lips were moving, but the ringing in my ears had taken over. Before I had a chance to say another word, my vision faded.

THIRTY
SIX

My eyes flickered open, and I had the weird sensation of being carried. When my vision focused, I was in Kenzie's arms, his eyes watching me as I absorbed where I was and what happened. I couldn't help the deep breath I took in of his scent.

We reached Doc's office only moments later, and Kenzie put me down on one of the open beds. A hobbling Tenason followed close behind, aided by Ainsley. I'd just noticed that Max led the way, opening the door for Kenzie when we arrived.

"What happened?" I looked around to my terrified friends surrounding me.

"You fainted," Kenzie said.

I frowned. All I remembered was the sudden heat and everything went black. My head was pounding, and there was a faint ringing in my ears.

Doc passed me a glass of water as he checked me over.

"You're burning up, girl. What were you doing?" he asked, shaking out the thermometer and trying one more time.

"Just sitting." I shrugged, pulling myself up to a seated position with Max's help.

"She's been burnt out all week," Max said. "Tired all the time, cold and shivering, but hot as hell." His eyes searched me.

I looked around and found the same expression on Tenason and Ainsley's faces. They were worried as well as confused.

In the corner of the room, Kenzie had sunk into the shadows. It seemed only I was aware of his presence. He, however, didn't look confused. He looked angry, his brow drawn and his eyes flaring with fire.

Before I could ask what was wrong, he stalked out of the room, startling everyone as the door slammed behind him.

"It's almost like you've got a cold or something," Doc said after he'd done his best to check me out. "Only that seems a bit odd given that your body isn't exactly human, but I guess if you can feel pain and hunger, why not sickness?"

For a moment my mind went to the Reeks and the possibility I'd been infected, but it hadn't surfaced on my skin in the way we'd seen Coleman, so it could have just been a cold like Doc suggested. It'd been days since we'd encountered them, and I would have shown symptoms sooner—wouldn't I have?

I sighed. I'd been feeling worn down and awful for the past week. I'd chalked it up to everything that happened and the adrenaline still pumping through me, waiting for Coleman to return. A lack of sleep didn't help, but I'd never considered it could simply be a cold.

"I doubt the medication I have would help you in any way. The best prescription I could give you is rest and lots of fluids," Doc said before he moved on to the rest of his patients still scattered through the room.

I was embarrassed with all the attention and the dramatics. When Max went to help me stand, I swatted his hand away. "I'm fine. Just need to get some food, I think. That's probably all it was. Lack of food and water combined with a bit of a cold. Nothing to worry about."

That did nothing to convince Max, but he didn't dare try to change my mind. Somewhere in the back of my mind the thought kept creeping in—those Reeks and the slash on my arm. I pulled up the sleeve of my shirt just to check, but my skin didn't even have a scar anymore, my Carbon healing had erased that. *You're fine, it's just a cold.* I didn't feel convinced either.

Three days passed, and I wasn't feeling any better. In fact I was getting worse. Max had me quarantined, hardly letting me leave my room. He waited on me, hand and foot. As much as it drove me nuts, I couldn't seem to even garner the effort to argue.

I coughed into my sleeve. A bright red stain splattered across it, and I did my best to wipe it off before Max noticed.

"When did you start coughing up blood?" Max asked from over his shoulder, as he soaked another towel in cool water.

I sighed. He'd always been observant.

"Just today."

"You tell Doc?" Max handed me the towel, and I draped it over my head.

"What's he going to do? I'm a Carbon. He doesn't have the medication or anything that would help heal me," I argued. "Just have to wait it out, I guess."

I tried to act tough. I tried to not let the panic inside of me show. I couldn't help being scared. I tried to ignore the lingering thought that this could be the virus. *It's not! It's just a cold.* My body was supposed to be superior. My powers were supposed to help me. Yet, I was as useless as a child, and knowing Coleman could return at any moment set me on edge.

I had been held up in this room for so long I hadn't had a chance to speak with Kenzie and ask him about the virus. I didn't dare mention it to Max, that would only cause more panic, and I didn't want that for him. I'd wait a few more days. If I wasn't better, I'd tell Max and ask him to speak with Kenzie.

"Any update from Adam and Sam about getting that shuttle ready for space?" I said, changing the subject.

Max shook his head. "Neither are well-versed in space travel, or how to get something up there without killing us all."

I sighed. "They'll find a way—they have to."

"That's not your priority right now, Sawyer. You just need to get better," Max chided.

I rolled my eyes. "Doesn't matter if I'm healthy or not. We stay the course, and we find a way to get to Coleman. *That's* our only focus right now."

"Yeah, we're working on it." There was a bite to his tone that told me to drop it. "Maybe Adam will have some idea of what's going on. He's studied the Carbons extensively. He's as close to an expert as we're going to get," Max suggested, as he sat on the edge of my bed.

I gave him a weak smile. "Thanks. For taking care of me. You're always taking care of me…"

He smirked. "Well, someone has to."

A knock sounded on the door. Theresa poked her head in with a steaming bowl of soup in her hands. My stomach grumbled in response.

"I'll let you eat." Max kissed the top of my head before he stood. "I'll go see if Adam has any idea what's going on."

Theresa placed the bowl on the table beside my bed. I sat up, leaning against the wall behind me for support.

"You don't look better. Have you been drinking the tea I sent you?" Theresa fussed, as she placed a tray on my lap with the bowl of soup on top.

"Yes, Mom." I winked.

Theresa rolled her eyes with the hint of a smile. "Well, go on then. Eat it all."

She waited until I placed the spoon in the bowl and took a big slurp. I continued until it was all gone. She watched the entire time with cautious eyes. I couldn't help thinking of my mom as I let Theresa take care of me.

"I think she would like you," I said.

Theresa tilted her head.

"My mom. You two would get along well."

Theresa gave me a kind smile. "Well, hopefully, she'd be

more useful than you in the kitchen."

I laughed. "She definitely would be."

Theresa gave my shoulder a squeeze as she grabbed my empty bowl. "If she's even half as stubborn as you are, she will be just fine."

I smiled.

"Now go on and get some sleep," Theresa said, as she pulled the tray away from my lap and headed for the door.

I nodded before my eyes could no longer stay open, and I fell back asleep.

The room was dark. I blindly walked through the room with my hands outstretched. The only sound was the soft clank of my shoes hitting the metal floor. A dim light shone ahead. I tried to reach it, but it felt so far away.

When I was in the center of the large room standing under the light, I found there was no end to this dark space. I was alone.

"Hello?" I called out. My voice echoed back. "Is anyone else here?" Silence was the only answer.

A sparkle in the distance caught my eye, and I moved out of the light and toward the side of the room. A small glimmer of light bounced off something shiny. As I came closer, there was a metal chain dangling from the wall it was attached to. I slid my hand down the smooth metal that danced in an invisible light.

A noise came from my right. I glanced up but found nothing. When I looked back to the chain, it was secured to my wrist. I tried to pull it off, but it wouldn't budge.

"You should have never come here," a voice slithered in my ear. I turned around, startled.

"Who's there? Who are you?" I asked, peering into the darkness. I continued to yank at the chain.

"I am darkness. I am silence. And I am death. And you shouldn't have come here," the voice spoke again.

My pulse thundered in my chest, and I jerked at the chain.

"There is no escaping me. Once I arrive, I do not leave... not without some form of payment. Your life will do." The voice laughed, and it echoed through me and into my bones.

I pulled and I tugged, but there was no escaping it. Death had come for me, and I was its prisoner.

I woke with a jolt, my pulse racing and a thin layer of sweat gleaming on my skin. As my breath steadied, I looked down to my arm where the chain had been tied to me. And this time, instead of a chain around my arm, a patch of black stood out against my pale skin, dark as coal and scaled like burnt fish.

THIRTY
SEVEN

KENZIE

Kenzie was careful to not make a sound as he slipped through a window at the back of his tiny room. It was dark when he heard the soft snoring of the guard positioned at his door. It took a few moments for Kenzie's eyes to adjust to the darkness; not even the moon provided him a sliver of light. Slinging his bag over his shoulder, he moved.

Carefully, he snuck behind the houses lining the village. The space was quiet and still as everyone slept. Even though he was certain he was alone, he took every precaution until he reached the edge of the forest and followed the trail toward Kuros.

The subtle crack of a twig breaking under a foot caused

Kenzie to pause.

"We give you the slightest bit of freedom, and the first chance you get, you run." Max stepped out from behind the tree he'd been leaning on.

"If I were running, you wouldn't have found me." Kenzie shrugged.

Max scoffed, "Waiting 'til the wee hours of the night, bag in hand, and sneaking through the village. If that isn't someone trying to run, then please educate me on what you're doing out here."

Kenzie avoided the question. "If you want to take me back, then by all means lead the way. Otherwise, just stay out of my way, Max." Kenzie went to step around him, but Max pressed a strong hand against his chest, stopping his movement.

"Do you see any guards here? I haven't raised the alarm. I don't plan on taking you back. But I'm sure as hell not letting you leave here by yourself," Max said.

Kenzie bit his tongue, wanting to get rid of Max, but not having the time or the patience to continue arguing. "Fine. Just don't slow me down."

Max let Kenzie go, and with a wave of his hand, he directed Kenzie to lead the way.

They were silent for some time as they walked through the dark forest on the single-person trail, worn and muddy. Max kept up with Kenzie as he steadied into a jog.

"So, do you plan on telling me where we're going, or is it supposed to be a surprise?" Max asked.

Kenzie clenched his teeth, already irritated. "Kuros."

"I gathered that from the trail we're taking, but where exactly in Kuros?" Max questioned.

Kenzie sucked in a breath between clenched teeth as he slowed his pace. They had reached the edge of the forest, and the ruined city of Kuros was coming into view. "There." Kenzie pointed to the large structure ahead of him.

It was a shiny silver metal circle the size of a city block, a structure with which he was very familiar.

"The ship those Carbons came in? That's where you're going?" Max stepped up beside Kenzie, as the surface under their feet changed from mud to broken cement.

"Yup." Kenzie didn't offer any more.

"Why?" Max asked.

"Do you always ask this many questions?" Kenzie rolled his eyes.

"This would go a whole lot smoother if you'd just tell me what we're doing here. I think I've proven more than once that you can trust me. It'd be nice if you showed a little of that back," Max said.

Kenzie sighed. This was the reason he hadn't told anyone where he was going. He worked better alone and preferred it that way.

They reached the dock of the ship, still open and eerily quiet. "Every sector on Coleman's space station is equipped with escape pods, should anything go wrong and someone needs to escape quickly."

"So you are getting out of here." Max narrowed his eyes.

"No," Kenzie said. "I'm trying to get up there." Kenzie

pointed to the sky, to the location he didn't know and couldn't see, but knew was there—to Coleman's space station.

"You can fly one of those things?"

"They fly themselves," Kenzie snapped. "And if I get one fixed, I'll show Sam how to control it from here if needed."

Max shrugged. "Still sounds like you're leaving."

Kenzie stopped and turned on Max, his fists clenched. Max had his hunting knife at Kenzie's throat before he said another word. Kenzie grimaced and stepped back.

"I am trying to get up there, so I can get the cure," Kenzie said before he continued into the sector, heading toward the back. "That shuttle they're trying to fix doesn't have a chance in hell of getting up there, not in the time line we need it to."

Max was still before he whispered, "What cure?"

Kenzie turned back around and could tell from the look on Max's face that he knew what the cure was for… or rather whom it was for. But he needed the confirmation. Despite not really liking Max, he'd been nothing but fair with Kenzie, and he was good for Sawyer, even if that bothered him more than he cared to admit. It was because of that that it pained him to be the one to say it.

"I've seen it before. Her symptoms are the same as his were… Coleman's." Kenzie did his best to be gentle as he spoke. "She's been infected by the virus, the same one Coleman had. And the only way we can save her now is to get Lena back. She's the cure."

It hadn't taken Kenzie long to figure out what was wrong with Sawyer, and even less time for the panic to settle into his soul in a way he hadn't ever felt before. That was a lie, the dreams he kept having told him he'd felt this before—and he'd sacrificed himself then to save her life, just as he would now. He was just beginning to get her back, to gain her trust again. He couldn't lose her, not now. He still had so many questions that he didn't know how to ask. Memories that kept flaring, and he needed time to figure this all out—to figure out why he needed her in his life, even when he knew he was so wrong for her. He couldn't let that feeling go.

So, he'd do whatever he could to save her.

Max was silent. He hadn't moved from the spot where he stood a few feet away.

Kenzie continued his way through the large warehouse in the ship to the back where several escape pods were lined up. "If I can get one or two of these working, we might have a chance of getting there."

Max moved, reaching Kenzie's side. Kenzie had put down his bag and pulled out a flashlight to check each pod. Many were heavily damaged, but they only needed one or two at best.

"How long… does she have?" Max whispered.

Kenzie's shoulders dropped, and he didn't turn to face Max. "I don't know. Coleman's change took a few weeks, maybe more, but he's… different—stronger than most. But so is she. We don't know when she was infected first, so it's hard to say how fast it's spreading."

Max nodded, his expression blank and solemn. He shook his head, coming out of his daze to look at Kenzie. "What do you need me to do?"

Kenzie shrugged. "Hold this flashlight? And don't get in

my way."

Max nodded and grabbed the flashlight, shining it against the wall behind Kenzie.

"Don't tell her yet," Kenzie said. "Not until we're sure we can get one of these things working. Don't give her hope just to let her down."

"I won't," Max agreed, and the two men silently made a pact to do whatever they could to save her.

THIRTY EIGHT

"I'm feeling better. I think I'm on the mend," I lied.

"Right." Tenason rolled his eyes, as he handed me a plate of fresh baked muffins, special delivery from Theresa. "And I'm gonna start running next week. We're both miraculously healed."

Ainsley swatted Tenason's arm, and he let out a feeble *ow*. "Why are you always so sarcastic?"

Tenason shrugged. "I thought it was what made me so charming?"

Ainsley tipped her head back with laughter. "You are not charming."

I chuckled and then hid the cough filling my chest. I had climbed out of bed on my own earlier and headed to Theresa's kitchen where I had found Tenason and Ainsley having breakfast. Max had left early in the morning, stating he had something to do for his dad, but that was a lie. He had said the same thing the day before. I had tried following him for a little way into the forest, but I lost him, too slow and tired to keep up. Today, I had just let him go.

"Well, I am feeling better." I tried to convince myself. I pulled the sleeve of my jacket lower. I hadn't slept much after that dream the other night. The black spot on my arm was still there. I wondered if my mother was feeling this same thing as her body surely transitioned just like mine. I'd been near the Reeks briefly—she was trapped in a warehouse full of them.

I tried to hide the shudder that ran through me. I knew what it meant, and I knew what was to come. But hadn't I always known I was going to die one day? Hadn't that been my fate for as long as I could remember? This might not be how I thought I'd go out, but I wouldn't let myself go far enough into this transition to turn into the monsters that haunted me. I wouldn't allow myself to become one of those Reeks. My days were always numbers, only now the clock had officially started counting down.

"You don't look much better," Tenason said. He received another smack from Ainsley. "What? She has to know she looks like crap. And might I add, you're probably overdue for a shower…" He ducked under another swing, smirking before the swift hand of Ainsley met the back of his head.

I chuckled. "Yeah, yeah, I know. You don't look so great yourself there, buddy. Look who's talking." I tried to redirect the attention back to him and it worked. Tenason and Ainsley argued over who looked worse.

"I should get Aelish to check you out. My grandmother will know what to do," Ainsley said.

"It's just a cold. Nothing she can do about it." The lie felt sour in my mouth. This wasn't just a cold.

Ainsley narrowed her eyes. "I'll let her decide that."

A few hours later, Aelish, Ainsley, Tenason, and Max stood around me while I lay on one of Doc's tables, feeling like a lab rat.

"Is this really necessary?" I argued but no one listened.

Max had been quiet since he returned from wherever he was only a few minutes' ago. Ainsley had sent a raven to find Max, as well as her grandmother. The leader of the Ladies of the Muted Forest arrived as quickly as she could.

"How long?" Aelish asked.

"Few weeks now," Max answered.

Aelish pressed against my chest with the palm of her hand. I coughed.

"How long?" Aelish asked again, narrowing her eyes.

Max frowned, but Aelish looked at me.

"Two days," I said.

She nodded, and Max looked between the two of us. "Two days since what?" he asked.

I sighed, knowing I couldn't hide it any longer. I pulled up the sleeve of my shirt. "Since this showed up."

An audible gasp came from Tenason and Ainsley. Max had gone pale and still. He shook his head.

"It's too soon," he mumbled.

"It's not," Aelish spoke. "There is still time."

It was my turn to be confused.

"We're not ready," Max said.

"Ready for what?" I asked, sitting up and turning to Max, who appeared lost in his thoughts.

"You will be," Aelish said, her face solemn. She gripped Max's shoulder before she turned to leave the room, pulling Tenason and Ainsley with her. "Ainsley will prepare a salve for you."

"What is she talking about, Max?" I asked.

He shook out of his shock and met my gaze. "We're going to get you a cure. You'll be fine," he assured me.

"What do you mean, you're going to get me a cure?" I asked, swinging my legs over the table. I sat up tall, so I could look him in the eye.

"Lena," Max said. "We're going to get her back. She can save you."

I was shaking my head before he had even finished. "No!" I said. "You have seen what he's done to her, what he's doing to her so he can live. I won't do that to her, too."

Max rolled his eyes. "I knew you'd say that, but this isn't your choice. We're going to do it with or without you. And I know Lena would do anything to help you."

I still shook my head. "She has been through so much already, Max. Can't we just let her be, let her live without constantly feeling like she needs to save someone? Protect someone?"

"Are you speaking about her or about yourself?" Max fired back.

I knew the answer but crossed my arms with a scowl.

"Then what would you rather do? Die?" Max growled.

"Yes."

"No! You don't get to choose that. You don't get to give up just because someone else will have to make a sacrifice for *you* for once. You do not get to choose her life over your own." Max was shaking, he was so mad.

"I am the only one who gets to decide," I argued. "You can't save me forever. We don't even have a way to get Lena back. That shuttle is nowhere near being ready for space flight and you know it. And even when it is, I'm not wasting all our resources on that. We're going up there to end this and hopefully get Lena back, but the goal is, and always will be, Coleman. There is only one choice… and I've already made it."

I went to storm past him, but he blocked my way.

"We're working on it. We'll get her back," he promised.

"How?" My eyebrows rose, waiting for him to continue.

He bit the inside of his cheek, as he looked down to his feet, avoiding my questioning stare. "Don't worry about how, and just know that we've got it covered. I've got you covered." Max looked back up at me, and a little of the fire inside of me dampened.

"You can't always save me," I whispered.

He smirked. "Yes, I can."

I shook my head. "Even if you get her back, which I highly doubt is possible, Coleman will come after us with everything he's got. If we take her and Coleman gets infected again, you don't think he'll send everything he's got at us to get her back? You saw what he did before. He will come at us with more, and no one will survive. I can't choose my life over everyone here. I can't put everyone in danger like that. And I am telling you now, I won't do that to her."

Max's shoulders dropped. "Why are you being so stubborn?"

"Me?" The fire rose again. "You're the one asking me to choose my life over every person here. I have lived longer than I probably should have in this world. And if I want to go out my way, then just let me."

"Sawyer, you're nineteen. That's not a long life," Max scoffed. "And don't you understand that without you, these people *will* die. You die, they die, that's how this story ends, if you don't just listen to me."

I sighed, draping my hand over my face. "I'm a curse to everyone here. Death has always followed me, and it will until I die. These people are no safer with me than they are without me."

Max stepped back and shrugged. "In the end, you don't have a choice in this matter. There's nothing you can do to stop me. I will not stop trying to save you, not ever."

The door slammed hard behind him. All that remained was silence.

THIRTY
NINE

No amount of convincing could change Max's mind, nor could he change mine. I was so frustrated with him that we'd hardly spoken in a few days. He left every night when the sun set and returned just as the sun was rising. He wouldn't tell me where he was going, and I didn't have the energy to follow him.

The virus spread and covered three quarters of my arm. It was a stark contrast against my pale, white skin. If it spread this fast for me, I was certain my mother would be going through the same thing where she was. I tried not to let that thought seep in. There was nothing more I could do here.

I covered it up as best I could with a long sweater, but there was no escaping the virus, an itch I couldn't scratch. It was a constant reminder that my time was going to be up soon.

Ainsley brought me some salve to put over the blackness. It wouldn't do anything to fix it, but it covered the smell that came with the scales on my arm. When I walked around, I smelled like peppermint tea.

The sun was waking up on a warm, spring morning. Orange and red streaks spread through the forest like little beams of light growing as the sun rose. A shadow walked toward me. His face wasn't visible against the sunlight at his back, but I knew who he was. His energy nudged my own before he came into view.

I was surprised to see him. He hadn't come to see me once since that day I fainted, and out of everyone I knew, he was the one person who could possibly give me answers on this virus. I hadn't sought him out either, though, and I wondered if we both avoided each other because that way it was easier to pretend this wasn't happening. That I wasn't going to die.

"How are you feeling?" Kenzie asked.

"Why does everyone keep asking me that?" I pouted.

He shrugged as he took the seat beside me, leaning against a tree. Not close enough to touch me, but close enough that I could smell his fresh, clean scent. "It's a common question to ask when someone is sick."

I rolled my eyes.

We were silent before I asked, "What are you doing up so early?"

He shrugged. "Couldn't sleep."

It was a lie, but Kenzie ignored my questioning gaze.

"You can't blame him for trying to help you," Kenzie said

after a few more moments of silence. "You would do the same for him."

I sighed. "Not if he asked me not to. I'd respect his wishes."

"Would you?" Kenzie's eyebrow rose.

I didn't answer.

"I know I couldn't sit by while someone I cared about was dying, especially if there was a way to help them," Kenzie said. His expression softened.

I ignored the small flutter in my chest and said, "But by saving me, he's dooming everyone else—you included."

"I've said before I'd sacrifice my own life for yours," he said, halting my thoughts before I even had a chance to comprehend what he'd said. The look on his face was unreadable, and I was unable to formulate words or even thoughts.

"You don't owe me anything, Kenzie," I said.

He smirked. "It's funny that you think I'd do it for you, even after I nearly killed you more than once."

My mouth gaped open, and he shook his head.

"Even without remembering it all, I know a part of me would die with you if anything were to happen. A part that even I don't understand," he said.

I nodded, knowing that feeling all too well. And even though I didn't say it and a part of me didn't want to admit it, I would also be torn apart once again if anything happened to him. He wasn't like I once remembered but he was here. That was more than I thought I could ever ask for.

Kenzie shifted as he turned toward me. "I know this is completely the wrong time to tell you this, and I'm sure you have enough on your plate, so just listen to me and don't say anything, okay?" He waited for me to nod before he continued. "I don't remember what we once had. And I don't know how much I hurt you, or if you could ever forgive me. But throughout this entire time, you have been the only constant thing in my life, the only truth I can hold onto." He glanced at his hands. "When I was a kid, I kept having this dream over and over again. A beautiful girl stood before me. Her long, dark hair flowed in the wind behind her. A lightning storm was overhead and all around her. And all I kept looking at, all I saw was her amber-brown eyes staring at me. Every night, I'd dream of her, and I'd hold onto that feeling of life, safety… and love." He glanced over to me, and my heart pounded even harder. "No one could have convinced me that dream was anything more than just that, a dream… until the other day when you stood before me, and that lightning storm we created was overhead, and all I could see was you."

My mouth was dry, and I didn't have the words to speak.

The corner of his mouth rose into a smile. "No matter what happens, no matter what has already happened, I have that image forever, and nothing and no one can take that away from me."

My mind was rattled and lost, but when I looked in his eyes, I felt… safe. Just as I had that day when we created a storm to save our people.

"I just wanted you to know that." Kenzie shrugged as he stood. He took a few steps away from me. "In case anything happens—to either of us—I wanted to tell you that you'll always be in my heart. You always have been."

"I've gained some access back to the space station but it's limited," Sam said to a room filled with attentive ears.

Murray had called a meeting to discuss what our next steps were. Lankey, Aelish, and Vance were all there with a few of their people. Max and Tenason sat on either side of me while Kenzie leaned against the wall in the back corner of the room. His occasional glance caught my eye, and I had to turn my chair to avoid staring, my mind still wrapped up in everything he'd told me.

"We've accessed their location and radar system, but inside the station we're still blind," Murray said from the front of the room, his hands clasped behind his back in a familiar manner. "We all know he'll be back; it's only a matter of time. So we need to beat him to it. We need to make an advance instead of sitting back and waiting. We've been working on something that might give us the upper hand." Murray nodded to Max, who stood up to my right, addressing the group.

"We've acquired two small escape pods that are almost ready to go. It will allow two small parties access to the space station, arriving mostly unseen. The plan is to layer out explosives across the station, set them, and then get out," Max said.

"How'd we be sure the pod ain't bein' located by Coleman?" Lankey asked.

"We've disabled the tracking system in it, and your Alatonion will help keep us invisible," Max answered.

"Even if you arrive unseen, Coleman will know when you're there. You can't just expect to walk through the halls setting explosives and not get caught," I argued. I wasn't happy with this plan, and I was well aware of the side mission Max was intending on completing while he was there.

"We'll patch Sam in manually to the security system when we arrive, so he can keep us hidden," Max countered, as he sat down beside me.

I huffed and crossed my arms.

"Who will go?" Vance asked from the end of the table next to Aelish.

I already knew the first two, Kenzie and Max. It was the other two that surprised me. "Ainsley and Tenason will lead the second pod," Murray said.

My head whipped to a guilty-looking Tenason, who had kept this from me.

"With my gifts, I am able to cloak us inside the station, keeping us invisible, so we can plant the bombs," Ainsley stated, keeping her jaw strong against my disappointed glare.

"I fear you will not be strong enough should you face those Carbons, Ainsley," Vance said. "I would request to join you."

"You don't need to do this, Vance," I said.

"Yeah, we can take care of ourselves," Tenason agreed.

But Vance kept his posture straight, as he said, "I am sworn to protect my people, and I owe you a life debt, Sawyer."

I shook my head and felt Ainsley ready to argue, but I beat her. "You don't owe me anything, Vance. You've already done so much for our people."

He stood up tall and strong, not a man used to being told no. "I will come. It is my duty as a Mountain Man and my job as a friend and a brother." He glanced to Ainsley, whose expression had softened. She nodded, and Vance turned back to wait for me.

I sighed. In all honesty, if Ainsley and Tenason would also be joining Max and Kenzie up there, a little muscle wouldn't be a bad thing. "Okay," I said.

Murray bowed his head in thanks. "Thank you for your assistance, Vance, you and all your men."

"What would you ask of us, then?" Aelish asked from the far end of the table.

"If the mission fails, Coleman will send all of his Carbons, everything he's got, down here as retribution. If we fail, then you can expect a war. And we felt it was only fair to have everyone aware of the consequences and potential outcome. And if anyone has reservations about that, now is when you should speak," Murray explained.

I didn't even get to open my mouth.

"There is a war coming no matter how you look at it," Aelish said. I wondered if she knew the outcome of this war. If she did, she said nothing.

"My men will be ready for whatever comes." Vance nodded.

One by one, everyone in the room agreed the potential consequences of this mission failing were still worth it. Everyone but me.

"Don't you guys get it?" I glanced around the table. "This is a suicide mission. The chances of it succeeding are slim to none.

And it won't be a matter of when or if he will come. Coleman *will* come, and we will *all* die because of it."

"He'll come regardless, Sawyer," Max said.

"There is a big difference between the attack of an annoyed bee and that of the entire hive raining down on you. If we just stay the course, let our people heal and prepare, we stand a better chance. Get that shuttle up and running, so we can send more people. We don't need to be going up there pissing him off now," I pushed back.

"Yes, we do," Max said between clenched teeth.

"Don't do this," I whispered so only he could hear. "Don't make this about me."

He shook his head. "It's too late. It's already done."

I looked around for support, for anyone to agree that we weren't ready, that we shouldn't do this, but no one spoke up. No one agreed.

Even Kenzie kept his gaze down when I looked for the one person who knew the consequences all too well to say something.

Murray cleared his throat. "It's decided then. We will prepare for the worst, but hope for success." There was a murmured agreement around the table. "You're all free to go."

I was the first to leave, unwilling to accept that everyone in that room made a decision that would seal their fate. I couldn't look at each one, knowing what they were agreeing to would lead to their death.

Behind me, swift feet approached, and a gentle hand gripped my arm.

Aelish looked so small and fragile standing before me. "I am sorry for the fate the stars have given you, but your story is not the only one written in the skies."

I tried to argue, but she stuck up her hand.

"It has been said before that to sacrifice one's self for the greater good is worth more than a thousand lives combined. But it is also said that one moment can change a day, one day can change a life, and one life can change the world," Aelish said. "Who are we to decide which life to sacrifice and which could change the world?"

My head dropped. Aelish didn't give me a chance to respond before she gave me a weak smile. She left me standing alone in the warm sunlight.

The rest of the group filed out of the headquarters, and I tried to leave before anyone else could put me in my place. Vance caught up to me, preventing me from hiding and sulking in my misery.

"I have heard of your illness, and I wanted to bring you something that may give you strength." Vance pulled out a small white vest, made from the fur of an Ice Bear. "This bear was one of our youngest but most fearsome bears. He sacrificed his life for his own mate on the day Coleman's Carbons arrived."

My heart sank, knowing that the bear whose fur this vest came from died for me and my people.

Vance caught my mood. "Do not feel sorrow for him. He'd do it a thousand times if it meant his mate could live. As all of us would."

I took the vest in my hands, feeling the warm, thick fur that was heavy in my arms. "Thank you."

"The Ice Bear's fur has always kept the Mountain Men's strength inside of them, strong and protected. This vest may do the same for you. When you are feeling weak, when your body is tired, the Ice Bear can be your strength." Vance tipped his head. "We will see each other again. Soon, Miss Sawyer."

I gave him a weak smile before he led his men back into the forest. I clung to the vest that gave me warmth, even if it was covered in death and blood.

FORTY

There was no use trying to convince Max to not do this, not any longer. He'd made his decision, and there was no turning back from it. I decided to take a different route.

"I'm going with you," I said from behind Max, who was packing a bag full of supplies.

"What?" He turned around so fast the bag nearly spilled over. "No, you're not coming."

"Yes, I am," I argued.

Max sighed. "You're too weak. You don't even know if you can use your powers or anything."

I nudged at my powers that may have felt weaker than usual, but they were still there. I picked up his bag with the flick of my energy, dropping it onto the bed. I gave him a crooked smile.

"We're going in quick. In and out, that's it. You can hardly stand, Sawyer," Max tried again.

I stood, did a hop on both feet, and spun around. Granted, I was a tad off-balance the entire time, but I didn't let it show. I was coming, and I was going to be useful. The vest Vance had given me was strung across my chest. And even if it was just a placebo effect, I felt stronger.

Max sighed and looked to the ceiling. "Why?"

"Because you need me. And I'm not about to let you go up there by yourself."

"I won't be by myself," Max argued.

He had let me know about the plan. Tenason, Ainsley, and Vance would set the explosives around the exterior of the station. He and Kenzie would find Lena and my mom, if they could, and set the remaining explosives at the center of the station.

Kenzie was the only one who knew the inside of the space station, so he had to go. That was the part I was most worried about.

"We don't know what Kenzie will do with Coleman there, if he takes control of him," I said.

"I know what I have to do if it comes to that," Max said.

"But what if you can't? He's strong, and with his arm… you might not be given the chance to do anything about it." I knew all too well Kenzie's strength. Even though I trusted him, Coleman would use him against us if he had the chance. And in the end, if anyone was going to do it, I should be the one to pull the trigger on Kenzie.

"Sawyer, why can't you just let me do this?" Max sat beside me, taking my hand. He twisted the small silver-and-copper ring around my finger. "I can take care of myself. I can take care of you. Just let me."

I didn't want to. Every fiber in my body was screaming no, but I couldn't stand the look on his face. If anything happened to him because of me, I couldn't live with myself. I was weak, and I knew I could become a liability, even if I didn't want to admit it. So if this one time I had to stand down and let someone else do it, that's what I'd do.

"Okay," I said.

He leaned in and gave me a long kiss. He stood up and finished filling his bag. Once he had everything packed, he slung it over his shoulder.

"I'll be back in the morning before we leave, promise." He gave me another kiss on the top of my head and he was gone.

It was still cold at night, even if the weather had warmed up in the past few weeks. I shoved my hands in my pockets and paced back and forth in the shadows. My body was exhausted, not just from the change going on inside of me or the virus taking its hold. The lack of sleep and the constant nightmares kept me in a state of nocturnal insomnia. The only time my body seemed to find it safe to rest was during the day.

I had waited until almost morning when I left my room. I'd been pacing in the tree line behind a row of tiny houses for more than an hour already, still waiting.

When I heard a small crunch of shoes over the shale walkway, I knew he'd returned.

Kenzie stepped around the corner but didn't startle when he saw me. Instead, he nodded to the door, which he opened for me first and followed behind.

"I was wondering when you'd come by." He dropped his heavy bag and kicked off his shoes.

I paced in front of him, still cold. I shivered.

"Are they ready?" I asked.

He nodded as he removed his oil-stained sweater. His shirt underneath lifted a sliver, and I had to look away before my mind wandered. *Focus.*

"Nearly ready. Max is finishing up a few last minute things while I download updated specs on the station." Kenzie pulled out his tablet from his pack and entered a few codes. A progression bar popped up, and he set the tablet on the bedside table before turning his attention to me.

"That's not why you came here." He narrowed his eyes.

I shook my head. "No."

He motioned to the seat beside him and I sat. My entire body slumped and relaxed into the soft bed, and my tired legs throbbed.

"I need you to promise me something," I began. "I need you to promise you'll watch out for him."

He nodded. "You know I will." He almost sounded offended I'd even ask him.

But I went on, "He deserves to live. And he will do everything he can to help me, I know this. He'll sacrifice himself if it means I'll live, but I need you to promise me you won't let him do that."

I waited for him to agree, and after a long pause, he gave a solemn nod.

I loosened a sigh of relief. "Thank you."

He watched me before he said, "Do you want me to come back?"

My pulse quickened. "Of course I do."

"And if I have to choose… if *you* had to choose…"

I shook my head. "That's not fair."

The corner of his mouth twitched into a sad smile. "You can't have it both ways."

"I want you both to come back," I said, and it wasn't a lie. I loved Max, but I cared for Kenzie, too, even this unfamiliar version of him. There was a bond between us that I couldn't remove, no matter how hard I tried. If I had to choose which one of them lived and which one died… I wouldn't make the choice. I'd rather die first.

Kenzie stood up fast, crossing the space of the room with a bottled-up energy I knew all too well. "Well, then, what will you have me do? Save him or save myself?" His eyebrows rose as he crossed his arms, leaning against the wall across from where I sat. "Or maybe it's neither. Maybe we're both crazy enough to sacrifice ourselves for you."

My face was burning, and I clamped my mouth shut. This was the last thing I needed. This wasn't fair. I wouldn't choose between whom I wanted to live more than the other. That hadn't been why I came there in the first place. Kenzie knew that, too, knew it was an impossible question he was asking me, so why? Why now?

"Stop trying to make sense of it all, Sawyer. I can see you trying to find a solution to something you have no control over." Kenzie shrugged. "I'll be sure to watch out for Max, that I can promise you. But I won't promise that I won't be fighting just as hard to come back to you as he will."

I froze.

He took a step forward, stopping only a few inches from me. He was so close his warmth seeped into me, and his breath tickled my neck. My gaze dropped to his lips for only a moment before I blinked, forcing myself to look him in the eyes. It was no better. His electric energy pulsed from him, and my own seemed to reach out for it.

"You asked me once before if what you had felt—what we'd had—was all a lie. Well it wasn't. It was real. And it's the only reason I am standing before you resisting the control Coleman still holds over me, because I remember." He pushed a strand of hair away from my face, and I don't think I was breathing. "I have fought against every instinct in my body screaming to hold you, touch you… feel you. I know you feel the same pull, you always have. That won't stop. Ever. And I will wait. I will respect whatever choice you make and whomever you choose. But that won't stop the pull… that won't stop this." Kenzie pulled my chin up, and I couldn't look away. That spark of his energy was on the tip of his fingers, and it caressed down my neck and across my chest, filling an empty space inside of me I tried to hide, even from myself.

For a moment, that pull drew me closer to him, and everything around me was nothing but space and time. All that remained was him—Kenzie.

I closed my eyes. "You died," I breathed.

"I didn't," he whispered.

My eyes opened, and I met his gaze. The fire inside of him burned through me, and his energy flowed inside of me. But I pushed it down, I pushed it away. "Yes, you did. You died, in my heart. It doesn't matter what I still feel. I can't forget what happened, and I can't forget the pain."

Kenzie's shoulders fell. "I will never do that to you again."

"You can't promise that. No one can." I tilted my head, my gaze following his jawline.

"What do I have to do to prove I am changed, that I'm not the same Kenzie as before?" he begged.

"You already have," I said, "but that's just it. I'm not the same Sawyer, either. And the one who lifted me from the ashes and ruins was Max. He is who made me who I am now, and who I would sacrifice my life for if you made me choose."

It pained me to say it. Every word felt harsh and unyielding but it was truth. I owed that to him. There was no denying a pull toward Kenzie, a want and a need to be near him. That didn't make it right. That didn't make it my destiny.

Kenzie's hand dropped from my cheek, and the cold air hit the warm skin where his hand had been. He said, "You are the one I'd sacrifice my life for. And nothing will change that."

"I'm sorry," I whispered.

"Don't. Don't be." He shook his head.

I couldn't be here anymore. I couldn't be this close to him and trust myself. I stood on shaky legs to leave, but my feet wouldn't move. Kenzie placed a hand under my elbow for support. That spark of electricity ran through him and into me, but it wasn't painful. It was comforting.

I felt dizzy and so confused, and all I wanted to do was run away, but I could barely stand. My entire body trembled like it was screaming at me. I tried to take a step away, but my knee buckled under me. Kenzie caught me, one strong arm wrapped around my waist and the other gripping my hand.

I tried to tell myself to run. I begged my legs to move, but I was frozen where I stood in Kenzie's arms. My face so close to his that I felt his breath on my lips. I looked up at him, my eyes meeting his, and I couldn't look away.

He bent lower, slowly, waiting for me to pull away, but I remained rooted where I stood. Not breathing. Not thinking. And then his lips were pressed against mine. His kiss was both foreign and familiar at the same time.

My eyes closed, and for just a second I forgot where I was— who I was with—even as my hand reached up to push him away. But then the click of a doorknob turning sounded, and my eyes flashed open to the figure standing on the other side. My heart stopped.

FORTY ONE

If someone could die of shame and guilt, I would've died right there. The look of devastation on Max's face broke me. He stood gripping onto the open door, staring at Kenzie and I, his arms still wrapped around me. I pushed him away, stumbling towards the door.

"Max…"

"They're ready. We leave in an hour," Max said before he turned and slammed the door.

I followed after him, trying to open the door before Kenzie reached around and opened it for me. I didn't dare look back at him, and he had the good sense not to stop me from leaving. I raced after Max.

"Max, stop," I called after him.

My legs still didn't want to work, and the effort it took to catch up to him had my lungs on fire. My head grew fuzzy. "Please, I can explain," I begged, but he didn't turn around.

I tripped over something. Maybe it was my own feet, but I pushed myself back up and chased after him. I was slow, and his anger made him much faster. I kept going, even when I could hardly breathe, even when my path was no longer straight, and my vision was blurred on the edges.

"Max!" I cried one last time. Something in my voice must've been different because he turned back around and caught me before I fell on my face.

He lifted me up with ease, shaking his head, as he changed his path to head toward Doc's office. "You stupid girl," he mumbled.

I tried to say sorry, but he shook his head.

"Save your energy."

Doc wasn't there when we arrived, but someone called him in quick. Max set me down on a bed, and I wheezed, trying to catch my breath again.

"What happened?" Doc asked upon entering.

"Two minutes of chasing me and who knows how long spent making out," Max said, as he shoved his hands in his pocket.

"It wasn't like that," I said, but my voice came out breathy and I began coughing.

Doc raised his eyebrows, but he didn't ask Max to elaborate. He placed a stethoscope on my chest and around to my back, asking me to take a deep breath each time. I did with difficulty.

Doc lifted the edge of my shirt where the black, scaled virus had spread once again. It ran down my right side from my collarbone to my hip. It was spreading faster.

"I'm not sure how much longer you've got. The virus doubled since yesterday, and your chest sounds like it's underwater," Doc said.

I sighed, closing my eyes. It was getting worse. Every inch of my body itched and burned.

"Can she last until we get back?" Max asked, showing more concern than he did a few minutes ago.

Doc shrugged, not the answer I was hoping for. "It doubled in less than twenty-four hours. At that rate, she could be covered before the sun sets, and there's no telling if it can be reversed at that time."

Max swore under his breath.

"Don't go," I said.

He glared at me. "Not this again… You can kiss whomever the hell you want, Sawyer, and I'll still go up there to get Lena and the cure."

"No, that wasn't what I… I wasn't trying to…" I could hardly understand myself what I had done, let alone try to explain it to him.

I'd just told Kenzie I was choosing Max. I'd made my decision, and then he kissed me. I'd hardly had a chance to even think, let alone stop him, before Max showed up, but deep down I knew I shouldn't have even been that close. I had made a mistake—a big one—and now the pain in Max's eyes was tearing me apart. *I did that.*

"I get it." Max sighed, his jaw tightening, as he struggled to

258

find the right words. "It's always been Kenzie, no matter what he does or what happens, you can't let him go—"

"I can. I did!"

"Don't worry about it, Sawyer. Don't try to explain it to me, and don't think this changes what I plan to do up there. This is about everyone here, not just you."

He was gone before I had a chance to blink.

With nowhere left to go and only enough energy to walk a short distance, I stayed in Doc's office. I waited for word that Max and Kenzie had left. Last I heard, they were getting things ready, and I wasn't expecting a goodbye from either of them.

Tenason entered the room a few minutes after Max stormed out. He wanted to get one last check on his mostly healed leg. He had kept me company while we waited.

"I know what it's like to feel useless," Tenason said, mistaking my silence for frustration.

"You're still useful. You're the one going up there to help end this," I said.

"Sure, because I couldn't let Ainsley go up there without me. Who'd she make fun of if I wasn't around?" Tenason gave me a goofy smile that I didn't return. "But when I was injured, if Coleman had returned, I'd have been powerless to help anyone."

I nodded, knowing what he meant.

"But sometimes, being powerless and relying on someone else gives you a chance to see who's really important to you, and that gives you strength. When there's nothing else you can do to help, who would you want by your side in that moment at the end?" Tenason shrugged, glancing out the window where Ainsley was helping prepare explosives they would bring with them. Vance was sharpening his knives beside her.

"If something had happened, Ainsley would've kept you safe." I winked and he chuckled.

"Yeah, if only to rub it in my face that I need her, and I'm just a little baby." He smiled. "But she wouldn't be wrong. I do need her, just like you need Max."

I sighed, knowing he was right, but I didn't want to bring up anything to him about what had happened.

Out the window, I caught Kenzie and Max having an argument.

"I'll be back," I said, brushing past Tenason. I headed out into the morning sun.

"There won't be enough time," Kenzie said.

"Then we'll go faster," Max argued.

"We can't go faster. We can only go as fast as these pods will take us, and even if we just went there and back, we might be out of time already." Kenzie's voice rose.

"We can't take her." Max shook his head. "It's not safe for her."

"What's this all about?" I stepped between the two, Ainsley close behind me.

Max gave me a hefty glare, but he waited for Kenzie to speak.

"I think you should come with us," Kenzie said.

If this had been even twelve hours ago, I would've wholeheartedly agreed, but I was weaker and I was dying.

"I can't come. I'd only slow you guys down," I said.

Max glanced at me, surprised I was agreeing with him.

"Sawyer, the issue isn't if you'll be in the way or not. It's the fact we may not be back in time for you. And I know it's gotten worse, so spare me the argument. Even if we went as fast as we could, even if everything went the right way, we might not make it in time," Kenzie said.

I understood what he meant. The virus could take over before they had a chance to return with a cure. I'd suspected this might be the case when Doc said it was spreading faster than he expected, and I'd already planned for it.

"Don't worry about me. I'll be fine," I said.

Max narrowed his eyes. "Define *fine*."

He knew what I meant. I didn't have to spell it out to him, but he was going to make me. "I don't intend to let this virus win. I'm not going to allow myself to be turned into one of those monsters. So when it gets to the end, if you guys haven't returned yet and Doc hasn't found another cure, I've asked him to do what needs to be done in order for that to not happen. He's agreed." I had asked—begged—Doc to not allow me to turn into one of the Reeks. It took a lot of convincing, but he respected my wishes.

Max threw his head back with a cynical laugh. "Why am I not surprised?"

"You can't kill yourself," Ainsley whispered. "The stars have not closed on your chapter yet."

"The stars have already done a terrible job at deciding what happens in my life, and now it's my turn to take control of my own fate. I am the decider of if I live or if I die, not anyone else," I said.

"No," Max said. "I told you before, and I will say it a hundred more times if I have to. You do not get to decide how or when this ends." He turned to Kenzie. "Can we find Lena in time?"

"Yes," Kenzie said.

"Then you're coming with us," Max said. I tried to protest but Max stopped me. "I will chain you to this pod if I have to, Sawyer. I trusted you a long time ago to keep fighting, and it seems you're in the mood to break my trust lately, so if I need to babysit you, then I will."

FORTY TWO

The pod wasn't meant for more than one person. It'd only been made to get a single occupant from point A to point B, not navigate from Earth to an orbiting space station. Regardless, the three of us were squished into the revamped pod with Kenzie at the controls and Sam navigating from the ground.

I could only imagine how tight it must've been in the other pod with Vance taking up more than half the room. I was careful to not say my goodbyes to anyone before we left, not wanting to admit that the likelihood we returned together was slim.

I was squished between a scowling Max and a stern, focused Kenzie. I was already sweating from the warm, tight quarters. The white fur vest didn't do much to quell the heat either, but it gave me a strength I couldn't understand.

"Sam will be on comms for as long as he can. You won't be able to contact the other pod until you've arrived. May the stars guide you back safely." A somber Murray rested his hand on the heavy door. "I'll see you soon, son." He squeezed Max's shoulder.

Max gave a weak smile. "Goodbye, Dad." Max pulled the door closed, and I noted the pain washing over his face before it returned to a scowl.

"The takeoff is going to be a bit rough," Kenzie said. He punched a few buttons on the screen before him. "Sam, you've got control of the pod. We're ready to go."

The Alatonion metal shell of the pod was smooth all around us. Three makeshift chairs had been placed around the inner layer, and harnesses had been outfitted and secured across our chests and over our laps. Our knees bumped into each other since the space between us was almost nonexistent. The panel beside Kenzie lit up green and red before the pod rumbled underneath us.

"Hold on tight, guys. We're ready for liftoff," Sam's voice sounded through the pod's speakers.

A lot of wires and added parts dangled from inside the already small space, and I was left wondering how Kenzie put these pods in the air. He'd always been good with computers and tinkering with things. I prayed this time he'd done everything right.

My knee shook, bouncing up and down as the pod rumbled, and the small, but powerful, engine roared to life.

"We're gonna be fine." Kenzie watched my knee bounce.

I gave him as brave a nod as I could manage, but that still

didn't stop my leg.

Max watched while I pulled on the harness straps once more to ensure they were secure. I gripped onto the edge of the seat, my knuckles already white. His scowl softened, as he looked me over. He let out a long sigh and grabbed my hand.

The gentle squeeze was all I needed for my thundering heart to settle. My knee stopped jumping.

"The stars will keep us safe," he whispered beside me, giving my hand another squeeze.

"Thank you," I said, knowing he didn't owe me any kindness. In fact I probably didn't deserve it. But just the feeling of his hand in mine sent a calm throughout my body. He was what I needed.

I wanted to say just that, to explain that what had happened between Kenzie and me was a mistake, but I couldn't find the words. This definitely wasn't the right place.

Kenzie was quiet beside me, but I couldn't help noticing his glances toward my interlocked hands with Max.

Before I had a chance to react or consider all the bad things that could happen, the small pod rocketed from the ground. My stomach dropped as one of my hands braced against the roof only a few inches from my head, and the other squeezed Max's hand so tight I was sure I was breaking his skin with my nails. I couldn't let go.

I squeezed my eyes tight. The pod shook violently, and my head spun from the pressure. The outer shell of the pod grew hot, and I hissed, ripping my hand away from the metal ceiling burning up against the pressure and atmosphere. Thankfully, the thick fabric against our backs kept the metal from burning us, but the tiny space was boiling. Sweat dripped down my cheeks.

I felt the pressure of a hand against my leg. When I opened my eyes, I found Kenzie holding my flaying legs in place. My body was too weak to hold itself. The grimace on his face told me it was a challenge to keep himself in check, let alone me as well.

Max was doing the same. His leg draped over mine, securing me down like another harness.

My ears popped next. The sound in the pod transitioned from deafening to a muffled silence in seconds. I had a moment's panic where I wondered if I was still alive or if my ghost had exited my body and was surveying what remained.

Just when I was sure the pod was going to break apart, and there was no way it could withstand the heat and pressure, the shaking slowed down. It stopped altogether, and I had a weird feeling like our pod was bobbing in a large body of water. There was only one small window on the door, but I could barely see through it from where I sat. The other pod jumped into view beside ours. There was no way to know where we were going. We were putting our faith solely in Sam, who had control of the pod back on Earth.

"That wasn't so bad," Sam's voice crackled into the sweltering space.

I glared at the speaker, wishing Sam saw me.

"We're all still in one piece, mostly," Kenzie said. He surveyed me once more before he took his hand away from its resting place on my leg.

Max watched every movement he made with what I could

only assume was loathing… or jealousy. It tore me apart, to see that. The two might never have been friends, but they had worked together on getting these pods running, and now I'd caused the rift between them. And the pain I saw in Max's eyes made me want to disappear, because I knew nothing I could say would make this better.

"It'll be a bit smoother until we reach the space station. The Alatonion should keep you guys off their radars, so they can't see where you are, but if I know Coleman, he'll be ready for you guys," Sam warned. "Still about ninety minutes to go, but it shouldn't be much longer."

I let out a breath and released my hand from its death grip around the chair. I didn't, however, release Max's hand.

"So what's the plan?" I asked to fill the silence. Since I was a last minute addition, I wasn't briefed on what we were going to do when we arrived.

"We'll land between Sector 7 and 8. A loading dock between the two should be fairly empty seeing as Sector 7 is… closed, and 8 was one of the ships sent down to earth," Kenzie answered. "Tenason, Ainsley, and Vance will take the outer perimeter of the station and set the explosives. It will be less guarded there, so they should be safe."

I nodded along, waiting for him to continue, but he didn't. He glanced at Max as the two had an unspoken conversation with each other.

I looked between the two. "And then what?" I asked.

They were silent again.

"Tell me," I demanded.

"Go ahead. It was your idea, after all," Max said with a tempered restraint.

Kenzie glared at Max before looking back to me. "We weren't expecting you to come, and it was too late to change the plans at this point…"

Max wouldn't meet my eyes.

I grew impatient. "Just spit it out already."

"After we patch Sam into the security feed and the others set out, we're heading to Sector 7… for your mom," Kenzie said.

My pulse raced again. *Why would they go to Sector 7?*

Max jerked his chin toward Kenzie. "Genius here thinks she'll be able to help us, if she's still alive." Max sneered but one look at me and guilt filled his features at what he'd said.

My breathing became uneven, and my head spun again. The chances my mom was still alive were slim. I didn't know if I could manage to see her like that, changed and transformed— into one of those Reeks.

"How would she be able to help?" My voice was quiet.

"She'd know where they're holding Lena. It'd take us hours to search that station on our own if we're forced to guess where we're going. Your mom is our only chance at a head start," Kenzie said gently.

"And what if she's already… gone?" I couldn't say the words out loud, knowing that if she was changed, that'd make finding Lena much harder, and might seal my fate right then and there. I could hardly sit up straight with my body feeling so tired and weak.

"Then we'll find another way," Max said.

I shook my head. "I can't… I don't…"

"I told you this was a bad idea. She shouldn't have to see that," Max argued with Kenzie.

"If you've got a better idea, I'm all ears," Kenzie said.

"Can't you hack into their system once we're there? Find Lena through that?" Max suggested.

Kenzie let out a long breath through his nose. "As I said before, that process would take a long time. It's not as simple as opening a computer and typing in her name."

Max shrugged. "You're the genius hacker getting us in there in the first place. I thought it'd be easy for you. Guess you're not so great at everything."

Kenzie rolled his eyes. "At least I was able to get us here."

That set Max off. He let go of my hand and aimed a fist at Kenzie, who ducked out of the way, causing Max to smash into the side of the pod. The sound rang in my ears. Max winced and shook out his hand.

"We had others more than willing to help us. You're not the only guy for the job. You just stepped in when you weren't asked, and I was nice enough to let you keep going," Max snapped.

My brows shot up as I spun on Max. "Stop this. He's just trying to help."

Max crossed his arms. "Right. That's all he ever does, just help."

"Max, you need to relax." Kenzie shifted in his seat.

"Don't tell me what to do." Max sounded like a child.

"This isn't the time to start not trusting people, Max. We need to stay focused." I rested my hand on his arm, but he shrugged it off. My throat tightened, and I felt my stomach turn to lead.

"Is that what you guys were doing last night? Staying focused on the mission?" Max wouldn't look at either of us.

I let out a frustrated sigh. "Max, please—"

"I don't need the details," Max cut me off.

"You're not letting me explain." I threw my arms up, nearly hitting Kenzie in the head because of the small space.

"Neither of you get to tell me what to do right now," Max said.

"Oh, come on," Kenzie scoffed. "Max, she picked you. Despite what you saw or what you think happened, she picked you!"

Max was silent. I didn't know how to respond. The hint of hurt in Kenzie's voice told me it pained him to admit that, to say the words out loud.

"She chose you and *I* kissed her. So if you want to hate somebody, go ahead and hate me."

Max still didn't speak. I wasn't sure if I was breathing. I had chosen Max, and Max had to know. I waited for Max to say something or for my mind to formulate the right words—words that wouldn't break one of them just to make the other feel better. I was caught in a mess of my own making with nowhere to go, nowhere to hide.

My mouth opened, but before I said anything out, I was cut off.

"Uh, sorry to interrupt, guys... I swear I didn't mean to listen in or anything, only I was on the comm still, and it was hard to not hear it all. I just... what I mean is," Sam babbled, and for some reason, heat rose to my cheeks. Kenzie closed his eyes with a frustrated sigh. "We're approaching the station's loading dock, so best be prepared. Landing is going to come in a bit hot to avoid being seen... hopefully."

To my left, Kenzie pulled out his gun. He rechecked the mag before sliding it back into its holster. I had my guns on my hips, but they felt more like weights than weapons.

Max still said nothing, and he wouldn't look at either of us. He pulled on his harness and prepared for a rough landing. Part of me wondered if it didn't matter that I'd chosen him—being in that room with Kenzie and close enough for him to kiss me was enough of a betrayal that he could never forgive me.

"Touching down in three... two..." Sam's voice cut out on "one" as the pod slammed onto the surface of the docking station.

We were tossed upside down and rolled like a ball against a bumpy surface. My head spun, and I didn't know which way was up or down. With a shudder, the pod came to a resting spot on its side.

Kenzie was the first to unstrap, gravity sending him nearly face-first into Max. Kenzie opened the pod door facing the roof of the station. We waited for a few silent seconds before Kenzie peeked his head out farther.

I unstrapped myself and stood on shaky legs behind Max. He gave me his arm to hold onto for support.

Kenzie was nearly out of the pod when the siren sounded.

FORTY THREE

I was slammed against a rough wall as Kenzie dropped back into the pod. Shots rang out through what sounded like a warehouse. Bullets pinged off the side of the Alatonion pod.

"How did they know we were here?" I screamed over the siren still blaring.

Kenzie shook his head. He offered me a hand up.

"Where's the other pod?" I screamed over the sirens to Sam.

"It looks like they've landed a few meters away from you guys, but their pod is on the wrong side. The door is stuck against the ground. You'll need to help them get out," Sam said.

Max was already pulling himself up toward the still open door. He lifted the heavy door to shield us and Kenzie took action. Squeezing past Max, Kenzie lifted himself out of the pod. From inside, I heard his feet hit the ground before his footsteps disappeared as he ran for better cover.

Max angled his gun around the door. Bullets flew past the opening, and I couldn't help feeling useless crouched inside of the pod.

As if answering my own question, my powers tickled on my fingertips. And then, I remembered I wasn't all together useless. I sent my energy out of the pod. It was slower than usual, just like me, but I detected the guard's stations a few meters away. Six Carbons in total, but none seemed to be the advanced versions. They were using bullets, not powers, to attack us.

I wasn't strong enough to reach them, but the energy inside of me felt each bullet as they aimed for our pod and for the hiding spot where Kenzie fired back with his powers. I grabbed onto each bullet aimed our way, holding them with my energy as they tried to push back. Weak as I felt, my powers were still stronger than the bullets. I flung them back to where they came from. All at once, six Carbons went down.

Max pulled himself out of the pod and reached a hand down to me. Gripping onto one wrist, he pulled me up enough that I was able to swing my legs over the edge and drop to the ground. Max caught me before my knees gave out.

Kenzie was already beside the guards, removing their microchips from the base of their skulls. Max and I sprinted to the second pod. It was tilted onto its side, but a lot less damaged than ours was.

I managed one step forward before my knees buckled. I fell to the ground, coughing up blood black as tar. That small use of energy took a lot out of me. Max helped me to my feet, his face full of worry. He held onto me tightly, and I tried moving on still wobbly legs.

An argument came from inside the pod. It shook from side to side as the occupants tried to flip themselves right side up.

"Hold on, guys! We're here," I shouted, but the alarm still blared, drowning out my voice.

Max and I pushed our weight against the pod. I used my powers only a little until we cleared enough space for them to open the door.

Vance shot out first, sprawling across the ground as he gasped for air. "I do not like flying!"

Tenason followed with a pale look on his face. Ainsley stepped out last with the biggest grin I'd ever seen.

"You'd think two grown men could handle a little bumpy ride." She chuckled. "I've never seen a grown man cry before."

Vance glared at her as he pushed himself to his feet. "I did not cry!"

Ainsley snorted. "Don't worry. Your secret, soft side is safe with me." She winked as she passed Vance with a playful slap on his back. She headed to where Kenzie stood by the door leading from the dock.

The sirens were still deafening.

"More will come if we can't get this damn alarm off," Kenzie said when we reached his side. He typed away on the tablet attached to the wall. He inserted the card Sam gave him to give him access to the security feed, but the alarms hadn't stopped yet.

I covered my ears and screamed, "How did they know?"

274

Kenzie shook his head. "They didn't… or don't. We just triggered an alarm at this loading dock when we arrived. It hasn't been sent out to the rest of the station, but it will soon if Sam doesn't shut it—"

The room became silent.

"Off," Sam's cheerful voice sounded from the tablet's speaker. "You should be all clear from here. I am patched into the security feed and am already looping the videos so you're not seen. I won't be able to communicate with you guys until you get back to the pod, but I'll be watching."

I glanced over my shoulder to our pod streaked with black burn marks, dents, and scratches all over. I inclined my head to our pod as if to say, "We're going back in that?"

"We'll deal with that when we get back," Kenzie said over his shoulder. He walked toward the only door in the large room. There were steel crates lining the entire loading dock around us, making me assume this was also a storage facility. That'd explain the limited security guards stationed here.

I followed closely behind Kenzie who lead the way. Max was right behind me with a hand on my back for support. I gave him a weak smile, which he didn't return. I didn't feel the cold distance between us like I had before, just somber focus.

"Max, I—"

He stuck his hand up to stop me. "It's okay. I shouldn't have… I'm sorry. I should've trusted you…"

I knew Kenzie listened as his body stiffened, but he didn't turn around or speak.

"No, I'm sorry." I struggled to find the right words. "I didn't

mean to hurt you. I just wanted to keep you safe, and then—"
I didn't finish my thought.

Max looked to the ground, as he said, "It'll all be over soon.
You will survive, Sawyer. I promise you that."

We reached the door, and I turned toward Max, but he stepped
past me and took up the other side of the door. Kenzie stepped
around to the far side. Vance took up the middle, ready to pry
the entire door off, but they all waited for a signal from me.

I stood back, sending my energy under the tiny crack in
the door. My power traveled out into the hallway in search of
anyone or anything nearby, but the hallway was empty.

Vance waited for my confirmation before he pulled open the
door. Kenzie was first to walk into the hallway.

"This is where we split up," Kenzie stated.

Tenason slung a bag over his shoulder as he stepped closer to
Ainsley. Vance took up the front.

"Stay in the outer shell of the station. This is one big circle,
and it will take you right back here. Don't wait for us when
you get back. Just get clear of the station, and we'll finish the
job," Max said.

"Be careful out there." Tenason nudged me.

"You too." I smiled back, not wanting to say goodbye for fear
it'd be forever.

Ainsley gave a nod as she cloaked her and the two men at her
side. Within seconds, they looked like nothing more than the
empty hallway.

"We'll see you soon, friends," Vance said before their soft
footsteps moved down the opposite hallway.

As soon as I turned back to the direction we were headed, I felt a weird sense of familiarity in the space. The hallway was long and curved, indicating it made a full circle around the station, as Kenzie had said. The metal walkway was cold and dimly lit. It smelled sterile and clean, but not in a refreshing way, in a haunting way. No matter how softly we tried to walk, our footsteps echoed loudly all around us.

When we reached another hallway and Kenzie led us down it, I knew where we were. Sector 7.

The lights seemed dimmer. The musky smell of mold, rot, and death filled the air, causing my stomach to roll, despite knowing I had the same scent all over me, even with Ainsley's peppermint salve masking it.

Kenzie stopped when we reached the end of the hallway and the large door before us. He hesitated before turning around to face me.

"Maybe you should wait here," he suggested, but I was already shaking my head.

"You don't need to see this. We'll be in and out quick." Max gripped my arm reaching for the door.

"No, I need to see her. One way or another, I need to know…" I said.

Kenzie and Max exchanged a look, but neither stopped me. I pressed the button on the wall, and the door slid open.

The stench hit us like a wall, slamming into us. Max nearly keeled over and Kenzie paled. I rolled my shoulders back, straightened my spine, and with whatever strength I still had in me, I stepped into the dimly lit room.

The walls spanned farther than I could see, and Reeks lined the edges, chained like animals. They pulled against their restraints as we entered, clawing at us. They groaned and screamed through hoarse voices, but my focus wasn't on them. I could only look at one thing in the distance.

A figure knelt in the center of the room. Its head hung low, arms outstretched overhead and chained to the roof. It was too dark to see anything but the outline of the person. I knew it was her—my mom.

As we walked farther into Sector 7, the Reeks grew rowdy and impatient. They tried to reach us, but we were too far away. They sounded tortured and angry, and the sound only grew wilder the farther we went.

The noise stirred the figure up ahead, and a pale face looked up from the slick hair draped over her forehead. She squinted as I neared. I would've run to her if I could, but my legs could hardly keep in rhythm as I moved toward her.

"Sawyer?" Her voice was barely a whisper.

I nodded, and a smile grew across my face. When I reached her side, I dropped to my knees and took her fragile face in my hands.

Her eyes watered over as she looked at me like I was a ghost. "How are you here?" she asked.

"We've come to finish this. And we've come for you. We need your help," Kenzie said, stepping around me. He snapped the chains around her wrists with a blast of energy. She dropped into my arms.

"You shouldn't be here. These things… this virus. It can

spread through only a single touch, through the air even," she warned. Her hands shook as she gripped me for support. I was hardly any better off than she was, but I stayed strong for her. I took the weight of her small frame with me as I stood.

Max took her other side, as she was hardly able to hold herself up.

"How long have they held you here? Have you eaten anything?" I asked.

She shook her head, and rage flowed through me.

Her eyes glanced to the Reeks around us. Their attention focused our way, as if they smelled us. We were fresh meat for them, and it seemed they hadn't been fed in a while, either.

"We have to go. You shouldn't be here," Mom said.

I gave her a weak smile. "It's already too late for that."

Her eyes widened, and she shook her head. "No, no…"

"It's going to be okay. We just need to find Lena. She can help us." I nodded and began making my way down the open hallway between the ravaged Reeks.

"How are you still here? How are you okay?" Kenzie asked my mother. I hadn't even had a chance to notice that she didn't have a hint of the virus in her. She looked pale and fragile, but she wasn't infected.

"Lena… she…" My mother shuddered and shook her head. Whatever Lena had done to protect my mother was too much for her to speak out loud, but I knew I owed Lena my life for what she'd already done, and hopefully what she was able to do for me if we reached her.

"We need you to lead us to Lena. Do you remember where

they're holding her?" Max asked.

"Yes." My mom nodded.

"Good, because I think we should hurry," Max said. He gestured to the wall of black surrounding us.

The Reeks had gone nearly feral, and with every step we took, the raspy, sickening noise grew louder. They pulled against the chains. I tried to pick up the pace, but my mom was too weak to go any faster. Max was supporting nearly both of our weight, but he couldn't take us both. We stumbled to the ground.

Behind us, there was the nauseating sound of flesh being ripped apart. I didn't have to turn around to know what it was. A Reek had torn itself free, and it was racing toward us with two stub arms swinging at its side.

"Move!" Kenzie yelled, as he pulled me to my feet.

Max reached down and scooped my mom into his arms. He took off, running as fast as he could. More chains broke loose, giving several Reeks freedom.

I tried to keep up. I tried to make my legs move, but I was slowing Kenzie down. Still, he didn't let go of my arm.

I stumbled over my feet and fell to my knees. Kenzie stopped and pulled me up, but those things were getting closer. I pushed my powers away from us, clearing a path as the Reeks in front of us joined in the chase. Max and my mom had reached the door, and he was now turning back for me, but Kenzie and I were surrounded and still far from safety.

Kenzie blasted through a few, but there were too many.

I sent my energy out, trying to grab a hold of anything, but there was nothing to grab. When I sent a wall of pure power toward the horde, it only stopped them up for a moment before they were back on broken feet, sprinting toward us.

"Come on." Kenzie pulled me again. He'd made a path for us to get through, but it was narrow. More were coming.

I searched for anything to help us, finding only my gun, which I emptied with little success.

I realized then that there was a clear path for Kenzie to run through. He was quick enough; he'd make it. But I was holding him back. I was too slow.

One of the things grabbed my ankle, and I stifled a scream, falling once again. I pulled back and kicked my leg free, pushing myself to my feet.

I ripped Kenzie's hand from my grip and pushed him ahead of me. "Go!" I called.

His eyes flashed at me as that small moment gave the Reeks enough separation to get between us. He tried to reach for my arm again, but I was too far away. They had us both surrounded, but Kenzie was closer to the door. He could make it. He had to.

I pushed my powers out, clearing a path to the door, but not for me—for Kenzie.

"Go," I yelled again, begging him to move. Hands clawed at my arms, pulling me back as their cold, scaled limbs wrapped around me. I was powerless to escape. "Please," I begged again, but he did the opposite.

His features transitioned from anger to pure rage in less than a second. At first I thought it was directed at me, but it wasn't.

It was for me.

FORTY FOUR

KENZIE

No, no. Kenzie let out a loud cry, and the energy building inside of him let loose. It smashed into the four Reeks between Sawyer and him, and they disintegrated into nothing but black soot. He continued, his power growing as it shot out between them, past Sawyer. His energy surrounded the Reeks with a blanket of electricity. White streaks circled the space around them like an electric current.

She had told him before that she would sacrifice her life for Max, not him, yet she was willing to die so he could escape. He wouldn't let that happen. It didn't matter who she chose—he had chosen her.

Kenzie arrived at her side and pulled her up into his arms. He pressed her against his chest and he was running. He felt Sawyer's energy pulsing around them, trying to clear a path, but there was nothing to clear. She looked toward where they moved and her eyes widened. Kenzie had annihilated every one of the Reeks standing between them and the door. There was nothing left in front of them but a faint black dust across the ground that stirred as he bolted toward that door.

More were still following behind them but Kenzie was fast. When they reached the end and barely slipped through the door, Max slammed his hand down to close it behind them. Kenzie fell to his knees, heaving for air. Sawyer was still in his arms on the ground as he knelt, gasping for air. He held her so close to him she could hardly breathe herself.

His chest pounded and he was trembling. His whole body was burning, and every fiber inside of him felt out of control. His powers filled him up, threatening to explode. *She almost died.*

A cold hand rested against his cheek, and he looked up and met Sawyer's gaze. Worry filled her face, but not for herself, not for what she just went through. For him.

"We're out. We're safe," she whispered.

His eyes searched hers, as if he didn't believe her at first. But then Kenzie's breath steadied, and he released his tight grip around her. Sawyer slid out of his arms but kept her hand on his cheek. He let out one last shuddering breath and his shoulders fell. They had made it.

Sawyer's mom sat against the wall, her breaths were labored and quick. A few feet away Max was looking at his feet, and

Kenzie pulled himself farther away from Sawyer.

"We should go," Max said.

Kenzie agreed. As he pushed himself back to his feet, he did everything in his power to erase the image he'd seen—Sawyer being consumed by that horde of Reeks, and the feeling of being powerless to stop them—until he wasn't. He let the rage take over, and nothing else mattered but her.

He helped Sawyer to her feet, but this time she walked on her own power. As she moved into stride behind Max and her mom, she glanced over her shoulder at Kenzie, who gave her a sharp nod and a silent thanks.

"They've kept her in a small room beside the Doctor… Irene," Sawyer's mom explained. A visible shiver went through her. "It's right in the middle of the station near Coleman's Office, and it will be heavily guarded."

Kenzie wasn't surprised that Coleman would keep his most prized possession close to him.

"Follow the plan, Max. I'll see you on the other side," Kenzie said, and Max gave a sharp nod.

Kenzie moved to head down the next hallway, but Sawyer grabbed his arm, stopping him, though he could've easily shrugged her off.

"Where are you going?" she asked.

"To create a diversion," Kenzie said simply.

"What kind of diversion?" Sawyer narrowed her eyes.

Kenzie shifted on his feet before he said, "I'm the diversion, Sawyer."

She was quiet for a moment, thinking, but as realization set in, her face fell. "No!" She shook her head. "No, you can't give yourself up."

"It's the only way," Max said from behind Sawyer. Max hadn't been keen on the plan when Kenzie had told him the only way to gain access to Lena was to give Coleman something else to focus on, or rather, someone else. "We need to give the rest of the team enough time to set those bombs, Sawyer, and this is the best chance we have."

"No," Sawyer argued. "We should all stick together. We can fight them off. We will find a way in, all of us together."

Kenzie shook his head. "The minute he realizes why we're here, the whole place will go on lockdown. There won't be a chance to get to Lena if that happens."

"So what, you're just going to walk in there and surrender yourself?" Sawyer asked.

"No." Kenzie gave a wicked smile. "I'm going to cause a big enough scene that they send everyone they've got at me, and I'm going to take out as much of this station as I can."

"He'll kill you," Sawyer whispered. Her voice cracked.

It took everything in him to not grab her and hold her tight. To tell her it would be all right. He couldn't, because this was for her, so she could live. She deserved to live.

"He won't. He still needs me," Kenzie said. He reached into the deep pocket of his jacket where he pulled out ten tiny metal dots. "Microbombs. Adam made them for us. They're the same ones the others have. If he tries to kill me, he just needs to be reminded that I hold the trigger. And if I die, I'm taking him with me."

Sawyer didn't look convinced. And in truth, Kenzie wasn't much convinced himself. The chances that another Carbon didn't kill him before he came near Coleman were slim. And even stronger were the chances that Coleman would see through his plan, knowing that there weren't nearly enough microbombs to take the entire space station down, but Kenzie would lie and bluff with everything he had.

"We should go with you," Sawyer said.

It wasn't just Kenzie who disagreed this time. Max and Sawyer's mom both said no before Kenzie even had a chance to say the same.

"But I could help. I don't think you should go alone," she tried again.

"I'll be fine. You need to get to Lena and fast. Especially now." Kenzie again shoved away the image of those Reeks clawing all over Sawyer.

Sawyer looked down to her hands, which were rapidly spreading with black scales. The virus was multiplying even faster than before, and her time was limited.

"We're wasting time," Kenzie said. He tried to shove Sawyer away, but she gripped onto his hand and pulled him close enough that only he heard her.

"Promise you won't give up," she said.

Kenzie couldn't look away. The words were on the tip of his tongue, ones he had spoken long ago to her, when he was a different Kenzie. When he was Sawyer's Kenzie. He remembered what she'd said to him. "I'll see you there," he repeated her words.

Sawyer smiled, and her eyes lit up at the memory. His heart nearly broke at the sight. "I'd better see you there," she said. All he could do was nod before he turned and sprinted down the opposite hallway. He wasn't sure if he could still do what he knew would have to be done if he'd stayed even one moment longer.

It killed him, to know that this was a promise he couldn't possibly keep.

FORTY FIVE

I watched Kenzie until he rounded the corner and was out of view. When I turned to find Max watching me, sadness was hidden behind his eyes. My heart sank with guilt, but I hadn't lied when I told Kenzie I didn't want to see either of them die, and I needed to make sure he still knew that no matter who I'd chosen.

"This way," Max said, as he continued down the hallway in the opposite direction of Kenzie.

I took a steadying breath before I followed. Long, narrow hallways were dotted with round windows looking out to the dark expanse. It was silent except for our footsteps over the metal, and everything smelled clean and sterile the farther away from Sector 7 we moved.

The words were on the tip of my tongue, but I didn't know what to say or how to say it. "Max..." was all that came out.

He glanced over his shoulder, and his face softened as he slowed down and gripped my hand. "It's fine, Sawyer. You don't need to explain anything to me. You don't need to apologize. You just need to hold on a bit longer until we get to Lena, that's it."

I wanted to say something. I wanted to apologize, but I didn't know how. There were too many things piling up to say sorry for. But I had to try. If this was the end, if I didn't make it, I needed Max to know everything.

"I couldn't let him leave thinking no one cared if he lived or died," I said softly, trying to explain, but feeling like I was failing and making it so much worse.

But Max just nodded. "I know. I understand," he said and gave my hand a light squeeze.

We moved into a light jog, as much as my mom and I could manage, both weak but determined to not stop. The hallways were empty so far, a few doors seemed to melt into the metal along the interior walls of the station, and the silence had me more on edge than if these hallways had been packed with Carbons.

"The guards don't patrol down here anymore. The virus can spread through the air, leaving them all paranoid they'd be the next one chained up to the walls of Sector 7," my mom explained, her words coming out staggered and breathy. "But the closer we get, the more there will be."

I glanced up to Max, wondering what the plan was to get

around them.

"We won't have many to worry about, not for long, anyway," Max said.

We slowed down at the next hallway, dim lighting hung from the exposed ceiling where ducts and pipes flowed across it. We peered around the corner, finding it exactly the same as the one we stood in, before continuing toward the center of the space station.

"How will we know?" I asked, not wanting to finish the question. *How will we know Kenzie had done his job?*

Max's face was grim, and he tried to hide it from me. "We'll know."

There was another intersection in the hallway, this time crossing with one of the larger main corridors that went down the center of the station. We slowed down, checking around both corners before we pressed ourselves against the wall. Max had his gun out, but I silently told him to put it down. His brow creased before he listened.

"Two down the left corridor, another three straight ahead," I said, after sending my energy out in search of something solid to hold onto. A light flickered overhead. The two Carbons to our left were heading our way. We'd be meeting them first.

"Silently," I ordered Max and he nodded.

My mom stayed pressed against the wall as Max and I crouched down. Two guards approached, their pace even and hurried.

Their casual conversation grew as they neared. Max and I took up a stance, ready to pounce.

They hadn't taken more than one step into view, when we attacked. Moving on near silent feet, I dove behind the first guard, wrapping my forearm around his throat and covering his mouth with my other hand.

The guard was taller than me. He leaned forward as he threatened to throw me off, but I laced my legs around him. With a sharp snap, I twisted his neck, and he fell lifelessly to the ground. My energy dropped just as quickly as the Carbon did, adrenaline fueling me in that moment. Max had the other guard wrapped up with his hand over his mouth as well, and a blade smoothly slid across the guard's throat until he, too, fell to the ground.

I removed the microchips from their neck, and we dragged them out of view, stashing them in the alcove of a locked door as best we could. There was hardly enough room for both of them, and blood stained the silver-colored floors, but it was the best we could do.

Silently, we moved forward, ready for more. The others weren't much farther down the hallway curving a little to the right, but they hadn't been alarmed or even noticed what had happened. The three guards stood side-by-side as they marched toward where we hid in the shadows. This time, I risked using up a little of my energy stores. I sent it out in search of those microchips that only my energy could detect.

Once I had grabbed hold of all three, I positioned myself in front of both Max and my mom, motioning for them to stay down and quiet. I stepped into the hallway as they came into view.

"Hey!" One guard started, but before he could question me, I ripped my energy out, and with it, three microchips dangled in the air. The guards dropped to the ground, eyes still open in surprise as the life left them. We didn't bother hiding these guards, there was nowhere to put three bodies anyway, so we just had to be quick.

"It isn't much farther," my mother whispered, as she led the way again.

We made it down one more intersection, passing an enormous floor to ceiling window that looked down on earth, before I felt the presence of more people, more Carbons.

I peeked around the next corner. A gasp caught in my throat before I turned back to Max and my mom. "Over a dozen outside the door. And I can see at least four more through the glass into the room." There was a large door that the Carbons stood before and a panel on the wall beside the door.

"We have to wait then. Too many for us to take on," Max said.

I wanted to protest. My powers could take all of them and more on a good day, but this wasn't a good day. I'd already used up a lot of my energy on just three Carbons.

I glanced down to my hand, which was black and covered in scales, and to the Alatonion cuff still glowing silver against the black. It was no doubt the only reason I was still able to use any of my powers, possibly the only reason I was still alive, that and the white fur vest tight against my chest.

"Vance, Tenason, and Ainsley will be done soon. Once this ship starts blowing, it will take everyone with them. Kenzie will do his part. He'll clear us a path," Max whispered.

I nodded, not wanting to think about how that was going to happen, or the clench it gave my heart to think about it.

We were silent as we waited in the shadows of a doorway for whatever sign Max was expecting from Kenzie to tell us he had succeeded in his distraction. The tension between Max and me was unfamiliar, and I wished I could wash it away. Max wanted to say something, but he just opened his mouth and quickly shut it again.

I watched him as he squeezed his hands tight in his lap. He looked up at me.

"Was he telling the truth?" Max asked. "That you chose me?"

I nodded. I expected his expression to change, for the heavy weight on him to settle, but it didn't. His shoulders slumped.

"Why?" he whispered.

My brow creased, and for a heartbeat I didn't know if I knew the answer, but I did. "Because I love you. You're mine—now and forever."

His eyes flashed up to mine, surprised at my response. They filled with tears before he blinked them away and swallowed. "And you're mine." He gripped my hand and held it tight, his thumb twisting around the small ring on my pinky. I felt his heart racing as it pulsed through his fingers and against my palm. "You deserve the world, Sawyer. You deserve the stars and the moon, and I'd give them all to you if I could. But mostly, you deserve to live. To truly live." He met my eyes, and I couldn't look away.

"So do you," I whispered.

He gave me a somber smile before he kissed me gently on

the cheek. "You have already given me more than I could've asked for. You are my world," he whispered into my ear before he pulled back.

I couldn't help the feeling that his words were like a goodbye, like he wasn't telling me something more, something he was hiding.

I opened my mouth to reply as the first bomb went off.

FORTY
SIX

KENZIE

Walking away from her would be the hardest thing Kenzie did, that he was sure of. He felt her eyes on him the whole way as he ran down the hallway and rounded the corner, but he was doing this for her. He was doing this for Sawyer. He wouldn't turn back.

As he walked down the wide, familiar hallway, Kenzie rolled his shoulders and set them back as he prepared himself. He placed the small microbombs at key structural points, hoping to inflict as much damage as he could with the small amount he had. The trigger was shoved into his pocket.

He diverted his path when he spotted another security

terminal, unguarded. Quickly breaking through the already broken firewalls, he sent off a message to Sam, hoping he received it in time.

"Make sure they see me coming," it read.

He didn't have to wait long to know Sam had received the message. The sound of soldiers stomping down the hallway and toward him was loud against the near silent space.

Kenzie picked up his pace, letting the electric energy flowing through him rise to the tips of his finger. He charged toward the pounding footsteps.

He sprinted around the corner and shot his hand up. Not even a breath went by before he unleashed everything he had. The front four soldiers were blasted back by the force, smashing into the line behind them, but the soldiers pushed the dead aside and kept moving.

He had their attention.

Turning, he sprinted down the hallway. He heard the heavy pursuit following behind him. Orders to stop echoed through the space, but Kenzie didn't listen. He moved faster. He paused only to position another microbomb before he took off again.

Hitting the next crossing hallway, he skidded to a stop. Another set of Carbons marched toward him, set on cutting him off. Kenzie turned down the still empty opening and sprinted as fast as he could away from where Sawyer would be headed.

They'd sent a lot of Carbons to track him down, but it wasn't enough. Not yet. He needed to get the attention of every one of them for his plan to work. He reached into his pocket and pulled out the trigger.

Only half had been placed and activated, but that would be enough to cause a little noise, enough to have Coleman worried.

He pressed the button.

The entire space station shook with the explosion, and even Kenzie was knocked off his feet. The lights flickered on and off before they turned black. Flashing, red warning lights replaced the extinguished lighting. An alarm filled the silence after the bombs had gone off. Safety airlock doors slammed into place, sealing off the exploded portions of the station from the rest of it. There would be more bombs coming. Much more.

Pushing himself back to his feet, Kenzie kept moving. He placed the remaining microbombs along the route as he went. A few Carbons from another posting had heard the blast, and they were sprinting at him. They didn't make it far since the second they raised their guns to fire, Kenzie blasted right through them. He aimed for their heads, destroying their microchip at the same time. They dropped to the ground, and he made quick work jumping over them, not wasting a second as he skidded around another corner.

This was the necessary evil he'd wanted to avoid, but he knew there would be no stopping it. He hoped to save as many Carbons as he could, giving them a chance to make the right decision on their own without Coleman's influence. But he was all too aware that there'd be sacrifices if he wanted her to live. And right now, nothing mattered but her life.

He was on the outer ring of the space station, back where he knew he was far enough away from where Sawyer was sure to find Lena. Kenzie hoped Tenason, Ainsley, and Vance were long gone. He positioned himself in the middle of the foyer, his back to the wall and his arm outstretched to the left hallway he had come down. His right hand held the trigger to the last microbombs he'd placed as he ran.

Footsteps sounded from both directions; they were converging on him. Kenzie hoped and prayed they had sent enough to give Max and Sawyer time to get Lena out. The Carbons to his left arrived first, slowing down as they came upon him, ready to fight back. They paused, and he understood they had been ordered to capture him, not kill him.

To his right, another group of Carbons filled the only space that had been his exit. They cautiously circled around him, waiting.

It didn't take Kenzie long to realize why they were waiting, or rather for whom they were waiting.

Coleman stepped out from behind the Carbons taking up the frontline, and he didn't balk or waver at Kenzie's stance, still poised to attack.

"You can drop the dramatics, Kenzie." Coleman smirked.

Kenzie felt the odd sensation of his arms growing heavy, and he fought against it. Sweat was already forming on his brow, as he held steady. Kenzie pushed against the control Coleman tried to exert over him.

Coleman's brows rose. "I see you've gotten a little help to try to resist me. But we both know your nature. We both know who you really are on the inside." Coleman's eyes flashed to the Alatonion cuff glowing on Kenzie's wrist.

Kenzie smiled through his grimace. "I don't need any help,

not anymore." His arms were shaking, but they didn't fail him. They didn't drop.

Coleman took a step forward, the corner of his mouth curving into an ugly sneer. "Don't you?" he whispered, as his finger grazed the top of Kenzie's fist, holding the trigger in it.

Kenzie's body burned, and his limbs grew heavy and throbbed. He tried to fight against the control threatening to take over. He tried to keep his body from betraying him, but he couldn't hold it any longer. He dropped hard to his knees.

His fist still clung to the trigger, and his powers still vibrated in the palm of his hand. His head dropped to his chin, and his body obeyed the order it was given. *No, hold on. You have to hold on.* Terror filled his body as the familiar feeling of Coleman trying to take control seeped in. He couldn't fail the now, not here. He had to hold on.

Coleman laughed. "That's what I thought. You're no hero— you're one of us. An obedient soldier who does as he is told." Kenzie's entire body shook as Coleman circled him, eyeing him down with a wicked grin on his face. "You can't play this game, boy. You're nothing more than a pawn piece on the board, and you've always been on my side—the winning side."

Kenzie's jaw clenched, and his heart pounded harder.

"Your worthless *friends* are never going to defeat me. They will all die, every one of them." Coleman leaned in so close that Kenzie felt his breath on his cheek, as he said, "And you're going to watch them die, son. You're going to see every one of them fail and lose, especially the pretty, little brown-haired girl who has you wrapped around her finger. She'll be the first one to suffer, and it won't be quick. Oh no, I'm going to make it last."

Anger filled Kenzie and his lungs burned. He felt like he was lifting a million pounds as he grimaced and battled with everything he had left. Slowly, he lifted one leg and planted his foot heavily on the ground and then the other, as he pushed his way back up to his feet. He towered over Coleman, who stood before him. Coleman narrowed his eyes at Kenzie.

A small bit of movement came against the wall across from him. He barely noticed it, but as soon as he did, he knew what it was. Quickly, he tore his eyes away and back to Coleman, keeping his expression as neutral as possible.

A slow panic ran through Kenzie, as just for the blink of an eye, he saw Ainsley's face in the back corner, tucked against the wall. They'd inadvertently been trapped here, and there was no way out.

If his job were to be a pawn, if that was what Coleman expected of him, he would take that role. He'd sacrifice himself, so his team could win. He'd give them time to finish the job because his sacrifice could change the game; it would change everything.

The invisible cloak Ainsley had draped over them moved closer. Kenzie only knew because they wanted him to know, so he put the play in motion.

"The only one who's going to suffer, Coleman, is you." Kenzie grimaced, as he nodded to the shadow across from him. "Now!"

Ainsley, Tenason, and Vance jumped into view, and Vance's fist connected with Coleman's head. Kenzie twisted and blasted through a set of Carbons standing in the path to retreat.

"Go, run!" Kenzie ordered, and Tenason gripped onto Ainsley's wrist as they ran. Tenason aimed his gun at the few still in his way fighting back.

Tenason paused, glancing over his shoulder and seeing that Kenzie wasn't moving. "Come on, we have to get out of here."

Kenzie shook his head. "No, you have to get out of here. Set those charges and get the hell off this station."

There was hesitation in Tenason's stance as he held onto Ainsley, both ready to drag Kenzie with them, but he knew the game. He knew the play Kenzie was about to make.

Tenason gave a sharp nod before turning back away.

There was a grunt beside Kenzie as two Carbons threw themselves on top of Vance, who was struggling to get up. They pinned him down with a strength equal to his own. Vance couldn't move.

Vance's eyes locked on Ainsley who had turned back, pulling against Tenason's grip to try to help him. "Get out of here," Vance yelled, but she didn't look ready to leave. "Please," he said. Tenason pulled her away, and in the blink of an eye, the two disappeared. When they could no longer hear their footsteps, Kenzie knew it was time. He could already feel Coleman's control trying to lock onto him once again, and he knew he and Vance weren't going to get away. He had to act fast before Coleman took full control of him. His eyes flickered to the trigger still in his hands and then to Vance who had followed his gaze. Vance gave a subtle nod.

"Do it. I am ready," Vance said.

Before Coleman collected himself, Kenzie pressed the trigger, setting off the last bombs. It sent a ripple effect, bouncing down the hallway across from him and blasting one after the other until it reached the last one only a few feet away.

The image of Sawyer standing before him calmed his ragged breathing, and he stood strong and tall as he awaited the inevitable. This was the only way he could ever make it up to her, what he'd put her through. He knew she wouldn't understand. She wouldn't know the pain he felt as each day a new memory of his past with her popped into his mind. He remembered every touch of her skin, every scar on her body. He didn't deserve her: he never had. The pain of knowing what he had done, what he would always be capable of being if Coleman were alive, that made this decision easy. Like choosing to turn on the light in the darkness, it made sense to him.

The last thing Kenzie felt was the burning pain of the flames as they slammed into him.

FORTY SEVEN

The second blast was larger than the first, hitting at the already weakened points in the space station. I could tell Kenzie had kept his word. He'd been the distraction we needed, and he'd opened the path to Lena.

The remaining guards who had stood watch in front of Lena's room charged down the hallway toward where the blast had originated, leaving only four to watch her.

Max stepped out of the shadows, his gun raised, no longer needing to be quiet. I tucked my mom behind me. I pulled out my gun, saving my energy for getting out of here, if that was even still an option.

Max loosed four bullets, and they each hit a target. Only two went down, though. The other two had enough time to move as the bullets hit one Carbon in the shoulder and the other in the back. The first Carbon turned on us. Without a weapon in its hand, I braced for whatever was to come.

I pushed Max out of the way as a hundred tiny metal spikes came shooting out of the Carbon's hands, aimed straight for Max's head.

We hardly had time to scramble to our feet before the metal spikes turned in the air behind us. Like a hundred bees swarming, they came straight for us, and I put up a small shield between us just in time, draping my body over my mom, who was sprawled on the floor beside me.

My breath was heavy. I pushed against each spike threatening to close in on us. A few made their way through, and I screamed out in pain. They pierced through flesh and bone, digging deep inside of me. My white fur vest became coated with dark red blood.

Another scream of pain leached out behind me as my powers faltered. Blood spread across Max's chest where the spikes had dug in. He winced but pushed himself to his feet. I held on for only a second longer, and he aimed his gun and hit the Carbon square between the eyes.

The spikes dropped to the ground in a chorus of chimes against the metal walkway.

The second Carbon didn't wait long to make his attack, but he didn't have any special abilities. Before he had taken two steps, Max dropped him.

I struggled to my feet, pulling my mom up with me. I hurried over to Max. His chest was speckled with red dots, blood trickling out.

"Hold on," I said, tugging on my powers and pushing them into the little slits where the metal had pierced through. I grabbed a hold of each one. Before Max had time to think about the pain, I ripped them out.

He screamed and dropped to his knees, but I caught him as best I could. He trembled in my arms, and I pulled him back to his feet. He gave me a grimacing nod of thanks.

"This way." My mom pulled us back, as we stepped toward the glass door the Carbons had been guarding.

The first room was filled with computers and charts. A small desk sat at the back, but it was empty.

"Through there." Mom pointed to a lone door at the back of the room, leading to another smaller room that was stark white and still bright under fluorescent lights.

I pushed the door open, peering through the small crack. Inside, the room was all white. A bed at the center of the room had a tiny girl lying on it. Lena. Her skin was pale yet bruised. Her chapped lips were parted, and the whisper of a breath came out sounding labored and harsh. There was no light in her eyes, and a dark shadow hung under them. This wasn't the strong princess I remembered. This Lena was broken in every sense of the word.

I held back a sob, rushing in. I knelt beside her bed. She slowly started, peeking her eye open, as her tired lids threatened to close again.

"Sawyer?" Her voice was nearly inaudible.

"Yes." I smiled, moving a strand of hair away from her pale

face. "We're going to get you out. It's going to be all right."

"No," she breathed. "She's still here…"

I didn't have time to ask whom she meant before I felt a calm sweep through the room. My body seemed to melt and relax at the warmth that filled it, coating every aching inch of me. It was then I noticed the Doctor standing in the corner of the room. I recognized her sandy-blonde hair tucked neatly behind her ears. Her glasses slid low down her tiny nose.

"She won't be going anywhere," Doctor Irene said. She stepped out of the shadows and moved with confidence toward us.

Max and I froze, our bodies both complying with whatever powers she wielded. Her abilities affected both of us, sending calmness which radiated through my body, and I had the weird sensation of wanting to move, wanting to fight back, but I couldn't. My body relaxed against the powers she threw at us, and I couldn't look away from her.

"Step away from my patient," she ordered. Max and I both obeyed, stepping back and pressing against the wall of the room.

My mom was at my side, already hiding behind me. Her hand gripped my waist as she pulled me closer to her.

"Please, don't hurt them," Lena begged. I wondered how Irene would hurt us? She felt so trusting and peaceful. There was no reason to think she would hurt us, was there? *This is a trick*, my mind screamed, but it was barely audible.

"Hush, child," Irene said, but she kept her eyes trained on us.

Irene stepped back toward the wall, reaching for the comm. She was poised to call for backup no doubt, but she was never able to.

A sound blasted and rang in my ears before I even understood what had happened. The minute it happened, I felt it—the instant release she had on us, the immediate end to her powers. The bright red hole in her forehead seemed to pause before thick blood poured down her face. She dropped to her knees, falling face-first onto the pristine white floors.

Beside me, my mom's hands shook. She held my gun in her hands, the one she had taken when she'd pulled me in closer to her.

Max cautiously grabbed the gun from her. My mom's hands fell to her sides with her eyes wide open. Not with fear, but determination.

"Thank you." I drew my mom's attention back, and she blinked, giving me a grim smile and a nod.

I reached Lena's side, helping her sit up. I pulled off the cables still attached to her. "We have to get out of here," I said with urgency.

Max positioned himself at the door, watching for any cavalry that might still be coming.

Lena glanced at my hands, completely black. I couldn't even hide it anymore. "You need help," she stated, looking past me to my mom, who nodded.

"I know, but we have to get you to a more secure place first. Then you can help me," I said, reaching under her arms to stand her on her feet. Her long, white gown draped over her thin body, and I saw the spark of life gone from her golden eyes.

She shook her head. "Not me. You don't need me."

My brows furrowed. I put her arm over mine and ducked

under her shoulder. I was hardly strong enough to help myself, but I let Max take the lead, as he was a better shot than me at this point. Guards still roamed the hallways, and we needed someone to protect us. For once, I could admit that wasn't me.

"Lena, you're coming with us. There is no fighting it this time. We've already got plans for your... Coleman. But we need to hurry." I tried to pull her along, but she was slow and stumbled. My mom took up her other side.

"He will come, he will find me," she said.

"He can't find you if he's dead," I said, but she still shook her head. "I know you said he can't die, but he can't survive if we blow up this space station, can he?"

She looked concerned, unsure. "I don't know," she breathed. I sighed.

How could anyone survive something like that? How could anyone live? But he'd have a contingency plan. He'd be prepared for anything, always one step ahead of us.

We walked into the next room where the computer screens were all flashing a warning. At first, I almost walked right past it, but my eyes caught something.

Across five screens were the words, "Sawyer, turn on the comm."

Max and I exchanged a look. It could be a trick. It could be Coleman, but I pressed the button.

"Oh, thank God! Sawyer, it's me Sam." His voice filled the room. "I've been trying to find a way to get a hold of you, as I can't really just announce over the speaker that I needed to speak to you. I tried hacking the room you're in and managed to leave that little message, and well…"

"Sam!" I yelled.

"Right, right, sorry. Here's the thing. There are five ships heading for Earth, sent from Coleman, I presume," Sam said.

I swore under my breath.

"How many Carbons?" I asked, not sure I wanted to hear the answer.

"Five times as many as last time." Sam's voice dropped. "Sawyer, we're not prepared for this. Everyone is running out to their stations, but there's too many of them, and not enough of us."

"Where are the others?" I asked.

"I've lost visuals on most of the station, but Ainsley and Tenason just returned to their pod. Their pod is still operational, I can bring them home unless… unless you need them?" Sam asked.

"No, get them to safety," I ordered.

"Will do. You can trust me, Sawyer," Sam said. "The last of the bombs are set to go off, giving you enough time to escape. I can remote detonate from here."

"Where's Vance?" I couldn't keep back the panic.

"I—I'm not sure. Tenason said to go without him, that it was too late," Sam stammered. "But Sawyer, these Carbons, we have to do something."

My heart sank. We'd already lost Vance, and we'd lose so many more if we didn't do something quick.

"What can we do, Sam?" Max asked.

"Maybe there's a way to stop the ships before they arrive? If there were a way, it'd be in the main control room. It's not too far from where you are. There might be a way to override their path from here. Or stop them long enough for you guys to get back here and help," Sam said.

Max nodded. "I'll go."

"We'll go," I corrected him.

"No, you get back to the pod, take Lena and your mom with you, and I'll meet you guys there," Max moved to leave but I stopped him.

"No!" I nearly shouted. "I'm not separating, and we aren't leaving you. We will all go and figure this out together."

Max let out a frustrated sigh. "I can't let you do that, Sawyer."

"You don't get to decide what I can and can't do," I said more harshly than I'd intended. "We go together or not at all."

I knew he wouldn't let our people die, and he knew that I wouldn't let him die. So despite all the reservations I saw running through his mind, he gave me a nod before saying, "How do we get there, Sam?"

FORTY
EIGHT

Red lights flashed through the dark hallway, casting shadows all around us and causing me to watch every corner I found. Max led the way toward the control room from the directions Sam had given us, keeping his pace quick as we went.

Lena's small body rested between my mom and me. We were both just as weak, but her body was so frail and light it was easy for us to manage. Her speech was quiet and confused, her skin pale and gaunt.

"You need to help me," she muttered.

"We're going to get you out of here, I promise," I responded.

"No, *you* can help me, only you." She glanced up at me where her arm rested across my shoulder. I followed her gaze to the stump at the end of her arm, the wound from where her hands used to be had healed and scarred over.

I tried to make sense of her confusing words. "I will. Whatever I can do, Lena, I will help you."

She shook her head. "No, not that."

I shook my head, trying to be patient. I kept most of my attention on our path ahead, watching for any guards lingering. Max had already taken out a few singles that were left, confused by the alarms and explosions. The space station shook with distant blasts, and the entire structure was moving; that was why we had to be fast, and why this discussion could wait.

"We'll figure it all out, Lena. It's going to be okay. When we get back, Doc will have a look at you. There may be something he can do," I whispered.

"No!" she said with as much fire as she could muster, causing Max to turn around. My mom and I almost stumbled into him.

"What is it, Lena? We don't have much time." I was losing my patience and my energy with it.

She glanced up at me, her golden eyes rimmed with tears that caught in the reflection of the lights blinking all around. "I am the reason he's still alive, I am the reason he is still here. Without me, he cannot live."

I caught Max's eye as he watched me. His mouth parted with words he couldn't find. I found them. "How?" There was fear in her eyes. We both knew it wasn't as simple as taking her away or getting her out of here. Coleman would search for her. He'd find her, and he'd destroy everything and everyone in his path.

Lena's eyes fell, as she said, "Only you can do it. You can be my mercy, my ending."

My head was already shaking. "I can't… I won't!" There was only one form of mercy in the world we lived in, only one way to make this all stop. Death was the only way to escape.

She turned her face to meet my gaze, and she held my stare. "Only you can do it. And you will… for me, you will."

I wanted to argue. I wanted to say no, that I couldn't do this. I wasn't strong enough and I needed her. But I think a part of me understood what she meant. I felt my powers stirring up inside of me, dancing on my fingertips. I gave her a sharp nod, setting my jaw, and kept moving. If the time came, I would do what I had to. For my friend, I would be her mercy.

Max hesitated, watching my body fall with the weight hanging over me, but he didn't move forward. Instead, he shifted toward me, gripping my face in his hands. "We'll find another way," he whispered. I didn't even notice the tear that had slipped out until it was running down my cheek.

He knew as well as me what Lena was asking. The only mercy Lena would ever find was in death, and she herself couldn't do that. I could. I had a power within me that changed everything. Even if I didn't yet fully understand how, I knew that if she asked me again, I wouldn't be able to deny that for her. My powers weren't just strong; they were all-consuming—even weak, I felt them throbbing deep inside my chest. The cuff allowed that, it allowed my powers to keep flowing, even as my body was ready to give up. When the virus fully took me, it would be gone, but right now, they could feel everything, be everywhere, even moving past a shield of protection.

Except to kill Lena and to provide her with that mercy, it meant my certain death. As the cure to the virus covering eighty percent of my body, my salvation would die with her.

The control room was empty. Two computers sat against one wall along with a chair in front of it. The rest of the wall had hundreds of buttons, all blinking red, green, and yellow. Some stayed solid, some flashed with clear warnings.

A wall of windows stood in front of us where we'd walked in, and nothing was visible but vast blackness and tiny dots of light in the far off distance. The room was dark with the flashing red lights, but at least the alarms were silent.

A loud boom came somewhere from the depths of the space station. It shook the entire platform, bucking both Lena and my mom to the ground.

"This thing is going down quick. We need to move," I said, reaching down to help my mom and then Lena, who rested in the chair behind her.

"The comms are down here," Max said.

He reached for a button on the wall but pulled away in time as a cracking spark hit the panel. The lights went dead. The entire room was black except for the glowing red light, blinking in the corner.

Max swore. "We have to get out of here."

"What about the ships heading for earth? What about Kenzie?" I asked, knowing he may already be dead, but Max and he had a plan. I prayed that included an escape.

"We meet back at the loading dock. Kenzie said there will be more pods stationed there, so we can get off this thing before it's torn to pieces," Max said.

"The ships… those Carbons. How do we stop them?" My voice cracked. I knew there was no way.

Max shook his head. "Maybe if we can get back fast enough, we can help…"

I read what he wasn't saying—help pick up the pieces of a broken and destroyed village. But still I nodded, knowing there was nothing more we could do.

I turned toward the door behind me as it flew open. I didn't have enough time to get my weapon up before a heavy hand smashed into my face. I fell to the ground, tasting blood in my mouth before I'd even hit the metal surface.

Max was at my side for only a second before he was picked up in one swift motion. He was thrown against the wall across from me. Blood trickled down his forehead, and he struggled to get to his feet. Heavy footsteps stomped over to him before he could, and the oversized Carbon pressed his foot down on Max's chest, pinning him to the ground and taking the air out of his lungs.

"Max—" My voice was hoarse as I tried to collect my bearings and figure out who was attacking us.

Another large hand picked me up by the collar of my jacket, nearly strangling me until I was able to get my feet under me. I had only a moment to glance up to the stern-faced Carbon behind me before he ripped my hair back and pinned my arms behind me. His face was identical to the one standing over Max.

They were both double the size of any man I'd ever seen before, twin Carbons who had superior strength to match their frames.

It was only then I noticed the body they had dragged in behind them. Vance lay unconscious by the door, and I couldn't tell if he was breathing.

The air had gone from the room. My mom knelt beside Lena, whose eyes were wide and haunted as she watched the figure walking into the room.

Sick, welted burns covered Coleman head-to-toe. His hair on the right side of his head was singed off, and his clothes hardly clung to him. He smelt of burnt flesh. But it was what he dragged behind him that made my world spin. My lungs lost all function.

Kenzie, his entire left side covered in the same burns Coleman had, could hardly stand as Coleman pulled him with a chain tied around Kenzie's neck. He shoved Kenzie into the room, and Kenzie fell to his hands and knees before Coleman yanked on the chain around his neck. Kenzie was forced to kneel before Coleman. My nemesis tied the end of the chain to the handle on the door, so Kenzie could barely swallow without choking himself.

The corner of Coleman's sickly burnt skin twisted up at his cheek—the skin over the bones nearly translucent—into what I assumed was meant to be a smile, but it looked more like a grimace. "Well, isn't this just a lovely family reunion?"

FORTY
NINE

"It's always nice to see you, Sawyer, my dear." Coleman sneered, as he gave his head a tilt in my direction, stepping over Vance's limp body.

"Sorry I can't say the same," I spat.

He smirked. "No, I would assume not, considering how many times you've been on the losing end of the stick from our many meetings." He took a step toward me, and his hand gripped my chin, tilting my head up so he saw the blackness growing across my neck. "Tsk, tsk. What a shame to see such a pretty girl like you turned into something as horrible as *them*. If only there was a way to fix that. But, alas, it will soon be fatal, and you will quickly be gone."

I spat in his face, red blood coming with it from the wound

on my lip.

He wiped it off with the back of his burnt sleeve, and his eyes narrowed on me. He leaned in closer. "I think you need to learn some manners, dear girl." He turned on his heels, striding toward his daughter who was shaking in the corner, glued to her seat. "My darling Lena, don't worry. Daddy is here now. I will take care of you."

Coleman rested his hand over her shoulder, pulling her in close to him. She could do nothing to get away. She was too weak and frail to even fight back, terrified into submission.

I sent out my powers, connecting with every inch of Coleman and lifting him from his seat. I pressed him against the wall, his toes barely grazing the ground, but he didn't balk. His eyes lit up as he smiled.

The shield surrounding him didn't allow me to get anywhere near him to inflict any damage. I couldn't break through it since it held strong.

"Impressive that you still have an ounce of power left in you, considering you're more monster than Carbon," he said.

The Carbon at my back pinned my arm behind me farther at an angle that was sure to break it if I didn't stop. My body burned with resistance, but I couldn't hold it any longer. I released Coleman who dropped to one knee before pushing himself back up to his feet with that wicked smile on his face.

The Carbon released my arm only an inch, still holding it tight, so I couldn't move, but it no longer felt like it was about to pop out of its socket.

"Shall we play a game?" Coleman asked, nodding to the

Carbon behind me who took a chain from the inside of his jacket. The Carbon wrapped it around both of my wrists. He placed the chain around my neck, tying the two together, so I couldn't move my head without the threat of dislocating my shoulder. Lastly, he tied the chain to a bar on the floor and stepped back.

"I wonder which one of your friends you will kill first once you've transitioned." Coleman circled around the room, glancing down at Kenzie.

Kenzie hardly held his weight up. His left eye was swollen, and he couldn't even open it. But his right eye wouldn't leave my face.

"Eenie…" Coleman glanced at Max being crushed under the foot of the twin Carbon. "Meenie…" Coleman's eyes fell to my mom cowering against the wall. "Miney…" His eyes rested on Lena. "Moe!"

I shook my head. "It won't matter. We're all going to die soon enough."

Coleman's brow rose only the slightest as he inclined his head. "Do explain how exactly *that's* going to play out."

"We're locked in on your location. You don't think Murray and his men have every bomb, every missile they have aimed at you, just waiting for a sign to strike," I bluffed, but looking for any way to stall him, to distract him. I quietly twisted my wrists against the chains around them. The black scales rubbed off like sawdust, and I ripped the skin around my wrist, prying them free.

"I think you lie, little girl." Coleman tilted his head to the other side, a predator watching his next victim. "But even so, there are thousands of my Carbons on their way down to have a little… chat with your Commander Murray. You think I would just sit here and watch my base get blown up? You think I wouldn't have ten possible escape plans, hundreds of more places to hide? Oh no, my dear, *we* will not all be dying here—only you and your companions will."

I swallowed back the tinge of fear, knowing he was always one step ahead of us. I had to be one step quicker.

My right arm twisted free, but I held onto the chain so the Carbon behind me didn't notice. To my right, Max followed my movements, knowing what I was doing. He made his own move as his free hand inched toward small shards of glass that had been scattered across the floor from the many explosions.

"But before the inevitable, how about we make this a little more fun?" Coleman said, turning back toward where Lena had her knees curled against her chest.

"I won't kill any of them. I'll kill myself first. I would never let that happen."

Coleman laughed. "And how, exactly, will you kill yourself, girl? With the gun you can't reach, the powers you can hardly control?"

I shook my head and leaned forward, pressing my arms back. I allowed the chain around my neck to tighten. It pressed against my throat, taking my air and voice with it. Max stirred, trying to say something, but the Carbon pressed his foot harder on his chest. All that came out was a wheeze.

"Stop, Sawyer. Please stop," Kenzie begged, his good eye widening, and his voice barely audible. It cracked with every word. He could hardly hold his head up, but he couldn't look away from me.

My eyes never left Coleman, determined not to play his game, not to be a pawn in his plans. He wouldn't give up the game that easily. He watched me while I gagged on my breath before he nodded to the Carbon still stationed a few feet away from me. "Release her neck."

The air rushed back into my lungs, and I coughed, glaring at Coleman. Kenzie's chest fell as he let out the breath he'd been holding. Fear still filled his expression.

"I would hate to have you ruin all my fun so quickly." Coleman smirked.

My arms fell loose against my lower back, giving me more room to work, exactly what I had hoped for. The Carbon pulled my head back as he made me face Coleman once again, and I gave him a devilish smile and a little wink.

"Back to our game." Coleman spun away from me. "Who shall it be first?" He grabbed Lena's wrist, pulling her out of her chair. She fell limp to the ground on her knees. She couldn't even stand on her own power.

Coleman lifted her to her feet, placing her only a few inches from me, within my reach if I wanted to. Her body shook, and she swayed where she stood, hugging herself. My mom moved to help her, but Coleman only had to look over his shoulder at her before she sat down, flush against the wall.

"I wonder how long it will take. I've seen some transition in ten minutes at this point. I give it twenty at the most." He slid back, moving into the chair Lena had been occupying. "Don't worry, my dear. You won't have to wait long."

I smirked, looking past Lena to where Coleman sat. My eyes picked up the small glimmer of a shard of glass in Max's hand. "I won't hurt you," I whispered to Lena.

"Oh, sure you will. That is what you do, Sawyer. You hurt the ones you love. Everyone you have ever cared about has been killed, injured, and scarred forever." Coleman crossed his ankle over the other knee.

"At the hand of you. I take no blame for the things you've done," I snarled.

"You're a curse, dear Sawyer, to everyone you love."

My heart stung at the words, but I kept my face neutral.

"Everyone around you seems to be dying or close to." Coleman kicked at Vance's limp body. It didn't move.

I clenched my jaw and said through my teeth, "Not everyone, not yet."

"Kill me," Lena said. Her voice was so tiny, but she was so close I heard her.

I met her stare. There was no longer fear in her eyes, no more trembling as she stood as strong as her weak legs would allow her. I narrowed my eyes and gave a subtle shake of my head.

"Please…" she begged. Before I could say anything, Coleman ripped her back, pulling her away from me. He slammed her back into the chair, and she winced from the impact.

"I change my mind. You're taking too long," Coleman said. Whether he heard what Lena had asked of me, I didn't know. His eyes told me she'd been a bluff. She was his prize, his property, and he wouldn't allow her to be hurt. All he wanted was to torture me, and he'd only just begun.

"We've got all the time in the world, don't we?" I raised an eyebrow. The space station answered back with a distant boom growing closer. The room tilted, as if the station itself were moving, and everyone was caught off-balance as we stumbled.

The strong Carbon behind me caught me quicker than I could move, gripping onto the back of my hair so hard I winced.

Coleman took a moment to collect himself, too, but when he looked at me, his eyes burned with fire. His arms shook, and I saw it in his eyes—the panic and the fear, threatening to consume him until he glanced to the floor where Kenzie still knelt. He didn't know how quickly this station would go down any more than we did. And if it blew up entirely, I doubted Coleman would live—but neither would we. His eyes lit up as he turned towards Kenzie, just before screaming filled the room.

FIFTY

Kenzie's scream was raw, and his muscles were tight with restraint. I couldn't see what was causing him so much pain, but he fought against it. My body flinched toward him, wishing I could stop the pain, but the chains held me back.

Coleman kept his eyes locked on Kenzie, as he took a step forward. "Stand up, boy," he said.

Kenzie fought it with every muscle trying to obey the order. His right leg stepped forward first. Kenzie braced his forearm against his leg as he struggled to his feet. He battled against the order the whole way. The chain around his neck kept him tight to the wall, but he was able to stand.

Kenzie glared at Coleman who smiled back.

"I think it's only fair we go back to that little game we were playing. But this time, I'm changing the rules. Let see how many of Sawyer's friends she gets to watch die before she turns," Coleman said.

"No!" Kenzie growled, as blood trickled down his cheek. The burns on his face and neck glowed red.

"Unfortunately, you don't actually have a choice, my boy." Coleman turned his back around, scanning the room to see whom he was going to pick first. "Hmm, it seems unfair to pick the poor human. They die so quickly. No fight in them." He motioned to Max still pinned to the floor. Max's fist was clenched so tightly around the shard of glass he hid that there was a small trickle of blood on the floor. "Maybe we should start with the ever-loving mother?" Coleman strode over to my mom, jerking her up by her arm.

I gritted my teeth, knowing the more of a reaction I made, the more it would please him.

Kenzie glanced between my mom and me. He didn't want to hurt her, but he was already so weak. Any resistance he might have had left would be used up. Coleman had already taken control of him.

Coleman placed my mother in front of Kenzie and said, "Kill her."

Kenzie's jaw tightened, and he closed his eyes. His arms hung limp at his side but his fingers curled. The muscles in his forearm twitched with restraint.

Coleman took a step closer to Kenzie. "Kill her," he repeated.

Kenzie shook his head. He tried with everything he had to keep his arm at his side, but it rose against his will. It stretched out in front of him, filling the space between my mom and him.

My mom quivered as her eyes darted between Kenzie and me, begging him to fight back.

Kenzie's hand trembled as it moved, positioning itself squarely in the middle of her chest.

"*Kill her!*" Coleman screamed.

There was a flash of light and the sound of my mom screaming before she fell to the ground.

"No," I cried but I couldn't move. I couldn't help her. I squeezed my eyes shut, begging for this to all stop, for it to all go away.

"It seems your aim has gotten a little worse lately." Coleman sneered. I opened my eyes. My mom was still on the ground, holding her shoulder where Kenzie's power had blasted through her, wounding her, but not killing her.

I sighed.

"No worries. I guess I'll just have to finish the job for you." Coleman stepped over my mom sprawled on the floor. He stood to face me. He reached down to my side and pulled out my gun. He checked that the safety was off, and the gun was loaded.

He stepped back to face my mom and pointed the gun at her head.

"No!" I shouted. "Please, just kill me. I'm the one you want. I'm the one you want to hurt."

Coleman glanced over his shoulder. "Begging doesn't suit you, Sawyer."

I clenched my jaw and forced the words out. "Do whatever you want to me. Just leave them alone, please."

He lowered the gun, the corner of his mouth lifting into a vicious smile. My mom cautiously dragged herself back to the wall beside Max. He struggled to move even an inch, reaching for her to pull her back, but the Carbon over him stepped down on his wrist.

"Oh, I will do whatever I want with you, Sawyer. Don't you worry about that. I know where to hit you the hardest. I know what will hurt the most." Before I had a chance to say anything, Coleman aimed and shot the gun, hitting Max in the leg. He screamed in pain.

My eyes welled up with angry tears. I tightened my jaw, but Coleman kept smiling back at me, circling around as he waved the gun.

"This is kind of fun, don't you think? I do love games." Coleman stopped at Kenzie's side and raised the gun to rest against Kenzie's temple.

Kenzie froze, his breath a ragged pant.

"You want to feel pain, dear Sawyer? Aim for her leg," Coleman ordered Kenzie.

His gaze darted to meet mine. He shook his head. "I won't hurt her."

Coleman pressed the gun against his temple. "Oh, yes, you will. One way or another, you will do it. Either you do as I say, or I pull this trigger. Either way, she gets hurt."

My eyes widened with fear. "Do it," I ordered Kenzie.

He shook his head. "I won't hurt you."

I tried to even my breath, to show him it was going to be okay. "Please, Kenzie. Just do it." Behind him, I noticed a pair of eyes looking up to me. I couldn't tell how long Vance had been awake, but the fact he had gone nearly unnoticed was to our advantage.

I quickly looked away from Vance as my eyes locked on Kenzie, but he knew I'd seen him.

Kenzie's hand shook as it rose a few inches. Coleman's smirk grew as Kenzie's hand aimed for my leg, and I braced myself for the pain I knew would come.

"Now," Coleman said between clenched teeth.

Kenzie let out a shuttering breath as he flexed his hand. His eyes stayed on me, as he said, "I will no longer be anyone's pawn." Before anyone had time to react, Kenzie brought his right arm across, driving his elbow up into Coleman's wrist. He knocked the gun out of Coleman's hand, and it flipped in the air before Kenzie caught it. With his right hand, he pressed the gun against his own left shoulder. The sound of bullets ripping through flesh and bone filled the room as he emptied nearly the entire clip until his left arm was dangling only by a wire.

FIFTY ONE

Kenzie dropped to his knees. Bright red blood poured out of his arm where exposed wires, bone, and muscle were torn away from each other. Only a thin wire kept his arm from detaching itself. His face had already paled, and his breath was labored, as he tried to keep his body from falling. His neck was still tied to that chain and his body shook.

Before Coleman had a chance to react, I did. Pulling my one wrist free from the chain, I drove my elbow into the midsection of the Carbon behind me. His heavy breath pushed against the back of my head, and I reached for another gun across my back. I shot two bullets, one in each leg, and he dropped.

Max reacted simultaneously.

The shard of glass in his hand was now deep in the calf of the

Carbon above him. The Carbon roared in pain. He lifted his foot only an inch, ready to stomp down on Max's chest, but my bullet hit him between the eyes first.

A fit of rage came from behind me as the twin Carbon swung at my head. His face was twisted with anger as he watched his twin hit the ground. I ducked in time, twisting onto my back, and I shot two holes straight through the Carbon's head. I rolled out of the way before the thick Carbon landed where I had been.

Vance had stood, aiming for Coleman, who reached for the gun at Kenzie's feet. I turned as the gun went off. I looked down to my chest, which should've been covered in blood with a bullet wound in the center, but there was nothing.

Standing in front of me and swaying on his feet was Vance. A blotch of red at the center of his chest slowly grew, filling the white fur vest wrapped around him. The strong Ice Bear fur had already been torn apart from the blast he'd taken earlier, and now there was nothing left to stop the bullet. He pressed his hand against the wound, his eyes flickered to the red blood coating it, before he staggered on wobbly feet toward me and fell. I stumbled, trying to catch him but we fell to the ground.

His eyes widened as he searched my face. I tried to press my hand against his wound, but the blood kept pouring out.

His breath was heavy, and his words struggled to come out. "Be strong…" was all he managed before the full weight of him fell against me. I had to drop to my knees, resting him on the ground. His chest rose one last time and stopped.

There was movement behind me as Max pinned Coleman's

arms behind him, the gun scattering across the floor. Max kicked the back of Coleman's knees, so he dropped to the ground.

"Thank you, my friend," I whispered to Vance, squeezing his hand before I stood. I did everything in my power to not let the weight of everything, the loss and guilt, take me. This was the burden I had so often felt. Death. It wouldn't consume me this time, not now. Not when I was needed the most.

The hot tears I expected didn't come, and I set my jaw, my glare filled with fire and wrath.

Blood flowed from Coleman's nose, his eyes following me while I walked over to where Kenzie hung. I released the chain from his neck. My mom raced to his side and pressed her sweater against the open wound where his arm dangled.

Kenzie could hardly keep his eyes open.

My blood boiled. I took my time removing the microchips from the base of the twin Carbons skulls before I slowly turned around to Coleman, my gun aimed at his head.

He smiled a bloody grin up at me. "So you think you've won, do you?"

I shrugged, glancing around to the two dead Carbons, making sure to not linger on the loss of my own. "It would appear so."

He chuckled. "You forgot one key thing, my dear." His eyes pierced through me as his smile grew. A crazed laugh escaped him. "I can't die!"

I was silent, trying to not allow panic to show. I knew he was right. "Then we'll take you in. A lifetime in a cell will have to do."

He continued to laugh. The menacing sound filled the quiet space. "A cell can't hold me. Nothing can hold me. I have a lifetime to wait and I will. I will wait forever if I have to. But in the end, I will always win."

A cold shiver slithered through me, and I tried to not let it show. I glanced to Max behind him, and his expression read the same as mine. This didn't feel like a victory.

Kenzie's breath was ragged and harsh, and my mom winced at her own wounds as she tried to keep Kenzie upright. She worked to stop his bleeding but there was so much.

I had to move fast. I had to figure something out.

Lena stopped me. "Kill me."

I turned to her. Even Coleman quieted at her words.

She took short steps toward me on wobbly feet. "Kill me," she repeated.

I shook my head, but she kept moving forward.

"He cannot live if I am dead," she said.

I frowned, confused, but Coleman stilled at her words.

"I don't understand," I breathed, the gun lowering to my side, as she stepped in front of him.

"When he created himself, he used a part of me during the process—my blood. We are tied together. It is why neither of us can die. I was the first Carbon created, so my shield that was formed when I was built is stronger than any other, and it lives inside of him, too. For me, it is an external shield that you can see and feel. For him, it flows within him like a living organism. He is the shield, and it cannot be shattered until the connection between us is broken. While I am alive, I breathe life into him. I protect him." Her voice cracked as she spoke, and tears filled the rims of her eyes. "The shield that protects me also protects him, but if that shield was gone… if it was broken…" Lena looked down to her arms where her hands once were. "I am the shield. I am what protects him. But if you destroy the shield, then it is gone in him, too."

I couldn't breathe. I shook my head, as my entire body screamed no. I looked into her bright golden eyes, glassed with tears, my eyes filling up. "I can't," I whispered. "You are my friend… I can't."

"You are the only one who can. Your powers… They can feel my shield, touch every part of it, and feel every fiber within me," she said. I remembered back to that day when she was so mad at me she locked herself in Doc's office. She wouldn't let anyone in, but I had ripped open the door. When she pushed her shield against me, my energy gripped onto that shield as if it were a physical object, a physical thing. I had taken it in my powers and I'd moved it. "Please, I want to see my beloved again… please." As if he was right in the room with us, Lena smiled at the thought of the one she had lost—Anthony.

"No!" Coleman spoke up from behind her, fear lacing his every word. "You can't kill her. She can't die. It's impossible."

Lena ignored him and gave me a nod. It was possible.

I glanced around the room, seeing what this monster had done to us. Kenzie was hanging on by a thread, and my mother was struggling to keep herself moving. Vance, gone, having sacrificed himself for me. Coleman had done all this; he'd destroyed everything I loved.

Max stood behind Coleman on one shaky leg. His eyes were wide with fear. He shook his head slowly. He knew the consequences of doing this. He knew what I'd be giving up.

Not only would I have to sacrifice a friend, but my life in the process. She was the only cure, the only way I could live.

But what Max knew, what I knew, was that I'd sacrifice my life for theirs. In a heartbeat, I'd choose them.

"Sawyer." Max's voice broke, as his eyes begged me to keep fighting, to find another way.

There was another blast, much closer than before, and we were running out of time.

"It's going to be okay," I said, trying to calm my racing heart.

"No, please," Max begged. He looked ready to move, to run to me, to shake me, or to make me promise to not do this, but he kept his grip on Coleman strong.

I looked back to Lena, and I gave her a nod.

I would do this, for her and for them.

Lena glanced to my mom, who looked as though she might break. There was no other way to stop the virus than the cure in Lena's blood. And soon, she'd be gone. "You will protect your daughter. You can save her." Lena's eyes narrowed, and my mom gave her a knowing nod, as a shuddered breath came out of her.

Lena turned to me, a sweet smile on her face. I couldn't help remembering how small and fragile she already was. "We will watch over you, from the stars above."

"I know you will," I said with a solemn smile, and then I sent my energy out toward her.

It was slow, dampened even, but it was mine, and it listened to my orders. The shield constantly surrounded her, even when she couldn't send it out. I felt for the energy pulsing from it. My energy gripped onto every inch, every fiber.

"No! Stop," Coleman screamed but I didn't listen. In my mind, it was only Lena and I.

I gripped onto the shield, feeling it as if it were in the palm of my hands. I was able to move it and mold it to my every whim.

And then I pushed.

Lena screamed with pain, but her eyes begged me not to stop and I didn't. The energy remaining in me pulsed, and I did everything I could to keep it going, to keep pushing.

My powers broke through the shield like it was a tiny eggshell. I slowly pulled back the layers, breaching through the strong barrier until I felt her inside of it all, and my energy swarmed past the shield and gripped onto her.

Her body quaked against my intrusion, and I pushed in deeper until I was holding onto the very molecules within her, the essence of Lena in the palm of my hands.

Lena's lips parted, tears running down her cheeks, but she kept her eyes on me.

My body grew weak and tired, but I couldn't let go. I wouldn't let go. This would be my last gift, the last thing I could do for a friend to whom I owed my life.

Back arched, I fell to my knees against the weight of it all. The room grew brighter as the shield still surrounding her broke away, and all that remained was a frail, young girl who had only ever wanted to be normal and loved.

SAVIOR

She was loved. More than she ever knew. She was so loved.

I held on for as long as I could before I knew it was time to say goodbye.

"I love you, my friend," she whispered and my brow pinched. I repeated those words back to her. My eyes closed, and with one last pull, one last tug on my energy, I separated every inch of her from itself.

The room became staggeringly silent, and when I opened my eyes, all that remained was a bright gold dust lingering in the room before me. Lena was gone.

Two labored steps was all it took for me to be face-to-face with Coleman.

"W-wait, just wait a minute," Coleman stammered, as I trained my gun on his head.

My eyes burned through him, and I fought back angry tears.

"Don't I get a chance to explain? Don't you want to know why I did all this?" Coleman whined.

"You never gave anyone else the courtesy of an explanation. Why should I?" I growled.

Coleman glanced to my mother, who was still at Kenzie's side. "You know why we did all of this, Russo. Peter was one of the few who really understood why this all had to happen."

I pressed the gun against his temple. "Don't you dare speak about my father. You tricked him. You used him. And he died without even being able to tell me what he really was, what you had done to him."

"I was trying to make a better world," Coleman spat. "When you are the only one capable of making change, you will understand the burden of making sacrifices. You couldn't possibly understand what I had to go through, what I lost to get here."

"Sacrifice? Is that what this was? Killing thousands of people, destroying cities and lives at the flip of a switch, that was a sacrifice for you?" I scoffed. "Everything you lost you did for yourself. I feel no pity for you. I do *not* care about your loss. You've deserved everything you're going to receive, and more."

Coleman's breathing became ragged, and Max had to tighten his grip on Coleman to hold him back. "They took her away from me!" he screamed, and I was certain he meant Lena until he said, "My wife died because they couldn't save her. They took away the love of my life and tried to take my daughter from me. I did what I had to in order to provide her the life she deserved, the world my Lena was meant to live in." His eyes glossed over with heavy tears, and his mouth quivered as he said, "Everything I did was to provide her a better life."

"And how did that work out for her?" I said with quiet rage.

Coleman tore against Max's hold, and his fury filled the room. I remained strong, and I didn't look away from the hate in his eyes. I had taken everything from him, and I knew very well what that felt like, to lose it all. But I wouldn't back down, not now, not ever.

I clicked the safety off the gun in my hand. Coleman stilled, and his eyes flickered to the gun, a few inches from his face.

"Do it. End this," Coleman whispered.

My finger trembled on the trigger. My heart beat so fast. I took one breath in and steadied my heart. One breath out, and then I dropped the gun to my side.

Coleman followed my hand, and the shadow of a smile crept onto his face. The wicked smile filling my face stopped him from breathing.

"A bullet would be too quick, too easy. You deserve to suffer for what you've done," I said.

My eyes found Kenzie, who knelt a few feet away. He fixed his gaze on me. He knew what I was thinking, what I was about to do. He nodded.

I glanced to my mother who took a step away from Kenzie. With a shaky hand, Kenzie reached out for mine, and the second our hands touched I felt the stream of electricity flowing through him. Though he had nearly removed the arm that released his power, it still lived inside of him. And now, it pulsed into me, my powers pulling them from his body to fill up my own.

My eyes glowed as I looked back to Coleman, who was on his knees. His body trembled at the sight of me, and Max took a step back, letting Coleman be the sole body standing before me.

"This is going to hurt," I said, placing my hand on Coleman's shoulder.

The electric current swam through me and poured into Coleman's body. The shield once there had been broken, and I had an open channel into him. Nothing left to stop me.

Our energy flooded him, and I felt the current, finding each vein and wire inside of him. My powers broke past any resistance his Carbon body tried to put up. I broke past every piece of him.

Coleman's entire body tensed and shook against the pain. His mouth was open, but no sound escaped his lips. The current, a combination of my power and Kenzie's, burned him from the inside out.

Blood poured from Coleman's nose. A black jagged line like moving ink crept up his neck and across his face. The electric current burned the wires it traveled through until it reached the microchip at the base of his skull.

I leaned in closer, my body shaking against the sheer power of Kenzie and me, but I wouldn't falter. I'd never kneel before Coleman again.

"Tell me," I whispered, and his cold eyes slowly found mine. "Was it worth it?"

I pushed everything I had into him, breaking the microchip and anything else left. Coleman's dark eyes locked on mine until the life left him. He thudded to the ground.

Coleman was dead.

FIFTY TWO

I let go of Kenzie's hand, and the power flowing through us stopped. I dropped to my knees, and Max caught me, pulling me into his chest. I sobbed as the weight of everything hit me. My chest hurt, and I couldn't breathe.

"It's over. It's all done," Max whispered into my ear. I clung to his shirt as he drew me into his body.

Kenzie watched me, and I knew the weight he felt was the same as my own. A different kind of weight, not like before. This weight didn't pull us all down with it. Kenzie nodded, and I couldn't stop the smile on my face.

It was over. Coleman was dead.

The space station still rocked and shook, the room tilting. I was suddenly aware this wasn't over.

"We need to go," Max said. He pulled me to my feet. "Can you run?"

I nodded.

Max reached down and pulled Kenzie to his feet, resting under his good arm. My mom stumbled to help.

Kenzie could hardly move, let alone speak, but the words that came out were simply, "It's done… it's done."

"Yes," I said. He seemed to relax at the sound of my voice, the hint of a smile filling his face.

"Come on, this way." Max pulled us into a hallway where the damage was much worse than before. The way we had come from was blocked, and the air had turned from cold to freezing as we stepped into the empty corridor.

"Which way?" I asked.

My mom spoke up, "This way." She pointed down the hall and we ran, all four of us limping and wincing with each step, but we didn't slow.

There was another blast, and I was thrown into the wall. Max stumbled trying to keep Kenzie up, and my mom skidded to the floor. I helped her up. We continued down the only open hallway left.

The next hallway was blocked, fire spitting from the wreckage. My mom turned around, trying to recalculate which way to go. "I think this way." She routed us back the way we came, but we took a hallway I'd missed when we ran past it the first time.

Another explosion sounded, and the entire space station seemed to fall, gravity pulling us to the side. We struggled to

341

stay upright, and the path before us was a mountain of debris raining down on us. We pushed our way through, nonetheless.

When we reached the end of the hall, I chanced a glance outside a window. The entire far half of the space station was gone, either blown apart from the explosions or torn apart by the force of Earth's gravity slowly pulling us closer. At this pace, Earth's gravity would grab a hold of the enormous space station and bring us down with it. The station was almost a mile in diameter. I didn't have to know much about physics to realize that an impact of that size on the Earth's surface would be catastrophic.

Max looked over my shoulder. "We're falling…"

I nodded. The ship was falling, and soon gravity would win this battle with no way to stop it.

We kept running.

"The loading dock you arrived at is gone, but there's another one just up this way," Mom said. She led us around the last corner.

A door stood in our way, cracked open only an inch because debris blocked our way.

Max put Kenzie down before we both started pushing and moving the steel and pipes blocking our path. I had no powers left in me to use and hardly any energy to lift, but as the space station creaked and shifted once again, I found a way to keep moving. I didn't know how much time I had, or if I would transition on the way back to earth. I wasn't even sure we should risk it now that Lena was gone.

Finally, we had cleared a path, and Max helped Kenzie

through the door. We entered a docking station where a few pods looked intact.

"How are we going to fly one of these things?" I asked, glancing down to Kenzie, who was barely conscious.

"Sam," Kenzie breathed, and Max moved to the intercom against the wall.

"Sam! Are you there? Can you hear us?" Max yelled.

There was silence before the sharp crackle of the intercom and then, "I'm here. Oh boy, is it great to hear your voices! We thought you guys were… Well, we lost most of our connection to the space station. All security feeds are down, so we didn't know where exactly you guys were."

"Sam, we need to get out of here. There's a few pods here, but we can't fly them," I said.

"Which dock are you in?" he asked.

I glanced around the room before I noticed a big number four on the wall. "Four."

"Great, if you guys can get the thing up and running, I can lock in on the system from here and guide you back," Sam said more cheerfully than I'd expected.

"Here, hold Kenzie. I'm going to check which one is still able to fly," Max said. I took the weight of Kenzie under my arm. He clung to my waist.

Max sprinted off to the closest pod before he ducked inside to check on it. My mom hovered behind him.

"Sam, how's it going down there?" I asked, wincing at the thought of what destruction might have already taken place.

"Uh, a bit weird to be honest, Sawyer," Sam said. "Well,

Murray will explain it all if he can, one sec."

"Sawyer?" Murray's voice filled the dock, and Max's body tensed before he moved on to the next pod.

"Yes, I'm here. What's going on?" I asked.

"Nothing, that's just it. Nothing is going on." Murray's voice was strained as he spoke. "Those ships arrived not too long ago, and we've set up a perimeter around them as best we can, but they haven't come out yet. No movement whatsoever."

I looked to my mom, hoping maybe she would have an answer. She shook her head; neither of us knew what that meant.

"No orders," Kenzie said before he coughed up blood.

"What do you mean 'no orders'?" I let him rest against my shoulder, and I crouched beside him.

"I felt it," he breathed. "When he died... The control, it's gone..."

My breath caught in my throat, and my mom's eyes widened.

"What's he talking about, Sawyer?" Murray demanded.

"Coleman. He's dead," I said.

An audible gasp sounded from Murray.

"The Carbons are freed, and they have no orders," I said. "No one is controlling them anymore."

There was silence on the other end before Murray said, "I think that's the best news I've ever received..."

I was smiling, too.

Max made his way back to us. "There's one in the back undamaged. It should fly."

I nodded and helped Kenzie back to his feet.

"Uh, guys." Sam stopped us before we'd moved. "We got

another problem, though. The remote detonator is offline. I can't blow the rest of those bombs from here, and that station is out of orbit, slowly falling toward Earth. If it hits us, well, it'd be like an asteroid hitting earth, one that would shatter anything in its path and send a ripple effect across the surface."

My shoulders dropped. *Why couldn't this just be easy?*

"Can we detonate them from here?" Max asked.

"Well, yes, but it'd have to be done manually, meaning someone would have to be close to the blast site. There's no chance anyone could survive a blast that close," Sam said.

"But if we did set off the bombs, would it work? Would it prevent the station from hitting Earth?" Max asked.

"If we can blow it up before it picks up too much speed, then I believe it may be able to push the station back into orbit, or at least most of it. That would keep it from being pulled by our gravity," Sam said. "It might just work, if we can find a way to detonate them."

Max nodded. He turned to where Kenzie was leaned up against me and pulled him up. Kenzie winced as we moved him toward the pod. My mom followed.

"What are you thinking?" I asked Max.

He didn't look back at me, as he said, "We need to find a way to detonate those bombs. But first we get to the pod."

I tried to catch his eye, leaning around Kenzie. "How do you plan to detonate them?" I asked.

He didn't meet my gaze. "Still working on it." I heard the lie in his voice. He was never a good liar.

My mom went in first before she turned and helped Max

guide Kenzie inside and into the only seat. These pods were only meant for one person, the ones we'd taken here had been outfitted with additional seats but there was no time for that. We'd just have to squish in, hold on, and hope for the best. Max pressed a hand to Kenzie's chest, whispering something before he stepped back. Max held the door open for me, motioning for me to get in next. I refused to move as he avoided my questioning stare.

"How do we detonate it, Max?" I asked again.

This time he looked at me and his eyes softened. He swallowed back whatever he wanted to say, whatever was burning inside of him. He gripped my face and kissed me hard. I didn't understand what he was doing until he shoved me away.

I stumbled into the pod on my knees, scrambling to my feet before the door slammed closed behind me. *No, no, no!*

Max was on the other side.

I pressed my face to the window of the door. My hands were shaking, and the pod felt as if it were crushing down on me. My breaths felt forced, and my heart beat way too fast as understanding hit me like a sledgehammer.

"Max! Max, what are you doing?" I screamed, shaking my head... But I knew, I knew what he was going to say next.

He stepped back, his eyes sad, as he said, "I'm going to detonate those bombs."

FIFTY THREE

"No!" My voice broke. I pulled on the door but it wouldn't budge. Max had locked it from the outside.

Max took a step back, his jaw tight, and he shook his head. "It has to be me. I have to do this."

"No, you don't have to do this. I should do it. It should be me!" I pressed my black hand against the window. "It's too late for me and you know it."

But Max shook his head. "I know, which is why it has to be me. You'd never make it. You can hardly move. And I know they'll find a way, Doc or Adam, they're close to finding a cure. They will help you."

"I could transition before we even get there. It's not safe for anyone—there's not enough time."

"I can do it," Mom said from behind me. For a moment, I thought she was saying she'd sacrifice her life for us, but instead she pointed to the warm blood seeping from the wound on her shoulder. "Her blood is in me, Lena's. It's how I survived in Sector 7. She knew there was a good chance I'd be found helping her, helping you. So she had me transfer some of her blood into mine..."

I remembered Lena's last words to my mom, "You can save her." I understood.

My mom nodded, but I still shook my head, turning to Max. "Don't do this. Please." Again, my voice caught, and I couldn't swallow back the tears filling my eyes. "I can do this. Let me do this."

Max bit the inside of his cheek, shoving his hands in his pocket, fighting back the urge I knew he felt to come back to me, to open this door, and tell me everything would be okay. Instead, he said, "You deserve to live, Sawyer. You always have."

"So do you," I whispered, pressing my hand against the door, pushing with all my might, but I was too weak, too broken.

"I think I've known for a long time now that this would be my fate. I was always meant to protect you, always meant to ensure that you lived. And you will." A faint smile grew on his face. "You're going to live a long life. You're going to know what love and happiness are. Live in a world that feels safe, not broken. You deserve that."

"I can't do it without you," I cried. Everything inside of me was breaking. I couldn't reach out to him. I wanted to feel his touch just one more time. "Don't leave me, please."

He broke. His head dropped, and his hands shook at his side, but he didn't move. His chest filled with heavy breaths, and he looked ready to run. When he gazed up at me, I knew he wouldn't be running back to me. Tears rolled down his cheeks.

"You can do this. You *will* do this," he said, his eyes never leaving mine. "You mean everything to me, you're my world, Sawyer. So you have to let me do this. For you…"

I shook my head, my chest caving. My heart was being ripped apart.

"They need you, Sawyer." Max nodded to where Kenzie and my mom sat behind me. "They need you to be strong, and they need you to hold on just a little longer. It will all be okay. You guys will have each other and you'll survive. You were meant for greatness, and I know you're going to be okay."

Max moved toward the window. I thought he might've changed his mind, but he leaned against the door and looked down to the spot where Kenzie sat. "Take care of her," Max demanded as he eyed Kenzie. Kenzie gave Max a sharp nod.

Max turned back to me, and my hand pressed against the window. He pressed his against mine. "I love you. I would follow you to the stars if I must, I'd go there."

My heart broke, and a sob escaped me. My legs didn't feel like they could hold me up any longer.

He waited, and I knew what he was waiting for. I almost didn't want to say it, just because it'd mean the end. It was like saying goodbye, but I found my voice. "I love you, Max."

He pressed a kiss into his hand and then pressed his hand against the window. He stepped back again. "Get out of here."

Behind me, Kenzie shifted. With his good arm, he was pressing buttons, and the pod came to life around us. I heard my mom strap Kenzie into his seat, and then she crouched down beside him and wrapped an arm around one of the straps to secure herself down. I couldn't move. I couldn't look away from Max.

He gave me a slight nod, his jaw tight with a thin smile on his face.

The pod leveled up, lifting off the ground before it slowly started moving out and away from where Max stood. *No, no. I'm not ready!* Tears flooded down my face, and I pounded my fist against the window, begging it to open, pleading for him not to leave me. *I can't do this alone.* I watched Max, not wanting to miss a moment before the pod sped up. He slowly disappeared out of my view.

I crumbled to the ground as I sobbed. My breath staggered, and I felt my mom's hands pull me closer, locking her arm around me as best she could while the pod bounced and jumped. My chin fell to my chest. Out the small window, I saw the space station still broken but there.

"I'm sorry," Kenzie said, and I glanced up to find pain written on his face. The pain for me, as he watched my heart breaking, and there was nothing he could do to fix it.

I blinked, but I couldn't take my stare away from the station.

My heart sped up, and I thought, *What if something went wrong? What if Max was injured or couldn't detonate the bombs?*

"We should go back," I breathed.

Kenzie shook his head. He knew we couldn't. Not only was

there no way to turn the pod around, but there was no time. "He'll do it," Kenzie whispered, knowing it was both the words I needed to hear, and the words that would break me.

Just before I was about to demand we return, just as I had a brief moment of both doubt and hope, it happened.

A small spark in the distance from the dock we'd just left lit up against the dark canvas of space.

Time seemed to pause, and everything became staggeringly silent.

A ripple could be felt across space. A visible wave ran through the space station, pulsing, before it pushed out, and the vibration was so strong it shook the inside of the tiny pod. I clung to the side walls, holding onto anything I could.

The entire station was torn apart. It flexed and then exploded into a million pieces. Everything that was once there disappeared in an instant. And with it, my heart fractured in two.

Blue flames sparked against the atmosphere briefly before it was all gone. The station. The threat.

Max.

Gone.

FIFTY FOUR

The pod landed softer than it had on the space station. People were already there, rushing to open the door. They pulled Kenzie out as he winced against the movement, thankfully still conscious.

My mom was helped out next, and I followed, shrugging off the help offered to me.

I looked up to the sky one last time where the broken station was visible against the dark sky, and I blinked in a trance before a voice took me out of my stare.

A hand was under my arm, and I nearly fell to my knees. The world around me seemed to be spinning. I heard my mom's voice telling me we had to hurry. My mind couldn't even comprehend why we were hurrying or where we were going.

He was gone, and it felt like I had gone with him.

I was pulled into a room just as my body started to shake. My limbs no longer felt like they were mine, and then my vision disappeared altogether.

I woke what felt like days later, but in reality it was only a few minutes. I lay on a cot, sprawled out with a needle in my arm and a tube coming out of it. The tube was dark crimson. I followed it with my eyes to see to what it was attached to. In the small bed across from me, my mom lay connected to the other end of the tube, and she was smiling at me.

"Where is he?" I asked.

"He's in surgery," my mom answered, knowing I was talking about Kenzie.

"Is he going to be okay?"

She swallowed before she spoke. "The young doctor said he's in bad shape… He's not sure."

I tried to sit up but my head spun.

The gentle hand of Ainsley, who quietly stood at my side, kept me down. "There is nothing you can do for him now but pray to the stars that they spare him."

I wanted to argue, but at the end of my bed stood Tenason, ready to help hold me down if I tried to move again. I sighed and nodded.

"I'm so sorry, Sawyer," my mom said, reaching out her hand to mine.

I gripped her hand, holding it tightly, as I noticed the black was almost gone from my arm. It was receding from my shoulder, and from the exposed leg of my ripped pants, the black was also gone from there, too. A dark red stain, where new skin was reforming itself, coated where the black once was, but that, too, was beginning to fade to a soft pink and eventually back to pale white.

"Thank you," I whispered.

My heart was in knots, trying to make sense of it all. I tried to understand the excitement outside about the news that we'd won while also feeling like I'd just lost everything. What would I say to Murray? How would I tell him his son was dead because he chose to save me? A crushing wave hit me again, and my throat felt like it was burning and raw.

"It's going to be okay. We're going to be okay," my mom said. I nodded before I rested my head back and closed my eyes.

Four hours later, I was able to move. I made my mom stay in her bed, knowing she was already so weak and had given me so much of her blood.

I walked into the back room where Doc was still working on Kenzie. His arm had been removed, and there was a machine connected to him, keeping him alive.

In a trance, I pushed the door open. Doc glanced over his shoulder to see me walking in. "You shouldn't be here," he said.

I stood on the other side of Kenzie, hesitating for a moment before I took his free hand in mine and squeezing it tightly. "I have nowhere else to go."

Doc paused, but he didn't argue and went back to work.

The damage was so extensive, not only to Kenzie's arm, but also to the internal system connected to him and a part of him. Adam was in the room, handing Doc a few items that looked like parts from one of the bots we used to fight.

"Is he going to make it?" I whispered.

Doc sighed. "We're doing everything we can to make sure he does. The system controlling his arm was connected to his heart. It was all damaged pretty bad. We have some parts to try to replicate what he had before, but we're just lucky he had any of this in him. If he hadn't, he'd be dead for sure by now."

I squeezed Kenzie's hand again, praying he felt it. I couldn't lose him, too. He had to live. I needed him to live, even if it was just to say thank you. Thank you for fighting. Thank you for giving us a chance to live.

I watched for hours as Doc took out parts of Kenzie and replaced them with the new pieces Adam had provided. The true test would come when he removed Kenzie from the machines still keeping him alive.

Adam was able to replace Kenzie's arm with a robotic one, but it was pure metal, Alatonion in fact, and the silver-colored metal was a sharp contrast to his tan skin.

Finally, Doc said he'd done everything he could do. It was up to Kenzie if he wanted to live.

I held my breath, waiting. *You can't leave me, too. Not again.*

The machine beeped for a few long seconds before the line jumped with each heartbeat. Kenzie's chest rose and fell, as I released my breath, letting the tears drip down my nose and onto his chest.

"He'll need some time to recover still, but I'll watch him closely. I promise," Doc said. I gave him a thankful smile.

Doc stayed with Kenzie while I made my way to the control room. I was met by a cheerful Sam, hugging me.

"You did it, Sawyer, you did it." He smiled, but I found it hard to return one.

Behind him, I sensed the same weight lying heavy on Murray. Sam stepped aside, and I didn't know what to say, how to tell Murray I was sorry I couldn't save his son. Murray did something I never expected. He pulled me in, hugged me, and wept.

"I'm so sorry," I whispered into his chest as tears found my eyes once again.

I felt him shake his head before he pulled me back. "No, don't ever say you are sorry. You gave him life. You gave him meaning. You are the reason he was even able to do that, to sacrifice himself. And I couldn't be more proud of the man he became."

I gave a weak smile. "Thank you," I whispered. That clenching in my chest pulled harder, an ache I knew would be there for a long time. He'd given his life for me—so that I could live—and a part of me wasn't sure I could do that without him. But I had to. I promised I would, and I'd keep that promise.

Murray pulled me into another tight hug before he stepped back, cleared his throat, and took a shaky breath. "They still haven't come out," he said, changing back to the Commander

I knew. "The Carbons are just sitting there…"

"I want to see them," I said.

Murray nodded and led me out the door.

I was still feeling quite tired and weak, but I kept my legs moving. I followed Murray out to the village.

In the forest separating Kuros and the village were five large, round ships. Trees had been flattened where they'd landed, and there was thick mud everywhere. A portion of the space station had crashed into a mountain within the Muted Forest, but outside of the ground shaking at the impact, we had been spared a far worse fate. Max had spared us.

Murray's men surrounded one ship. Aelish and the Mountain Men had returned from the forest and surrounded another. The men watched me pass, and each one pressed a fist against their heart and bowed their head to me. They knew what had happened to Vance, the sacrifice he made so I could live. I didn't see sorrow in their eyes, but instead I found pride, a strength within them that was heightened for what their leader had done for me.

I kept my chin high as I passed, swallowing the lump in my throat, knowing they didn't want pity or an apology from me. I gave them what Vance deserved, a hero's salute. I pressed my fisted against my chest, against the stained white fur vest I still wore.

There were more soldiers stationed around each ship, all armed and ready to fight, but with no idea what to do.

Tenason and Ainsley stood near Aelish, whom I approached. They, too, had their fists against their chest, a silent thanks for all I'd done and everything that had been sacrificed.

Aelish stepped forward and said, "The stars map out all of our paths before we are even born, and Max is now among them, watching over every one of us. His life was full and with purpose, and he will not be forgotten. He would expect you to keep your promises to him, and live your life to the fullest."

I swallowed and gave her a thankful nod. She squeezed my shoulder before turning back to the ships looming over us.

"Is there a way I can speak to them? Could Sam patch me into their ships?" I asked Murray.

He radioed over to Sam, who said he'd have it done in a jiffy. Murray handed me the radio.

"Okay, Sawyer, you're on," Sam said.

I pulled the radio up to my mouth. I took a deep breath and said, "We have all lived most of our lives under the tyranny of one man. One man who felt he was the decider of who lived and who died. A man who thought he could cheat death and live forever." My voice was loud against the stark, quiet forest. All ears heard me, both inside and outside of the ship. "That man is now dead. And with him, the terror and fear we have felt is gone. We have nothing left to fight for. We have no reason to fear each other. I am proof that Carbons and Humans can live in peace—that *we* can live in peace." This time I glanced around me, seeing every eye watching me. "It's time to put down our weapons, time to forgive, and start living a new life, a life we all deserve." I swallowed back the emotion quivering in my voice. "We have all lost many people that we loved, have sacrificed so much just to survive. But now, we must not just look to survive, we must all strive to live."

I waited. My heart beat fast. I prayed my words had meant something.

Outside of the ship, the sound of weapons dropping sounded in unison. A breath later, there was a subtle hiss. The door to the first ship opened and then the second and the third. All five doors were opened and scared Carbons stepped out, tentative at first. I held my breath, but they stepped out and walked unarmed toward the crowd. It wouldn't be easy. A lot of hearts and wounds had to be mended, but it was a start.

Aelish was still at my side and she smiled. "That, my dear girl, is the reason you were meant to live. The reason fate placed you in the arms of a protector. Because only you could be both of them and yet different. You are a storm and a calming wind. And you have brought the wolf and the lamb together in peace."

As I watched the two worlds collide, Human and Carbon, warrior and soldier, friend and foe, I couldn't help feeling Max was smiling down on me.

FIFTY FIVE

KENZIE

Sunlight shone through the window, telling Kenzie it was morning. He'd been awake for an hour but hadn't wanted to wake anyone. He lay still and silent as he watched Sawyer sleep in the chair beside him, her hand still clenched around his.

The porcelain white skin coating her was the first thing he noticed. The odd feeling down his left arm came second. A white sheet was tucked under his chin, covering the view he wasn't sure he wanted to see. He already felt his arm was different; his powers were gone. But he wasn't sure he was ready to *see* it gone.

Sawyer stirred beside him, and he watched as her eyes

fluttered open. Her hand squeezed his, and she stretched her other arm out before she noticed his eyes on her.

She straightened up. "How do you feel?" she asked.

He thought for a moment. "Odd…"

Sawyer gave him a small smile before it quickly disappeared, as if that small movement was too much right now with everything she'd lost. He could see it in her eyes, the pain she was trying to hide. She stood and motioned to Doc on the far end of the room, half asleep at his desk.

Doc came over, asking the same question Sawyer had. Kenzie gave the same answer, "Odd."

Doc chuckled. "That's not surprising." He reached for the sheet covering Kenzie's upper half and pulled it down to his waist.

Cool air hit the bare skin on his chest and right arm, and he took another steadying breath before he glanced down.

"Now, I know it's not what you're used to. And sadly, I have no special abilities to give you, but it'll do all the usual things your other hand will. Adam's working on some sleeve or skin to cover up the metal if you'd like," Doc said, as he pointed a finger to Kenzie's chest. "Inside, however, we had to do a little… rewiring. You'll find things might feel a bit different, but it all works the same. Though you're a little more machine than before, your ability to heal fast is still there, luckily."

From his shoulder down his left side was a metal replica of what his other arm was, only the metal was in smooth rods that slid between each other. He moved his fingers first, feeling them tingle all the way up the entire arm and into his chest. He rotated his wrist, seeing the metal rods twist and turn seamlessly with each other. He lifted his arm off the bed. It felt both different and familiar all at once.

"How did you…"

"I can't take much of the credit. It was mostly Adam who came up with all of this. He's been working on different prosthetics for some time and finally had a chance to use it. I just put it in place," Doc said, moving on to check the burns still coating the side of Kenzie's face and neck. "Just be gentle with it for a bit."

With an encouraging smile, Doc left. Kenzie's eyes fell back on Sawyer. Though she was smiling, her face was sad and broken. It destroyed him to see it.

"How are you?" he asked.

"Fine. I'm good," Sawyer lied.

Kenzie tilted his head to the side in disbelief.

"I will be," Sawyer said. "It'll take time but I'll be okay."

Kenzie nodded, knowing it'd be a while for everyone to adjust, but all that mattered was that she was still here. Broken and sad, but still alive.

He'd give her time and space. He'd be a friend if she needed it, someone who understood the pain and loss she felt. He didn't need anything more than to know she was safe. She was alive. What mattered now was that they had it—time.

"It should've been me. I should've been the one to—" Kenzie started, but Sawyer shook her head, stopping him.

"There would never have been a right or wrong person in that moment. The pain would be here no matter who was there— me, you, or Max. We all deserved to live, and that sacrifice would've felt just as painful had it been you," Sawyer said.

It didn't make the guilt go away. It never would. Kenzie remembered her words before, *Max is who I'd sacrifice my life for.* And now he was gone, and Kenzie couldn't change that. He would never replace Max—he wouldn't even try—so for now, all Kenzie could do was hold his promise to Max and take care of her in any way he could.

"You'll get through this. We'll do it together, if you want," Kenzie promised, and Sawyer nodded, a look on her face that broke his heart.

"Together," she repeated.

Sawyer reached into her pocket and pulled something out. She examined it in her hand before she placed the shiny item in Kenzie's hand. "This was given to you a long time ago. And you once asked me to hold it for you, but now I think it's time you had it back."

She placed the small star-shaped pendant, attached to a keychain, in his hand. Kenzie rubbed his thumb over it, feeling the sharp points and smooth surface.

"The stars will keep us safe," Kenzie said.

Sawyer reached up to the identical star-shaped pendant on the necklace resting against her chest. "Always."

FIFTY
SIX

I stood in front of the makeshift grave as strong as I could, keeping my head high, so he'd know I was doing what he asked—living. Someone had placed a star-shaped stone in the ground that I stood before, and across it I had etched:

He waits in the stars,
always watching over us.
And he lives in the wind,
whispering while he waits…
I love you.

Kenzie stood a few feet away from me. Tenason, Ainsley, and Aelish were at his side. Murray stood on the other side of Max's grave with his jaw tight, his emotions in check as best he could. I did my best to not look up to him for fear of breaking once again.

"Though his body is gone, his heart will always beat strong within each and every one of us," Aelish said.

I nodded, unable to form the words out loud, but I spoke them to him in the silent moments when it was just he and I. "Thank you," I said to him, "for saving me. For pulling me out of the darkness and into the light I didn't know was still there. You will never be forgotten, and you will always be missed. But I promise to keep moving, I promise to never give up. I will live, for you and me both."

Murray placed a small stone beside the headstone, and the others followed until there was a small mound of rocks. I placed the last one against my lips, kissing it softly before I rested it on top.

The week went by slowly and my feet dragged. Kenzie was healing quick and getting stronger, and my mom was already up and helping whoever she could, taking quickly to Theresa who welcomed the help this time.

There was an odd excitement throughout the village, an energy that had kept everyone moving, no matter what or who they were. Carbons and humans were intermingling in a way I didn't think anyone could've imagined. But without someone ordering them or telling them what to do, their true natures came out, and it was peaceful, not the horrors we thought we knew.

Tenason and Ainsley didn't leave each other's side, and I found them sitting together near an open fire as the crisp morning sun peeked over the horizon.

Tenason slid over, so I sat beside him. "How are you doing?"

"As good as can be expected," I answered.

"It gets easier." Tenason nodded his understanding. "It will never go away. The pain… the loss. Not a day goes by that I don't think of Ethan, but it gets easier. I promise you that."

I gave him a weak smile. "Thanks."

"Has Aelish found you?" Tenason asked, one arm around Ainsley, but not for support this time. He pulled her in tight, and she leaned into him with a smile she couldn't hide.

"No, not yet. Why?" I asked.

He grinned. "I'll let her tell you." He nodded behind me where the old woman was walking toward us.

I waited as she neared, not noticing the odd thing in her arms until she was closer.

"You were looking for me?" I said.

She nodded as she lifted the item in her arms and pushed it toward me. I blinked, staring at the small, furry animal in her arms. It tilted its head to the side.

"It is said that when someone passes, their spirit goes into the animal that is most like them." She shoved the small puppy into my arms. "Max had the fierceness of a beast, but the loyalty of a dog." Aelish nodded to the puppy trying to lick my face. "He is yours to love and care for. His spirit is not gone."

My throat tightened. I looked down to the fuzzy dog, limp in my arms. His bright green eyes stared up at me. His brown-and-white fur was thick like a Dred Wulf's, but soft as silk. I rubbed my hand over his head and down his back. He whimpered and curled his nose under my chin, snuggling in tight and warm.

Aelish, Tenason, and Ainsley were still watching me as I stroked the sleeping pup's head.

"What will you name him?" Tenason asked.

I didn't have to think for more than a second. "Max. His name is Max."

With nothing left to fight and no one left to protect, everyone fell into rhythm with this new life. Six months passed before anything felt normal again, but slowly it did. The pain in my heart lessened, and I allowed another to put it back together.

It took time for me to let Kenzie back in, but gradually I was. He gave me as much space as I needed. It was all new to me, this weight that had been lifted, and the constant threat having disappeared. We had to get reacquainted with one another, becoming friends again first, and figuring out the new people we had both become. But it came naturally, easily. There were times when all I could think about was Max, and on those days, Kenzie never pushed me. Guilt churned when I did let myself feel happy, because how could I be happy when he was gone? But I knew that wasn't what Max would want. It was hard, not to think of him constantly, but Kenzie remained by my side, listening or just sitting silently beside me just so I knew I wasn't alone.

Time was the one thing we had on our side. With the threat no longer looming over me like it once had, this Carbon body had given me something I didn't think I could ever have: time.

I would live in the same body forever, an eighteen-year-old girl for the rest of my life, but I would *live*—and that was all that mattered. I might be broken, but in time I would heal.

With Kenzie and my mom by my side, I was no longer afraid of my future. No longer afraid of what was to come.

Captain Lankey had decided that to honor his princess, Lena, they'd return to the United Isles and rebuild it until it was once again the haven it'd been before.

The village was too small for the numbers we'd grown, so work began on rebuilding Kuros. The abandoned city that spread out past the dense forest was still broken and in ruins, but it could be restored. Carbons, with their special abilities, made quick work of the rubble, and progress was beginning. It'd take time, like everything else, but it was coming back to life, just as I was. Adam and Doc had made a cure for the Carbons using my mother's blood to ensure the virus never spread again, and I could see each person—like me—was slowly finding a way to live in this new world.

Walking into the forest, I watched my little bundle of fur hop ahead of me, bouncing through the leaves and tripping over branches and thick roots. A hand brushed against mine, a silent request, and I laced my fingers through Kenzie's as we made our way deeper into the woods, following a familiar path.

The roaring water sounded before we reached the edge of the river. We found a spot against the tree where we sat, watching the water flow by.

"Come here, Max," I called to the clumsy pup. He sauntered over to me and jumped onto my lap, trying to lick me as he leapt. I giggled at him before he settled into my lap and curled up, content to watch the water flow by.

"Have you ever felt this?" Kenzie asked into my ear. I leaned against his shoulder, and he wrapped an arm around me, pulling me closer.

"Felt what?"

"Peace. Calm. Quiet," Kenzie said.

I thought for a moment. There'd never been a time when a threat hadn't hung over my head, when I hadn't feared for my life or the life of others. I shook my head. "No."

"I have," Kenzie said.

I glanced up at him, frowning in thought.

"I remember a moment that seems so long ago," Kenzie said. "One I can hardly even remember, but I find myself constantly hoping and praying it's real. We were in this forest, together. And for a moment, only a brief time, nothing else mattered but you and me. There was only peace, calm, quiet, and us."

I smiled up at him, remembering that same day, that same feeling. "It was real," I said.

I rested my head back on his shoulder, closing my eyes as the sound of water filled the silence between us. I knew that somewhere, up in the stars, Max was watching over both of us. And I held on to that image and allowed myself this moment of peace, to just be here, with Kenzie, who my heart had always loved, and with Max watching over me, who my heart would never forget. He'd be glad to see me now.

Living…

Alive.

EPILOGUE

50 YEARS LATER

Though so much time had passed, I still reveled sitting in the open air, high above the boulevards. The sprawling city underneath me was buzzing with life, even in the dark of night. The crisp breeze reminded me that winter would soon be upon us again, but for now, I'd enjoy the warm air and the stars that shone brightly in the dark sky.

Cytos had grown to more than double the size I first remembered. No longer broken and war-ravaged, but a metropolis of life, the hub of the new world.

Its citizens were made up of both humans and Carbons, all living in harmony with one goal in mind—peace. We'd succeeded for fifty years, but I was certain it wouldn't last. The remaining ruins, the scars and memories, reminding us of how bad things once were, and how far we'd come, would one day fade. But for now, we were strong and there was peace.

Many Carbons, like myself, still remembered those days, when the world wasn't the haven it had become. I made sure not to forget that for one moment. I never took for granted what we'd been given—time.

I remembered those days when I sat on these same edges, looking over a city torn apart. I would wonder when my last breath would come. But as my legs dangled over the edge, I didn't feel any fear or worry, only hope. Watchers still spread out through the city, now set on keeping the peace and ensuring it lasted, not fighting to keep the human race alive. They were the figurehead of survival and protection, and they'd live on long after even I was gone.

Soft footsteps arrived behind me, but I didn't stir.

Kenzie took up the empty space beside me as he wrapped a blanket around my shoulders. I looked up to his face with a smile, the face that in the last fifty years had hardly changed. When Doc saved Kenzie's life, he didn't just change his arm, but also his entire body had been affected. The mechanical parts inside of him kept his body almost ageless, much like my Carbon body. Though he'd eventually die—he couldn't outrun death forever—for now, he was here and he was mine.

Though time had worn on us, age and life hadn't yet caught up. The man who sat beside me looked the same as the day I'd met him. The same smile, the same perfect blue eyes. He was mine.

"You're going to catch a cold out here without a jacket on," Kenzie teased. "And I'd rather not have to take care of a sick wife who refused to listen to her husband." My heart still fluttered when he called me his wife.

"That's impossible." I smirked. He flicked my nose.

Still, he wrapped his arm around me and pulled me in. I rested my head on his shoulder.

Looking out over the peaceful evening, I wondered, "Do you think this is what he intended? Coleman? Was this the world he was trying to create?"

Kenzie thought before he spoke. "I think this is what he thought he was trying to create, but his views of how to achieve this were always flawed and rooted in vengeance and self-preservation, rather than what was good for everyone."

I nodded.

Kenzie gave my shoulder a squeeze as he kissed my temple. "Don't stay out here too late," he said. He stood to move back into our apartment across from the rooftop I sat on. "Oh, and your mom sent an e-link. She says hi from the United Isles, and that it's still sweltering hot there."

I smiled. My mom had become an ambassador to the new world, bringing together all the people who had experienced life under Coleman's tyranny. Given the same opportunity that both Kenzie and I had, a lifetime to make things right, she set out to do just that—bridge the gap between those who knew our history, and those who had experienced it. She traveled the world bringing peace wherever she went.

I turned back to the dark evening sky, watching the stars sparkle as I did most nights. And every time I did, I always thought of the one person who made sure I had this life with

Kenzie, this peace I felt. The one who'd sacrificed his own life so that I could live—Max. My Savior. Not a day went by that I didn't thank him for that, for giving me a reason to live, for being the reason I lived.

After everything that happened.

After all that we had lost…

I was still alive, and he still watched over me.

WANT MORE FROM THE WORLD OF WATCHER?
FIND OUT WHAT HAPPENED AFTER THE EVENTS OF SAVIOR IN...

EVER MARKED

BOOK ONE OF A NEW YA SCIFI SERIES
SET IN THE WORLD OF WATCHER.

ABOUT AJ EVERSLEY

As an avid reader from a young age, it only made sense that one day I would write my own stories. I grew up in a small town in central Alberta, Canada where there wasn't much to do but read, cheer on the Oilers, and endure the long cold winter months with copious amounts of hot chocolate and tea. After high school, I attended college where I played 4 years of college basketball and eventually went into Recreation as a career, but stories always held my heart. I began writing Watcher after an injury forced me to find a new hobby outside of sports and recreation, and you will find much of my writing is influenced by my background in how the body moves, through fight scenes and training. What started off small, quickly turned into something bigger than I ever could have imagined, and continues to grow every day. Still living in central Alberta, I spend my days with my loyal dog, and co-author, Moto, and my amazingly supportive husband. Every day I get to do what I love, and I couldn't have asked for a better team to help me along the way. I will continue to write more stories and worlds and can't wait to share them all with every one of you.

Keep up with my journey through my social links below or join my newsletters to be the first to know what's happening in the world of AJ Eversley.

INSTAGRAM: @AUTHORAJEVERSLEY
FACEBOOK: AUTHOR AJ EVERSLEY
TIKTOK: @AJEVERSLEY
WEBSITE: WWW.AJEVERSLEY.COM

Manufactured by Amazon.ca
Bolton, ON

32927984R00212